70

WITHDRAWN

JUN 1 2 2012

D1280023

keeneland

Alyson Hagy

SIMON & SCHUSTER

NEW YORK LONDON SYDNEY SINGAPORE

Simon & Schuster
Rockefeller Center
1230 Avenue of the Americas
New York, NY 10020

Simon & Schuster and colophon are registered trademarks
of Simon & Schuster, Inc.

Designed by Jeanette Olender

Manufactured in the United States of America

10 9 8 7 6 5 4 3 2 1

Library of Congress Cataloging-In-Publication Data
        Hagy, Alyson Carol.
    Keeneland / Alyson Hagy.
        p.   cm.
        I. Titl.e.
PS3558.A32346   KK44   2000
813'.54—dc21
99-046967

ISBN: 0-7432-4269-6

For information regarding the special discounts for bulk purchases, please contact Sim
Schuster Special Sales at 1-800-456-6798 or business@simonandschuster.com

*f*or Kim

who has the laughter and the sass

keeneland

CHAPTER 1

i was on my way to the race secretary's office when I was way-laid by the sight of crotchety Reno hosing down a high-hocked chestnut mare. He shouldn't have been there. Alice Piersall's barn had always been down the hill, closer to the track kitchen. I'd been sweating blood about running into some people, the wrong people, before I got my story straight, so I hadn't bet on having my first sparring match of the morning with that sour old man. I could've turned around, eased the corner at the next shed row, and mazed my way up the hill to where the hustlers were eking out their deals. They wouldn't care why I was back from New York without a husband or a horse to my name. But I'd had a bad moment when I parked my car, knowing I was going to endure a lot of hot eyes and tattling before I had my legs under me again. I'd pulled into Jack McClellan's reserved spot because I knew he wouldn't be up here until after the big race at Gulfstream. The hand-lettered *Reserved* signs hanging on the whitewashed fences didn't mean squat until the meet was open and there were races to be lost and won.

A long, bad moment. I'd stepped out of the Chevy only to

feel my ribs go squish against one another like the gristle in a picked-over turkey carcass. I'd pounded them pretty good when I took the fall from our mare Sunny during her workout three days before, a stunt my husband, Eric, had planned as a gift for the creeps who'd bankrolled him into trouble. The odds on Sunny were supposed to go way up when word got out about her panicking in the gate and dumping her rider; that had been jerk Eric's plan. After being laid up with an injury, Sunny was due to run her first race in months at the end of the week. If I had any guts left by then, any meat shred of pride, I wouldn't pay attention to that race, no matter how much I loved that perfect horse. I'd forget about it. Flip right past the tout in the *Racing Form* and everything.

So my ribs were hurting, and my neck and thigh where Eric had punched me in some kind of speed-freak gangster desperation, and the foot which always went dead when I drove any kind of distance, a problem that went back to being stomped on by a bird-shy colt when I was still dumb enough to hotwalk horses in sneakers. I was hungry, but not the sort of hungry that waters your mouth with any idea of what to eat. I was tired too. None of these complaints was new—except maybe the punches from Eric, which pissed me off even as they brought into my head a kind of cold, shrunk-up worry I hadn't felt before. What was new was the whittled sadness I had to swallow when I set foot on that swept pavement and took in a long, dewy breath of racecourse air. Cherry trees, budded dogwood, the low purr of a truck hauling fresh straw to the sheds. I thought it should cleanse me right then and there. Sweep away New York. Broom away Eric Ballard and the good love that was still French-braided with the bad. But it didn't. The foam bedroll stashed in the back of my car still looked like my ten-year-old bedroll. My two saddles, one uncracked helmet, cooler, duffel, lockbox, bridles, dress boots, and parka still looked like exactly what they were: hard-worn leftovers of a leftover life. I was a gypsy. Which made me no different than two-thirds of the folks working the backside of the track right that minute. It made me very different from the gal who'd left Kentucky two years before, though. The assistant trainer with a string of hotblood horses. The gleaming wife. The optimist who thought she could beat the game that beats *everybody, every day, amen*. I was back from the tough, year-round tracks of New York, the land of milk and big money, with nothing but lousy stories to tell and a box of stolen cash I couldn't bear to think about, much less touch.

It was a low-rent, prodigal return. No lookouts at the fancy stone gateposts. No messenger cries. I was just another saddle-sore working girl boomeranging back to where she came from.

And I run into Reno.

He was Alice Piersall's foreman and had been for a long time. I'd heard he was head man at one of the top barns in Florida when he was younger, but there'd been some kind of trouble there. He'd done piecework on the fairground circuit for a while before he fell in with Alice. He was too good for her grade of horses, and her operation was too small, but for all the years I'd known him, or known of him, it was clear that Reno was exactly where he wanted to be. There were bushels of stories about the man. How he'd been a famous child preacher in the Everglades, soloing in purple velvet and gold lamé. How he'd worked in the boiling cane fields with his brothers after his voice changed and the dove-spirit of the Lord left him for the tender throat of some other dark and shining boy. How he nicked a white boss man with a knife. How he ran a big-time trainer out of his own barn, following him right into the private dining room of the clubhouse and shouting the whole way be-cause the man was messing with a horse's stone bruise and pretending that horse was ready to run. He'd lost his job over that one. I'd ridden for Alice off and on before I left with Eric for up north. I had a few Reno stories of my own. Most of them revolved around the legend of his temper and the fact that I was the kind of person most likely to set that temper off.

Now, this minute, there was no getting past the man. He had the mare half on the grass and half on the soaked gravel of the road, his tapered back to me while he doused her joints with cold water. I took a couple of dragging steps forward.

"Watch the rogue horse," he said as the mare shook her head, then lowered it to look at me. I almost laughed. The mare was no more rogue than a puppy was, but a man like Reno—bossy and gruff—couldn't resist the play. He probably hoped I was a high-heeled tourist.

"She won't hurt me, will she?" I downshifted into a spoiled belle accent. "I just want to feed her some sugar like Daddy lets me do the ones back home."

He froze for maybe two ticks before his oval, close-shaved head rotated in my direction. He was careful to keep one hand under the mare's ticklish chin and the other on the red industrial hose, cooling the horse, always doing his job. His eyes didn't show anything once they focused on me—not surprise or dislike or even one unswept grain of pleasure. I expect I looked the same to him I always had: tallish, half dirty, my hair in a muzzy yellow braid down my back. He certainly hadn't changed. He was wearing navy blue work clothes, long in the leg, short at the sleeve, mildly faded at the pressed creases. No watch. Thick-soled army surplus boots he kept polished. And that same thin rawhide strip of a belt that featured no buckle to speak of and which always failed to cover the copper tab of his fly. His face was the deep, burnished brown of fine walnut furniture, the kind my mama coveted. He had high cheekbones and a long jaw, a wide clamped mouth. I could see the whites of his eyes were bloodshot, which was not a good sign. It meant his mood was simmering.

"Found you a daddy up north, have you? Ain't that always the way." He spoke to a point off to my right, then rotated back to his business, unconcerned, like a rattler surveying the desert from his rock.

I had to hand it to him. He knew how to wrist-snap his punches. My smart-aleck talk hadn't slipped past him. Hoping we were even, I headed uphill, where I trusted Joanie, the race secretary's assistant, would pour me some free coffee. I gave Reno a half wave as I went by, a movement akin to brushing sawdust from my jeans, but I didn't look at him again.

"She want to see you."

I stopped. Waited for him to go on.

"I know you looking for work, like everybody else."

I heard him drop the hose and swing the mare around for the walk back to her stall. Her hooves chittered on the wet gravel.

"I didn't ask. Okay?" My fingers, still throbbing from the long drive, began to dig into my belt.

"Yeah, you did. She scream us both red if you don't come on."

He led the mare forward, her flanks whirling orange in the morning light, his shoulders square and head high as though he alone transmitted the grace and power of her breed. His deep ease with horses was a thing I envied.

I coiled the hose beneath the rust-collared faucet, then fell into step behind them. The sun had cleared the manicured fields of Calumet Farms and was flashing off the barracks rows of barns, glinting on drainpipes and halter buckles and toppled pails. I caught the chuckle of radios turned low, the clang of a trailer dropping its ramp. Reno talked to his mare as they slipped

through a gate, tilting his head gently to the right while he ca-
denced a language I wouldn't have understood even if I could
have heard it. Reno had his secrets—his whispered sermons to
his horses was just one of them. He was also goddamned proud
as hell. I thought about the uncoiled hazard of the hose, how
he'd left it for me to tidy up. Catching on to what he'd done
made me laugh—my first true laugh in days—and I considered
that being bullied and enjoying it might be exactly the treatment
I needed to start my life over again.

Alice Piersall was a fat woman without excuses. She'd been
around horses most of her life and had gotten her trainer's license when I was still exercising hunters for rich girls busy with
country club tennis and their hairless boyfriends. As far as I
knew, Alice had never apologized to anybody about anything
that mattered to her. She'd been born near Versailles, where her
father had the gall to own a tag horse or two that he ran at
Churchill Downs when he felt like it. I'd heard Alice call him a
gentleman farmer, then laugh like the devil about it. He appar-
ently operated a bunch of service stations in the central part of
the state, swapped some real estate, had the expected taste for
barrel-aged bourbon. In any case, she caught the bug from him.
When he died, so I'd been told, he left his only daughter a small
farm and enough money to breed and raise a few thoroughbreds. She'd gone hell-for-leather on her own from there.

   She had a reputation on her hometown track which was well
deserved. She wasn't the only woman in the state who ran a
middling string of horses—there were a few of those—and she
wasn't the only one who'd been known to vise-grip a man's
balls. She just did it with lather. She loved to claim horses off
trainers she considered number one assholes, and she'd put in a

claim for no reason other than sheer spite. She was also known for being patient with young horses. The touts had learned to watch her. When she sent a colt out to break its maiden, it would be ready to win. And so would the shrewd money.

It was hard not to admire Alice Piersall.

After lifting two gates and sidling around a muddy corner, I saw Reno lead the mare into an empty stall in a partially occupied barn. Six horses, it looked like, with room for a half dozen more. Reno clipped some white webbing across the mare's stall, then slipped a monogrammed sheet from the rack. He'd hang a hay net, recheck the mare's stifles and cannons for heat, maybe mix up one of his foul Everglades poultices for a compress. Or he'd move on to one of the other lean and restless animals in his care. I wasn't his concern. Most people weren't.

Alice ran an organized barn. She was good to her animals, and Reno was probably better than that. But Alice wasn't super slick, so her operation didn't catch a person's eye. No brass plates on the tack room door, no matching blankets, no team windbreakers for the grooms to wear. Each owner outfitted his or her animals however they liked. If an owner wanted pink pom-poms on the mane for race day, that was fine, but Alice's own stock was usually wrapped in mismatched bandages and whatever gear she could trade for or repair. I figured the raggedy approach was Alice's way of regulating expectations— the owners' and the competition's—but she never admitted as much. She just insisted that decoration was foolish, even though everybody knew the racing business was more than half decoration, whether you were comparing tack rooms or bloodlines or the estimated price of the designer clothes worn by your wealthy clients.

The woman herself was sitting in a canvas-backed director's

chair in the shade of the freshly raked aisle. She looked like she was asleep. In fact, with her olive green coveralls, pink goose-down vest, men's work boots, and large, lolling head she looked like she was trying to discourage attention, even as she attracted it. Vintage Alice, I thought. Always issuing a challenge.

She began talking at me before she opened her eyes. I wondered if I was giving off a smell—some sort of Empire State stink—the way folks were onto me before I had a chance to open my mouth.

"Have a sit down," she said, slinging a stubby arm at a bale of straw that lay near her chair.

I sat, fighting the dizziness of fatigue. Alice opened her hazel eyes as though she needed to be absolutely sure it was me, then closed them again. It was like being blinked at by a hungry owl.

"Where's that tea? You like some tea?" She took in my face once more, then my clothes, then my face again. "Bet you haven't had breakfast."

"I haven't. Tea's good."

"I bet you just pulled off the highway, driving like a bat out of hell. I bet you don't have a good penny in your pocket."

Alice had a peculiar way of injecting exactly the right kind of static into a person's blood to make it buzz. She knew how to get under your skin. "I got money. Don't think I broke any speed records getting here."

"But you're back." She shifted her weight from one drumstick thigh to the other. "The tea's herbal mint, by the way. All I got."

I nodded.

"Don't have that fella—that what's-his-name, Ballard's kid—with you, do you?"

I pulled my tongue back from my teeth, thinking I should fuss with her assumptions about my marriage. But I stopped

myself. There wasn't much reason to quarrel about what was true.

"I heard y'all had one tolerable year up there. Good and bad horses. Good and bad runs. You must be back here because it didn't work out. Which I might have predicted." She huffed a little under her breath, her way of laughing, then put her hands on her wide knees as though she had good cards to lay on the table.

"Meet opens in three days. I can give you a few horses now, with another three or four in a week when I decide to yank them off the farm. I'd give you the whole string to ride, but I promised Red Flora I'd let this bug boy of his have a try. It's not much. And I got nowhere for you to sleep." She pushed her long, free-hanging brown hair behind her shoulder and leaned over her folded gut as well as she could. "You could do worse."

"You get right to it." I thought of the poker games I could slip into or the rides I could catch at other barns. If I decided to stay here and join the game again, I was going to need money, clean money. "I didn't ask for a job."

"You didn't, did you?" Alice slumped backward and glared into the concrete-block room at the shed's end that usually bunked hotwalkers and grooms. "I could go out there in the road and holler. Five or six Mexican boys would run right at me. But I know you. You'd take the job even if you didn't need it—I expect you *will* take it—because you love to exercise horses, even ones as sorry-assed as mine. You're hooked. Deep. You left one track for another. And I need a good hand."

I shook my head and stood, trying not to gasp at the clawing pain in my ribs. I was taller than Alice even when she was up-right, so it steadied me some to look down on her flushed, smooth face, directly into the bronzy eyes that sparked with mockery or laughter, I couldn't tell which. "Hate to think you believe leaving New York has made me pitiful. I came back because things are usually good for me here. Not lucky. Just good."

"Those tracks up there don't make anybody pitiful. They're rat-ass rough, but livable. Bugs me to see you glued to the saddle, is all. I've seen it too much. That man of yours—if he's still your man—is an empty pair of shorts, just like his oil slick of a daddy. You ought to be running your own string by now, or shacked up with somebody who's got real money." She stopped and let her nostrils flare. "I don't like to watch a girl go down."

Her words smacked. I'd left the touchables of my life— horses, furniture, husband, bills—up in New York, but not any good part of myself. Or had I? Alice Piersall seemed to think I was missing a few hard white bones in my spine. She sat there like her brand of survival, which was mostly combat and loneliness, was the finger-slick brass ring a Kentucky girl should reach for. Sure, I'd take the horses she had—I'd take *any* horses. But I hoped that didn't mean giving up on respect.

"Might be some of us are just born to be muckers." I glanced beyond her at a skitter of brown sparrows pecking in the dust. "I'll ride your horses if you need me."

She huffed again, then tossed a wink down the aisle toward where Reno was silently rolling bandages. "You'll do fine for me, Kerry. Always have. But I want to know a few things. Are you free and clear? Will that little bastard come bother you?"

I imagined Eric Ballard sauntering through these paddocks in one of his crisp seersucker suits, greeting his father's friends with their gold watches and fizzing mimosas, tossing his head in that bursting, coltlike way he had because he knew where he belonged. He'd been at his best here, where racing was as much style as business.

"Don't think so," I lied.

"You owe him money?"

"No, I got nothing of his." Which was the truth.

"All right," she said, levering herself against the arms of her chair. "I was hoping you'd robbed him blind, but we can't have everything. I'm not going to ask if he slapped you around either, because that's an old story. You come here, I'll show you the horses you can have and let you meet somebody. He's the one's supposed to be making that goddamn tea."

Alice shook the matchstick chair free of her hips and headed up the aisle in the quick, close-kneed walk that was the only pace she ever kept. She was a marvel in her way. Nosy, prone to snap judgments, marginally successful. She was also honest, and angry about it, and I could appreciate that. At five bucks a ride, which was all I could expect her to pay me, I'd need the appreciation.

The bunk room wasn't empty, just more sparsely decorated than usual. It held two camp beds—one of them still folded shut—a tiny portable fridge, a hot plate, and an ugly square window fan somebody had left unplugged. The unfolded camp bed was made up with a sleeping bag and some kind of yolk-colored, blotchy sheets. Leaning against the far wall near the single slot window was a man reading a book. The coils of the hot plate were a bright smoking orange. A white enamel kettle hissed with steam.

"Damn it, Danny," shouted Alice. "Quality shouldn't take so long."

Danny looked up from his thick paperback and acknowledged Alice with a tilt of his shoulders. He was average in height and build, dressed in a plain white T-shirt and jeans, his wavy, sandy-streaked hair pulled back in a ponytail. I pegged him as a groom, one of hundreds who would roll through Kentucky over the next few weeks as the horses left their winter barns in Florida and moved up the coast.

"Haven't forgotten you, boss. Might've got a little caught up in my story is all." His voice was low and plain sounding except around the vowels, which were chipped and nasal enough to prove he wasn't southern. He set his book in the windowsill and lifted the kettle above the refrigerator, where he'd laid out a small black pot and two glossy cups without handles. He filled the pot with water. A thick, leafy smell clouded the air. "I got another cup if your friend wants a taste."

"She can have yours right now." Alice put herself in front of Danny so he'd know what she said wasn't a request.

"Sure." He shrugged slowly from the elbows up. "It needs to steep. I'll bring it out."

"Good. Then you can rewrap that white-foot filly for me and check her temperature. Kerry will be riding her in the morning."

He looked at me for the first time then, sorting my freckled, windburned face from all the other faces he'd seen in the few days he'd been here. He was trying to guess where I stood in the pecking order—whether I rode horses, shoveled their shit, or wrote them off on my tax return—though I doubted he was the kind of man who lost much good sleep over such distinctions.

I gave him just enough smile to let him know I hadn't been completely buried by Alice. I also hoped the smile hinted that I knew herbal tea when I smelled it. Whatever he was brewing in his shiny Japanese pot was not what he claimed. Then I followed after Alice, opening my ears to her catalogued knowledge of her horses, letting my usual wonder about new people fade with the sweet, mossy scent of Danny's room.

"He says he's worked Ak-sar-ben and some tracks in Califor-

nia, though he's probably lying about that. Also claims he hasn't
been to prison, like they all do. Knows how to handle his three
head, however, which is all I care about." Alice stopped at the
last occupied stall, which was outfitted with a high half door.
"Danny's cute enough, which I'm sure you noticed. It's the
other boy I worry about. Skinny black thing that Reno's made
his project. You can imagine how that's going to go."

Reno was in earshot, of course, as he always was, and I wondered again at their long-term ability to tolerate each other.
Running a barn was harder than marriage, as I knew, but Alice
and Reno had pasted together almost ten long years with spit
and bile. They were a flint-eyed team. Maybe it was better if
you didn't have bed love for the other person. Maybe it worked
if you never paused while you were stirring hot mash to lay your
hand on top of your partner's. I wished I knew.

"If I don't go bust this time," said Alice, who'd been clucking
her tongue into the murkiness of the stall, "this will be the reason why."

I watched as the horse inside pivoted toward daylight in that
droopy, awkward way they have, rotating with the care of an
elephant on a circus stool. The liver-colored head that finally
swung over the gate was strong boned and big eared, with a
prominent brow and a nose just long and curved enough to be
called Roman. The thin white streak that began between the
horse's eyes looked like a badly patched crack in a wall. His
withers were narrow and very high, and though I couldn't see
his legs or rump, I guessed he was a distance runner, a stayer
with English or Irish blood in his scribbled veins.

Alice caught the halter and stroked the animal's muzzle.
"Don't know him, do you?" And I didn't. But the brass plate on
the halter set me straight. I reached up and touched his warm
jaw. Twilight Flare. An older gelding with a knack for the turf.

"If you didn't have your miserable head up your butt, you'd know we won a Grade Three at Turfway last week. Beat Niall Riordan's sheik horse and some other classy boys."

I looked at the sleepy-eyed gelding again. Like a lot of good ones, he didn't appear to have enough energy to carry schoolchildren across a hay field, though I knew that would change when he was pointed at the track. "You had him two years ago?"

"For a while. He finished about ninety-fifth in the Derby because Mrs. Stronheim wanted to run him there. Then I convinced her to have him cut and try him on grass. She's old and willing to believe me. We won fifty grand last year, lightly raced. This year, we turn him loose."

It wasn't unusual to see Alice proud of a horse, but it was rare to hear her speculate with any optimism. She'd grown up cagey. Most of us learned not to admit our affection for any one animal. Liking a horse didn't make it faster. Loving one, as I knew, could put a whole lot of things at risk. I shivered, thinking of Sunny, imagining how she was doing without me. Then I slid a hand down Twilight Flare's neck until I felt the slow thump of his pulse. He could run twice in the next three weeks, in top company. If he did well, the praise and offers would come across the yard like rain. I wondered how Alice would handle it.

"Reno won't want me to put you on him. Rogelio, that bug boy I mentioned, worked him at Turfway, and we'll keep it that way for now." Alice tugged at the big gelding's sparse black forelock. "I think it's the damn chicken myself."

"Likes birds, huh?" I hadn't heard any noise from the stall, but it was common for thoroughbreds to latch on to unusual companions. They were as eccentric, maybe even as superstitious, as human athletes.

"I don't know what the hell he likes. Had a damn nanny goat that lived under his feet all last year, and when it died from eating everything that was bad for it I thought I'd shoot myself. The big fellow went right off his feed. Then Reno tossed that dirty rooster in there—" Alice stopped, turned broadside in the aisle, and sputtered into a full guffaw. Her eyes got creased and wet. "This business," she roared. "It breaks me every day."

CHAPTER 2

*t*he next morning Charlie was up at the in-gate mounted on his hangdog sorrel, same as always. He was the first person I'd seen since I left my bedroll willing to speak a word that wasn't a curse. I eased Alice's white-footed filly off the side of the road to let a gray BMW whine past, and she took it well enough, tossing her chin once and half hitching her hindquarters for good measure. I waved to Charlie. He looked good—slim, leathery. He nodded back and spit a cigarette free of his lopsided smile. By the end of workouts, the ground around the gate would be splintered with half-smoked Pall Malls.

"Kerry, girl," he rasped. "What brings y'all back? Yankeeland getting too cold for your ass?"

I shrugged in my windbreaker, hoping he wouldn't ask about Eric. "Money. Ain't that what keeps you old-timers stuck in this sweet Kentucky horse poo?"

Charlie whacked at his saddle horn with a gloved hand and snorted. He'd always enjoyed laughing at me, maybe because I allowed for it. His sorrel mare didn't move an inch even though my filly was giving her the walleye, just waiting for a fight. It was filly's first time on the big track, and Alice had told me to take it super easy. I dug my right heel into her ribs to square her up, but laid off the whip.

"What you got there? One of Roy's prize bitches? I heard you was riding for his buddies up at Belmont." Charlie put another Pall Mall between his lips and gave the filly the once-over. As clownish and leached out as he acted sometimes, nobody ever questioned Charlie Hamner's eye for horseflesh. He'd seen too many. Been an outrider at the track for a million years.

I wheeled the filly to face the gate, trying to ignore the people clumped along the rail to my left. I knew most of them. The clockers who were pacing in the frostbitten overhang of the grandstand, waiting to time the scheduled workouts. The jockey agents who were hustling the grouchy half-awake trainers for rides. The crew from the secretary's office and the guys who worked on the grounds. I thought about the story Charlie had heard about me—how it was mostly wrong—and how there'd be more stories about me on the grapevine in a few short minutes. They'd all be wrong too. And I had no good reason to correct them.

Charlie held the gate until two horses turning in a brisk blow cleared the pole. They thundered by throwing dirt like it was rat shot. I recognized the deep green saddle blankets—Three Pines Farm, an old ride of mine. And who the hell was aboard the lead colt but Louisa Fett of Frankfort, Kentucky, a twiggy, back-stabbing witch I'd known since high school. She'd stolen a hand-stitched bridle from me once, and I'd never forgiven her. My empty stomach flipped and furled. She would hate seeing me back in the territory.

"This one's Piersall's," I said to Charlie, reminding him I

needed to go through the gate. "She's straight off the farm, got some Native Dancer blood Alice mentioned, so don't say a word about her hocks. I just got in last night."

"Not riding for Roy, then?" His leaky, red-rimmed eyes slid sideways. I knew he was calculating my chances of lasting the week.

"Nobody but Alice right now." I snapped my chin strap and stretched upward in the stirrups, clucking the filly into a trot. "Why don't you tell everybody I'm looking for good rides?"

I heard Charlie slap at his saddle again, and I spent a second trying to remember how many fingers were missing inside those grimy doeskin gloves. He'd been a helluva jock before his mount shattered a leg and dropped him under the hooves of the pack.

Alice wanted me to jog a half, then canter a half in hand. I was to find space on the rail and let the filly soak up the sights. Easy work if I was careful, though it would have been easier if my bruises hadn't been so deep. My ribs were moaning. Once we cleared the first turn I felt better, though. It was like being pasted into a giant silent movie. Mist cradled in the sloughs to the west, cottoning the rough trunks of the hundred-year oaks and maples. A clear, winking sunrise. The stone grandstand simple and clean in the dawn. The skin across my back prickled as I balanced above the familiar runway of the backstretch, watching the color-daubed horses and riders swing in front of me. The sight made my heart change gaits. Churchill Downs got all of the attention because of the Derby, but this place—the track of my home—was a better place to run horses, cut deals, or do anything that didn't involve a TV camera. Before I left here I'd had a full-time job breaking and exercising horses for Billy Tolliver at Three Pines. I'd been his assistant in all but name; I'd shared an apartment with a friend who worked in a bank; I'd known that daybreak on horseback was a gift. Some-how I'd convinced myself it wasn't enough. I fell for Eric Ballard and the advertisements we broadcast about ourselves, how we'd be richer, more ambitious, better at every task we tried. I'd let all this get away from me.

I kept the filly on the bit, letting her spook just enough to get the kinks out while we jogged along the outside rail. A Panamanian kid I recognized loped by on a big-boned black colt. He was talking nonstop the way a good exercise rider will, his bright teeth clenched with effort. I could practically feel the burn in his knotty, compact thighs. The colt moved well, and his deep, rhythmic snort made me wish I was on him, that I was the one breaking that cold, wind-streaked sweat. Riding like that, being on the muscle, was what I loved and what had always kept me going when the rest of it was mud and ache and shit.

We took our time on the far turn. It was only when three horses broke past us going hard and a rider's nylon jacket ballooned with air, soaring free of his belt, that the bad shadows swept over me. Eric had been wearing a cheap raincoat when he charged at me, and it had filled with frantic speed as he bulled down our barn aisle, fists swinging. I was already stiff from the fake fall I'd taken off Sunny, and I was too stunned to duck. I remembered the flimsy hiss of the coat, how the coat didn't go with his khakis and collared shirt. How he grunted. How his eyes flicked off and on. I remembered the way he slugged me where the bruises wouldn't show, like he'd thought about his moves beforehand somewhere in his pinned and wriggling mind.

Filly bunched the muscles in her back—I could feel it through my saddle—and broke into a choppy canter. She'd felt me go tense and responded the only way she knew how. By running. I looked over my shoulder and found a horse we could fall in behind, a rib-sprung gray that was striding loose. I nudged the filly onto the rail after him. She was more comfortable right away, rocking and eager. I dropped my weight back and began to hum a nonsense tune over the crest of her neck. An old trick of mine that was good for me too, better than any string of words.

Alice was easy to spot. She claimed the same slatted bench in the grandstand every morning, above the rail, just past the finish line. Sat there in her puffy pink vest with her coveralls zipped up to her chin and her hands empty. She left her workout book at the barn, where she thought it belonged, and she never let anybody see her in public with a *Racing Form*. Ever. No cup of muddy tea either, only a quick thumbs-up as we cantered past. That was my signal to finish smooth. There was another horse waiting at the barn.

I got a better look at Louisa Fett when she rode by again, cooling down. I didn't recognize the redhead with her; she was heavy in the hips and sat too far forward in the saddle for my taste, but she seemed confident enough. Louisa looked the same she always had, rat faced and bottle blonde. I watched her whipsaw her bay colt back into a walk—she'd never had light hands—then I dug up my good manners and gave her a nod, though the redhead was the only one who returned the favor. Louisa stared right through me, which was just as well. I didn't have one word to say to her. Besides, Billy Tolliver would be filling her big ears before long. I knew Billy T., had even been half in love with him once. He'd scorch Louisa for riding that colt so rough.

By the time I worked the filly back to the gate it felt like she'd grown up a little, like she was less daisy cutter, more racehorse. I guessed she'd do all right in a few races, probably be dropping foals by the time she was four. *If* she had some heart, which she most likely did if she was in Alice's barn. I rubbed the hot slope of her shoulder to let her know I thought she was just fine. I'd exercised better horses and more than I could count that were worse.

I raised my whip to Charlie on the way out. "This place is tops," I told him. "I've missed it."

He lifted his scuffed reins to eye level. "Hell, the Arabs and Japs done come and gone, bought everything that eats hay since you were here last. Gotten so an old fart like me can't hardly park his pickup on race day. Too many limos."

"But you're still here, Charlie. You and that cozy fleabag you're sitting on. Foreigners don't have much chance against that."

Charlie hawked and spit. "But the goddamn money does. Not a soul in this town that'll turn down a dollar anymore. The real horse people went and died. 'Cept Miz Waddell and me."

I blew him a dry kiss, something else to make him laugh.

The area around the gate was even more crowded with horses, trainers, grooms, and hangers-on than before. I saw Red Flora, the jockey agent, launch himself from the secretary's office with a clipboard full of curled papers, his suit pants twisting around his knees like they always did when he was in a hurry. I saw a leggy girl I knew gather the reins on a gorgeous roan that wore a saddle blanket from the most successful barn in the country. She was getting instructions from an assistant trainer, leaning forward to finger the buckle of one spur. It was like she had nothing else to think about but that roan, its speed, its storm-weather attitude. Then I thought I glimpsed a silvery shock of hair near the corner of the grandstand. I was afraid it was Billy T. I knew I wasn't ready to see him yet, especially in the middle of that circus, so I swung the filly downhill. I hadn't seen a groom, decided maybe Alice hadn't bothered to send me an escort. It would take a little longer to get to her barn if I dodged left, but the crack at solitude seemed worth it.

I was sniffing the morning air and reminding myself I should enjoy the buds of spring when I realized I'd worked my way to the edge of Roy Delvecchio's kingdom. Roy always tried to snag barns near the main paddock because he thought it made a ritzy impression on his owners. Over the years his operation had become large enough and successful enough to deserve the prime location. In fact, the only thing that hadn't improved in the ten or twelve years I'd known Roy was his character.

Everything on his shed row was perfectly coordinated as always—the blankets, the feed tubs, the wasp yellow-and-black webbing on the stalls. And there on the snipped green of the yard was the scrawny, mustache-sucking SOB himself. He was flipping through a blurry sheaf of X rays while his foreman, Thomas, saddled a horse on the path behind him. Roy had a guy peering over each shoulder, thick men with blow-dried hair and Bermuda tans. They wore sunglasses and shimmery jogging suits with glowing white sneakers. Definitely not horse people. Nouveau owners, I guessed, up from Boca or down from D.C. Knowing Roy, they might even be orthodontists from Louisville. If they were in with Mr. Delvecchio, however, they were likely to be in over their heads. The man could snake-charm money from a bookie's pockets and do it in a way that made the bookie feel smug and happy. Then again, Roy didn't appear to like what he saw in those X rays. He was scowling, and his knees were locked stiff like he was holding in a scream.

I nodded to Thomas. I'd first hotwalked for him on this track when I was barely sixteen. He'd been the one who made me care about the whole slave-driving business. My mother had moved down to St. Pete to dry out my stepdad, but I'd stayed behind with cousins to finish school and exercise jumpers for some kids I knew. While things around me changed, I stuck to the simple things I understood. Horses seemed simple. When I heard that locals could clear good money during a meet, I came looking for work. Thomas hired me and spent time teaching me some practical things about thoroughbreds that were trained to race. He also warned me about his boss, how Mr. Delvecchio liked his girls pretty, slim, and quiet. "I work for the man," Thomas said. "He knows his horses. But don't let him pull you into that, treating you like stock. Not unless you want it that way."

Thomas waved, a snap of the hand that got snappier when he actually recognized me. I saw him glance at Roy, who was smooth-talking his customers back into their smiles. He gestured at me to stop by sometime, and I knew what he meant. I should come by at night when Roy was in town with the wine-'n'-dine crowd. We could catch up. I made a promise to myself to buy Thomas a package of ribs at the grocery after I got paid. He worked wonders with his hibachi and his secret barbecue sauce, Thomas did. Every unleashed dog on the backside came to sit at his feet when he cooked.

Danny had my next ride ready for me when I got to Alice's barn. Reno and the new kid they called Dawg were busy tacking up Twilight Flare, or trying to. Flare, as they called him, had turned into a hoof-stomping twister. It took two men, one levering a chain shank across the bridge of his nose, just to hold the gelding still enough to cinch the girth. Reno was singsonging and shouldering his weight against the horse, working to calm Flare's body with his own, but even that wasn't enough to make things easy. A small young man leaned against a post with his arms across his chest watching the whole tap dance with a flat, private expression on his face. I figured he must be Rogelio, the apprentice jockey, or bug boy, that Alice had hired. He seemed to be studying the big horse's style, every rump tuck and spin, analyzing his balance and his habits. He did this without making any move to help the others, however, and I guessed he'd scouted the veteran jockeys in the locker room as closely as he scouted his rides. He already owned the tightly held mouth, the brown eyes that gleamed with a pinpoint challenge they tried not to express. Jocks had their own rules, most of which accommodated the sawed-off, explosive egos that were attracted to the pressures of the job. Alice said Rogelio was good. I didn't doubt that he rode well. Only time would tell if he was tough enough to stick. He'd be hazed by the veterans on the track and off. He'd break a few bones or bust his head in a fall and be asked to remount before he had a chance to measure out the pain. He'd have to deal with groupies, gamblers, pissed-off trainers. He'd have to handle his money if he was lucky enough to make any. I could see he'd already laid in a store of cowboy poses for the long months ahead. They wouldn't do much good if his guts weren't up to his intentions.

My second ride of the morning was a $15,000 claimer Alice had picked up at Turfway. He was four years old, thin, long in the pastern, with a marbled fleck in his left eye. A below-average prospect, but Alice thought she could salvage something by changing his diet and sharpening what little speed he possessed. Danny had done a beautiful job turning him out, and I told him so while I slid my saddle and pad across the horse's back.

"Yeah." He smiled. "Boss man is fairly picky, and I didn't want to ruin his morning. Besides, this fella ain't much sensitive about his bandages. He's easy."

"Hope he stays that way," I said, slipping my boot into a dangling stirrup.

"He will for you. I asked him special."

I pretended I hadn't heard him. Flirting was part of the regular give and go at the barns. That was something else I'd learned around Roy's crew too many years before. Talk was talk, and you could expect some of it to be thrilling and some of it to be raw. Most of it was wolf-whistle harmless. Yet Danny caught me out, and it wasn't because I hadn't noticed him that morning. I had. He was wearing old jeans, beltless, with a plain red shirt tucked in at the waist. The back pocket of his jeans was branded with the faded circle of a snuff can. His sneakers were the kind that had been popular when I was real young—black high-tops with a childish white rubber toe. His hair was held back by a bandanna. He didn't seem to have any great big tattoos, and when he brought me the horse, I'd noticed he smelled clean.

He unclipped the lead once I was up, then turned to the filly, who needed to be washed and scraped and rubbed. The alarming smile he'd given me faded as quickly as it had come. But it had caused a tug and I wanted to pinch myself for that.

I rode across the yard toward the end of the shed, where a glimmering trailer truck had parked to unload. We were getting company. By day's end whatever stalls Alice hadn't reserved would be occupied. I took in a long breath, tasting the warm stew of grain, straw, and manure, and it came to me that what I wanted was company. Lots of it. I looked forward to full barns, a teeming grandstand, high hopes, and hot tempers. I looked forward to a place in the show. Maybe Danny's words would be halfway good for me. Maybe I could use them to chisel some of the old Kerry loose. What more could I ask for? Chewing on that question, I squeezed the claimer into low gear and headed uphill into the colorless, lifting sun.

C H A P T E R 3

i was finished by eight-thirty, $20 richer and a little deeper into the burrow of old habits. I offered to help Reno bathe a three-year-old Alice was training for some lawyers in Cincinnati, but he shooed me away, cussing me for spoiling the boy he'd hired to do the slop work. "Come from nowhere over in town, says he wants to learn the horses." I looked at the kid Danny had nicknamed Dawg because of the Georgia Bulldogs cap he wore backward on his narrow head. He was young and bony and peat colored, his long legs swishing in a pair of black nylon sweats. His untied sneakers smacked the sawdust as he tried to keep up with Reno's drill sergeant orders. "He want to learn horses," continued Reno, "I teach him the truth from they asses forward." I wondered if the kid would split for his neighborhood in town once he got his first pocketful of pay. He'd made it through two days because he kept his mouth shut and because Reno tolerated the boom box he set up near the stalls as long as the sound was kept low. He looked like a watchful kid. For all I knew he would become a lifer. You could never be sure which of us would get the curse.

I wiped down my tack and stored it with Alice's stuff, where it would be safer than in the back of my car. The door to Danny's bunk room was open, so I stuck my head in, wanting to prove I was capable of being neutral but friendly. Danny was there, leaning against the wall with his back to me, his body a trim layout of gray shadows and blue. His book was splayed open on the high windowsill. But this time he was talking to somebody on the other side of the dirty, half-opened window. His words were whispered and enthusiastic. I couldn't tell much about the other voice except that it was high-pitched and probably female.

Danny was savvy. It was okay to mingle with friends at the barn, but you had to be careful doing it on the boss's time. Reno would have Danny flipping manure until noon if he caught him goofing off. As I backed out of the door, I wondered who she was. I could have strolled around the corner and seen her standing on her tiptoes in the wet, untrimmed grass, chatting and stifling her giggles, but I didn't. I stayed squarely where I was, trying not to react to the flush I felt running up my backbone. Bits of the conversation seemed to be in jostling, tumbling Spanish. I figured that was more than I needed to know.

My Chevy was where I'd parked it the day before. Somebody had pulled a perfectly waxed Lincoln into the space next to mine, the one reserved for a hotshot trainer from California. Somebody else had sketched the name of that year's Derby favorite—a horse the California guy didn't have in his barn—on the dew-silvered windshield of the Lincoln.

I had nowhere special to go. I thought about driving over toward Frankfort to look up my cousins. I'd lived with them when I was sixteen or so. They'd survived me. I thought about parking in the lot of the branch bank where Michelle, my old roommate, worked. I could buy her lunch and check out the possibility of sleeping on her couch. In the end it seemed better to stay out of those lives until I'd at least eaten or had a shower. So I cranked up the car, killed the guitar grind of the radio, and headed out. I saw one attendant, a milky-eyed old man dressed in starched khakis and the official dark green cap of the track; he was weeding a fence line in the rolling parking lot. He waved me past even though he looked confused by his own instinct. I saluted him back.

I grabbed an early lunch at the Food Mart up the road. Cheese sandwich, Mountain Dew, a half pint of soggy cole slaw for vitamins. I ate the sandwich on the hood of my Chevy Citation, enjoying the sun, then spent five more dollars on food I could keep in the cooler. It wasn't until I was rummaging around in the back of the car, shifting my lumpy duffel so I could repack the cooler, that I realized why I'd left the track when I could have stuffed my face happily enough at the track kitchen. It was the money. The dirty brick of profit I'd taken out of the house before I left Eric. The money was in the dented lockbox, which was wedged in the tire well along with an oily tangle of jumper cables and old towels. I couldn't actually see it; it was carefully hidden. But I knew it was there.

For a short second I thought about throwing the money away, just dropping it in a ditch near the entrance of some billionaire's farm, where it could rot untouched and unneeded. But it was mine, or part of me. I needed it. I hadn't brought much to the marriage other than a strong back and enthusiasm. Eric was the one connected to money, the one who had prep school style and friends and a history even strangers were familiar with. His father was a developer in New York and New Jersey; his mother came from Oklahoma oil money just old enough to be acceptable. Yet the thing that had drawn us together was how plain we seemed to each other. When we met, Eric was learning to train from an unpretentious old crank who made sure Eric did all the muck work. He never mentioned his family, so we talked horses. The romance was long and slow, just like the sex. And that's what drew me in: the bond seemed honest and undecorated. I hadn't counted on the extravagant wedding gifts, the impatient clients drummed up by my in-laws, the perils of going too far too fast. Neither of us had. Our love, which had been plenty real, if new, was no stronger than a yearling's sesamoid. It didn't take long to crack it under stress.

The way I remembered it, I'd dumped about $2,000 into the joint savings account after Eric and I traded promises and rings. Some of the crinkly bills in that lockbox were mine. Problem was, I'd walked off with a good ten grand, all of it owed to other people. I was so mad, so fire brained, I'd taken an heirloom necklace too, just to show Eric I knew how to pop the top on my own scheme. I thought it would serve him right to feel just as cornered as I had when he swung at me in the barn. Now I couldn't bring myself to touch the stuff. I got queasy when I thought about it. The electric thrill of the rip-off was dead, fizzled out. It was like everything Eric and I had breathed on was poisoned—including my own body, my confidence.

Still, I couldn't get rid of the money. I'd be a fool to start at the very bottom again, no matter how much Alice seemed to like me, or how well things were going so far. I'd seen what happened to the chronic losers in this business. They lived in trailers or tilted shacks just out of sight of the mansions and heated barns. No more useful than stranded hoboes, they eventually shriveled away to nothing, victims of cigarettes, bad bets, and brief glories.

I wasn't going to be like that.

I slammed the car shut. Anger heated my skin. I was in trouble I hadn't caused. Jamming the key into the ignition and squealing onto the smoky gray ribbon of Versailles Road, I talked to myself in my head like I hadn't done since my night-mare gallop out of New York. I swore that I'd get shut of Eric—every picture, every finger touch and memory—before the meet was over in a month. That was the thing to do. Kill my feelings at the root. Get him out of my life for good. Use the money and necklace to make myself into a thick-skinned racetracker who could withstand manipulators like him.

My flooding frustration drove me far enough west to see the rebuilt rock walls of Three Pines Farm. Like a homing pigeon drawn to the roost. A spasm of good sense allowed me to swing left down a tiny lane before I actually passed the house, though I could see it rising above the pruned magnolias and evergreens, a wedge of chimneys and coppery roof. For a moment I was sure I'd been seen, that everybody would come sprinting from the barns and offices to stare at me before they ran me off the prop-erty. Then I felt stupid for thinking I'd ever been that important to anybody. Billy T. and his crew were still at the track; they'd be there all day. And while it was true that dear Stacey might be seated in the main office of the big house, filing her nails be-neath the oil portrait of Seattle Slew, there was no way she'd trouble her big-haired head about me. Troy was busy in the stud barn, getting mares teased and serviced, keeping a sharp eye on the millions of dollars of retired horseflesh in his care. And the way I'd heard it up in New York, Billy T.'s wife, Chan-tal, was gone, shacked up with some broker type she'd met at Hialeah.

I drifted up the lane past honeysuckle, pin oak, the roadside trickle of a spring. As I crested a low hill, I could see the octago-nal stud barn and its large, secured paddocks. I saw the equip-ment sheds, the bright brick of the summer kitchen where Billy had his office, the distant smudge of the broodmare barn. I felt a knuckle punch of loneliness. I'd spent a good long year here before I left with Eric, and the damned beautiful place hadn't changed. I imagined Louisa Fett working in the new barn. I imagined her halter-training my foals and saddle-breaking my yearlings. The whole idea stuck sharp as a stick in my craw.

I pulled over at a gravel road that had once been the broodmare entrance. When Billy T.'s investors built the eight-sided stud barn they hoped would one day hold eight of the world's top-producing sires, he'd rerouted van traffic to the west end of the farm. The road I was on was used for feed deliveries or the occasional shortcut. I pulled close to the fence, making sure I couldn't be seen from the multipaned windows of Three Pines. Looking across the green meadows, I somehow knew what I needed on this floating, silent noon. I needed to know this kind of life was still here. That there were good people in Kentucky —like Billy, like Troy—who made honest calls in a roulette wheel business, even if I wasn't yet fit to join them. That would be my dream: to be as plain and certain as I had been before my marriage.

Dreams. The long, sweet one I'd had about Sunny began right here. Billy owned Sunny's dam—a solid daughter of Mr. Prospector—and he teased me about the favoritism I showed her new foal by Sun Chief. I'd hang over the paddock fence between chores and watch her, her coat still fluffed with blonde, her overlong legs still a mystery. She strayed from her mother's side with curiosity and purpose. There were lots of beautiful babies in the fields that year, and I enjoyed them all, but Sunny's certain eyes drew me in. Maybe I was ripe for the bond, needy and daring all at once. I don't know. I did know I shouldn't get too attached. Thoroughbreds are commodities. Sure enough, Sunny was sold as a yearling, a business move Billy halfway apologized for. Eric was the one who brought her back to me, buying her with his father's money and giving her to me to put under saddle. An engagement gift, he called it. Better than a polished diamond. Better than anything. She would be proof of our desires.

For two years, and a race record that made you want to shout, she'd been just that.

I reached into the backseat and tugged my bedroll free from where I'd slept in it the night before, ignoring the stink of socks and bad money. I spread the bedroll on recently mowed grass near the fence, lay down, closed my eyes. The engine of the Chevy ticked along with the tick of occupied insects. I heard flies and the dull irritation of a crow. I smelled limestone and the mild heat of morning. I couldn't hear the horses in their square paddocks, but I had seen the lazy, full belly amble of a few mares before I lay down. I could taste a milky warmth in the air. Those things, a few thoughts about Sunny, lullabied me away.

i woke to find a platoon of ants snacking on my ankles. My back was a little stiff from napping on uneven ground, but once I brushed a couple dozen persistent soldiers off my skin I didn't seem any worse for wear. I'd had a pretty good nod. My ribs bothered me when I stretched, though they'd held up damn well when I was riding. Which just goes to show something.

I sat on my bedroll for a few minutes, mainly to work the crusty taste out of my mouth but also to tally the day's score. It was restful to be out here, but if I wasn't going to spend the chunk of change I had—and I couldn't, not yet—I needed to make some more money. That meant brushing my teeth, wiping the glum look off my face, and getting back to the track. It was time to hustle more rides.

Of course the first body I laid eyes on after I got back to the track belonged to stringy old Louisa Fett. She was dawdling against the side of a green customized van with a large cup of lemonade in her hands. I got out of the car and looked straight at her. Neither one of us had ever missed a chance to hassle the other in all the years we'd been in the business.

I lathered up a fakey sweet drawl. "Nice colt you had this morning, Lou."

She didn't miss a beat. "Yeah, Billy's give me his best ones this spring." Took a noisy sip of her lemonade. "This here is Billy's van. I'm waiting on him so we can meet some owners for drinks. The Vanderhavens. In town."

I didn't believe her for a second. I'd had my differences with Billy T., big ones, but he was too much of a class act to take Louisa to a business meeting. It was barely possible he was screwing her now that Chantal had split, though Billy wasn't a natural tomcat. And Louisa was no kind of date, even with a skirt on.

"What about you?" Louisa twisted her scrawny arms into a bad-girl shrug. "Heard you were shagging rides at Charles Town."

"Never been stuck in West Virginia yet. More like New York, riding my butt raw on my own horses."

"But you're back. I don't reckon Piersall's slow boats will be too hard for you to handle." She arched her plucked eyebrows. "Won't get in over your head again."

My hands and feet started to tingle. I thought of Three Pines and the cold, cracked-stone shed rows in New York. I thought of Eric and what he'd lost for both of us. "I guess I missed the healthy air down here," I said, "and the lovely sight of you yanking the shit out of a horse."

I ducked when she threw the lemonade. It flew by, wetting the side of my face before it exploded on the trunk of the car behind me. I threw my hands up, whooped into a belly laugh, and Louisa was on me a half second later trying her damnedest to slap me and pull my hair out at the same time. I'm sorry to say I let fly. I saw all kinds of ugly things in her face—sharp splinters of Eric, my mama's impatience, Alice's disapproval—and I went after them. Socked Louisa in the stomach, took a few finger-nails across the face, leaned in and hit her again, hard. She gave a burping yelp and crumpled to the asphalt behind Billy T.'s gleaming van. I looked at her retching on the pavement, her big, gnarled feet twitching in her sandals, and I knew I'd done wrong. Fighting Louisa was a bad choice. What I had to won-der, as I stood there with my cheek feeling germy and sore, was how much misbehavior it would take to learn to make better ones.

When Billy T. showed up I was yanking a bath towel from a paper bag in the back of my car. Louisa had wormed her way into the front seat of the van, then tattled on me the second she had the chance. I dropped the towel and raised my empty hands in surrender. "Give me hell, Billy. I deserve it. That bitch just drives me wild."

He watched me for a second, kept his distance. I could smell the dusky syrup of his cologne.

"Me too," he said finally, smiling in a tense way. He looked as good as he ever had. "Don't know why I put up with her."

"I do." I scanned his drizzly blue eyes. "She's a known factor. That means a lot around here."

His forehead wrinkled, the lines going deeper than they had the last time I'd seen him. I felt us drift into an achy, uncomfort-able pause. We'd parted on poor terms two years before, mainly because we liked each other too much. Sleeping together hadn't been enough, and working together got to be more than we could handle, especially once Eric tangoed onto the scene. Now we were here, face-to-face again like two hell-raising cousins all grown up. I could tell Billy wasn't sure whether he approved of what he saw or not. I watched him chew on his fleshy lower lip. He was thinking about offering me my old job.

"I'm okay, Billy. I need work, maybe a little time to get my head on straight, but I'm getting there. Just tell Louisa I'll stay out of her way if she'll stay out of mine."

The muscles in his jaw got tight like they did when his horses ran poorly. "You're the best I've had, Kerry. At the barns, I mean." His neck started to heat up with a blush. "I'd be lucky to get you back."

I tried to look at him straight on, without hiding behind my eyes or my words. What I had to say wouldn't be easy. "I was the lucky one, to be there when I was. I'm not ready for it now."

"Is Eric on his—"

"Eric's out of the picture, which won't surprise you a bit. Might surprise you to know he hasn't ruined that Sun Chief mare yet." I choked up a grin at my own joke, tried not to think about how I'd left Sunny in desperate hands. "She's supposed to run in a few days."

Billy fanned his fingers across his turquoise-patterned tie, then did it again. "I never had much against Ballard. He worked his horses all right. I just wasn't for you leaving like you did . . . for my reasons . . . not the business."

"I heard about Chantal," I said.

"Yeah, it's been a bad winter. Had to put a colt down last month and I God-to-Christ hated it." He looked up from his feet, shook his hair off his face. "It's good to have you back."

"Good to be here, I think. I'm riding some for Alice."

"I know." He threw a look at the van. Louisa wasn't in sight. "I heard about it. You could do worse."

"That's what she said, boss man." I laughed. "Y'all got your act down perfect."

He chuckled a little in return, finally giving me a face I remembered from the easy, private times. "If you need any-thing—"

"I'll be around," I said, cutting him off. "You'll see me. Let's do it like that."

He slipped his hands into the pockets of his tailored slacks and gave me a sort of curved bow from his shoulders. He did look fine. Dark eyebrows under his thick salty hair, full lips and blue eyes, simple clothes that signaled he knew how to speak for himself. In a lot of ways he was what Eric aspired to be—successful, independent, and understated about it. But Billy was a strip miner's grandson, one generation from the mountains, and he'd made that work in his favor. He was tough, well grounded. He never let the glitz get inside his head. I watched him disappear behind the rhino flank of his van. Even his walk, limber and preoccupied, got to me.

I grabbed my chaps from the car so I wouldn't show up on Roy's shed row empty handed. I'd had my little two-step with pride at Louisa Fett's expense, and I suspected it was more than I could afford. I needed to make my living. Like I'd tried to tell Alice the day before, a living—not even a life—was what a person had to aim for first. I couldn't work for Billy; my heart wasn't up to that. I'd have to earn a new future, another shot at a place like Three Pines, the hard way. Roy Delvecchio was the biggest certifiable bastard on the grounds, and he always needed riders. This time I was going to be the one he hired.

Roy had already left for the day, of course. The slumped old man holding down the fort at the end of the aisle told me I'd find Thomas at his bunk. I was partly relieved. It would be better to deal with Roy in the morning.

Thomas was sitting on his bed thumbing through a small stack of mail. He stood when he saw me and reached out his hand for a shake.

"Bet you looking for the man."

"Not really," I said. "I'd just as soon see you."

"Ain't much to say about me. I hadn't changed a bit, and it looks like neither have you. Got a letter from my boy in Tampa today. He's growing fast." Thomas held up a square blue envelope decorated with rainbow spirals. He was lucky to get any mail on the road, and he knew it. "Already talking about working with his daddy, though I tell him to take his time. He likes horses."

"How old is he?" Thomas had two kids he never saw enough of.

"Just turned five." He planted his hands at the base of his back and stretched. "Got to hold him off awhile yet."

I pulled up the milk crate that seemed to be the guest chair and saw that Thomas was right. He hadn't gone for much change. As foreman of a big operation, he didn't have to share his room so he used the space to outfit a card table as a desk. He was in charge of feeding, exercising, doctoring, and protecting at least two dozen expensive horses. I saw the payroll book at the back corner of the table, the expandable file folders, the framed pictures of toothy children. Roy would have gotten Thomas a small camper for his quarters, but Thomas didn't want one. He liked to be in his barn.

"How's the husband?" he asked, using his low gospel voice.

"Not around," I said. "Lot of pressure this spring with some new colts and all. We weren't agreeing on much."

Thomas flattened his mouth. Lives were always falling apart at the track, coming together on a run of luck, then falling apart again. It seemed to be a rule, and there was no reason for anybody to act surprised.

"You bring horses down?"

My insides banjoed when he asked that. The right question,

and the toughest one. I'd left them all with Eric, somehow thinking the split was only about us and not the horses. Maybe I'd made a mistake. I might not deserve those animals, but neither did my husband. Or his gambler friends.

"Might not have been easy for you," Thomas said, sidestepping his way to the door. "That boy's good enough to them. Might be trouble for you if you brought them down."

"I'm already in plenty of trouble." I spoke to the flaking cement between my boots.

There's a kind of code on the backside like the one they have in prisons, where you don't ask a guy what he's in for, ever. Around the horses you don't dig much into a person's past, and you never pester them about their problems. Not unless they bring it up first. Maybe not even then. Thomas had hired his share of college girls and road trippers and carneys. He'd also dealt with bikers, drunks, whores, and bail jumpers. Some of them were handy with horses and some were not. The one certain fact was that a foreman didn't need a piece of anybody's woes. He had plenty of his own.

"I got a fever to check on down yonder. Why don't you come along if you want." I looked at him braced by his fingertips in the doorway, a big man in beige work pants and a short-sleeved polo shirt. His skin was three shades darker than his pants, his neck and chest thick. He'd been known to joke about his high yellow Creole blood on nights when he played cards and it was a thing he could laugh about. He'd told me he was from Louisiana and Missouri both, but I'd never asked him exactly what that meant. All I knew for sure was that Thomas would never protect me from what was hard. He'd always be honest and readable.

"I'll give a hand," I said. "Anybody alive can see I need more to do."

Thomas made his way through the crosshatched shadows of late afternoon, pausing to speak to the bent old man I'd seen on my way in. I could tell the man was a boozer; that fact hummed in his nervous gray hands. He'd been sitting at the far end of the shed in a logo-stamped chair doing what he was supposed to, keeping folks away from Roy's horses. After Thomas spoke to him, the man gratefully shuffled off in the direction of the track kitchen. Permission to go have a smoke, I guessed. Or a cup of coffee. Or something stronger if he could find it.

"Jake's working out good enough." Thomas lifted an elbow in the old fellow's direction. "Don't play at poker, though, only pinochle, and trying to drag me into that shit. So far I'm staying strong."

The colt we visited looked plenty sick. Listless and hollow necked like he'd been off his feed. The urine smell in the stall was extra sour. The infrared lamp rigged above the door cast a gooey glow across his dull eyes. I eased in and held his halter while Thomas took a rectal temperature. The colt didn't even have the energy to nuzzle my offered palm. Thomas showed the numbers to the colt's groom, a hard-faced woman in a NASCAR shirt, and asked her to check his temperature again in an hour. He'd track down Roy because it was clear the horse needed to be shipped out of the barn.

"Man will have my hide if that spreads. I told him not to bring that colt in here yet. Came on transport from California, needed to be watched. I told him." I could see Thomas quarreling with Roy in his head so he could get it out of his system.

"What's the vet say?"

"We always use Marcus when we're here, you know that. He was in this morning drawing blood. Said to watch him, and all the time I'm seeing sickness floating in the air. Horse needs to get on home, ain't gonna run here anyway. Just about got bucked shins."

I thought about the thin-boned animal I'd seen and touched. The colt was a blue blood, probably purchased as a yearling for a couple hundred grand. The pressure to race money horses like that early—to make them worth even more—was enormous. A lot of them couldn't take the pounding. Tendons bowed, sesamoids chipped, cartilage tore, and the horse would be out for months, if not forever. Filling your barn with green horses was a high-stakes gamble, but Roy liked it that way. The young ones were unmarked by failure; they could still be the next Secretariat or Winning Colors or Affirmed. Their owners could be plied with hopes, cocktailed with dreams, billed for their anticipation. A nice game, if you could survive it. Eric and I had proved how wretched it could be to play that game with the wrong people's money. We bought horses for the hasty, then for the crooked. Injuries, bad weather, bad luck—they all put us in the hole. The horses didn't win enough; the bills stacked up; the owners either left us or put us on the griddle. The pressure had made Eric a cheat. Me, a deserter.

Thomas invited me back after he'd checked in with the vet. "Just you and me and Granddad," he said, referring to his brand of whiskey. "We got to figure how to make the man hire you at top dollar, then I can tell you about the two pair last week that won me two hundred dollars." Thomas's fox red eyes went wet with a gleam. He was a lousy cardplayer from way back, and he knew it. But he fibbed as well as anybody on the shed rows.

I told him it was a deal.

"That Reno man's been sitting in some is what Jackie down at the Maple Leaf barn's telling me. Supposed to be right sharp at the table."

I shrugged like that wasn't news, although it was. I'd never known Reno to relax, much less gamble. "Everybody's got money to lose," I said. "That's the racetracker's first commandment."

Sunset. The heat-rinsed colors of the horizon. I wandered up the parade route taken by horses on race day, thinking to myself. There were no velvet-trimmed outriders or squeaking trumpets yet. Just damp, jagged stone and squared hedges. The track surface had been dragged smooth for workouts the next morning and was as unmarked as a beach after high tide. I scooted into the abandoned grandstand and watched the last of the starlings rush to the black magnets of the trees. One more day rolling by. I was twenty-seven years old, more or less healthy, more or less single, technically broke. But I didn't feel rock bottom. The track kept me from that. The races, the yearling sales—pageantry came and went in a rhythm here. Folks like me could straggle behind the fancy pageants. If Roy hired me, I'd live on the cash from my rides. I'd braid some manes and cover for some grooms at night to make more. I'd recover from Eric. As I watched the sun collapse beneath the hard hand of dusk, I figured my future would post itself on the tote board whether I was calculating it or not.

It seemed natural to drift by Alice's place to say good night. Her barn was my current anchor. It wasn't until later that I realized what a mistake it was. Alice Piersall was famous for hanging around the shed rows far longer than she needed to, offering up cocoa and snacks and her brand of shoving companionship. Most days she didn't drive home until midnight, only to be back before 6 A.M. The blind sounds of the barns, all that flesh and temperament, comforted her—or so she said. It was an atmosphere she loved to guard.

She pinned me down before I even saw her. "Got a question," she bellowed. "How much college did you get in the bag?"

I found her in the tack room standing over a small, hooded reading lamp that gave her chins a smoldering red glow. "Thought I'd come peek at the filly," I said.

"Well?"

"Two years, give or take. At the community college."

"I knew I remembered you taking classes, in bookkeeping and that management crap. I told Reno that this evening."

"No big thing." I breathed in the twilight that was sluicing over the stalls. "My roommate Michelle liked me to keep her company in class."

"So you didn't do it for yourself? To get smarter?"

Alice was worked up, hot and bothered about something, although I didn't know what. I doubted it was me. She was no longer wearing her vest, and the zipper of her coveralls had slipped low enough to reveal a plain gold chain at her throat. The chain seemed to ripple in the campfire flicker of the lamp. "College doesn't make you smart. I've heard you say that yourself. It just gets you organized and planes down your edges."

"Damn." Alice snuffed. "Been here one day and you're already throwing my own turds back at me. And this"—she pointed at a plywood workbench that held some unlabeled glass bottles and tobacco tins—"this voodoo doctoring of Reno's is stinking up my office. I believe I'm surrounded by crazies."

I offered my news as a distraction. "I had it out with Louisa Fett today. You hear about that?"

"You know I did. It's on everybody's smacking lips. Make you happy?"

"No."

"Mention it because you think it'll make *me* happy?"

I hesitated. "Maybe."

"Haw." Alice brayed like a burro. "And you'll be telling me now that's one reason to stay out of that college. So you can keep the Fayette County fighting edge."

I shrugged automatically. "I didn't enjoy it much. It was my fault."

"Nobody likes that girl. She should've gone off and married some dipstick by now, started training ponies for the 4-H fairs, which is about her speed." Alice shuffled through some invoices on her desk, looking busy. "You'll be all right."

"I won't blame her for coming after me."

"There's plenty of blame around here already," Alice said. "My life is salted with it."

I watched her deal out the pastel invoices once more as though she couldn't find what she was looking for. She was definitely on edge. I asked what was wrong.

Alice stopped moving for about five seconds, then spread her feet and lifted her arms from her sides like she did when she wanted to be even larger than usual. "There's nothing about it that's your business."

I shrugged and walked out. It would have been better for both of us if I'd kept walking, showed up the next morning for work with my helmet on and my mouth clamped closed. But I stopped, reeled myself backward a step or two, and apologized.

Alice deflated until her cheeks hung slack on either side of her tired mouth. "The secretary wants me to fill a race on opening day, and I hate that shit, I'm just sick of it. Like I'm their favorite two-bit operation to come to when the card's not full. Like my barn's loaded with ready-to-order, ready-to-fly dog meat. But they'll be good to me and Flare when the time comes, and I could use that."

"You really need the favor?"

"Yep. This time I do."

I knew she despised being thought of as low-rent, but help-ing a track fill races—even if it meant running your horse sooner than you planned or against fancier competition—wasn't always a bad rap. Some trainers took the request as a compliment, recognition that their horses were fit and game. And the favor would be returned; the race secretary would see to that. But Alice seemed to be considering something else, a worry with more bite. Money problems, I figured, like every-body else.

She switched off the lamp. The close darkness in the room became smells, a strange ointment of Reno's medicines, my breath, Alice's unsummoned evening sweat. "Do me a favor, Kerry. Come back with me to the farm tonight. Talk. Rest. I've got a daybed all set up."

I made another mistake. Even though the offer was a good one, one that could help me, I did what skulking track gypsies always do. I went ice cold at the thought of a plan that wasn't mine. I'd been to Alice's place. It was cluttered and mud tracked and warm like a home ought to be. But I couldn't help see the invitation as the first awkward step up a long, creaky ladder of obligation. Alice would suck me into whirlpools; she'd make me some kind of girl mascot. She'd want a loyalty I didn't have to give. My hesitation was enough.

"Get your ass out of here, then, if you don't want to come. I need to lock up." She went for a false cheerful sound in her voice that let me know just how bad I'd made things.

"Good night." I worked up a late whisper.

"Reno will start you at six," she said, charging off at almost her usual speed. Her words sounded like they were squirming from between clenched teeth. "I won't be here."

So I was left to descend into the backside on my own. I'd blown it somehow; that fact sawed sharp at my breastbone. But what was I supposed to do? Be a comfort to Alice Piersall? A comfort to anybody? I didn't have enough heart red blood cells left for that, not after Eric I didn't. And maybe I never would again. All I believed in right then, under the shotgun pattern of the stars, was work I was good at, animals whose speed I could control. Humans seemed to be creatures I could barely handle. I made my way into the muttered sounds of the track—the rustles and sighs, the drone of a far-off portable TV. It was like walking the unlit hallways of an old aunt's house, familiar and strange all at once. I held my hands out to the side for balance, and thought hard about what I'd already managed to buy and sell, lose and gain, on that hoof-cut springtime ground.

CHAPTER 5

*R*oy made hiring me as humiliating as possible. *Old times' sake,* he said. *Been dying to see you.* He stood next to me with his hairy hand snaking across my shoulders, then down my back to flick at my belt. *Want to hear all about it,* he said, how I rode for his *good friends up north.* He'd be taking a batch of horses there after the Derby. Maybe I could come along too, and didn't I look *fresh as a daisy.* I corralled his wrist just below the Rolex and gave it a hard squeeze. Roy was smart enough. He knew exactly how much crap a person would take before they slapped him or spit on his New Zealand boots. I could see that Thomas, who was supposed to be in conference with Roy's copycat assistant, was about to bust a gut. I'd picked up more horses, good ones, and the fact that riding for Roy meant I'd be four feet taller than him most of the time helped me keep my cool. I thought about what Alice would say when she found out I was exercising for Delvecchio again. How, in a weird way, she might even approve. "Sweat in the saddle," she'd say. "You do live for that."

You couldn't call it a normal morning. The meet opened the next day and workouts were beginning to take on an edge. I'd shown up to find out that the zigzagging claimer I was riding for Alice would be in the number two race. Alice had decided to help the track fill its card. I also found out she wasn't at the barn—just like she'd said—and Reno was running the show. We do-si-doed around him, all of us. I worked the claimer in blinkers, breezed the little filly three steady furlongs, then took a nice, solid mare out as a rabbit for Rogelio and big old Flare, who blew by us like he was turbocharged. The air was cold and damp, making the backstretch mist as dense and layered as mountain shale. The horses spooked some, then loved it. They cut through the pewter light like falcons from the sky.

When I finished my heartburn visit to Roy, I went back to Alice's to help out. She was still running a hand short even though a new hotwalker, a pale smiling woman named Jenny, had just signed on. I cooled out two horses, which gave Danny time to tinker with the portable whirlpool that had gone on the fritz. Jenny and I circled the frosty oval of the yard for twenty minutes with tired horses on shanks, our eyes open for any signs of lameness. Walkers from the barn across the way turned on some salsa music and mixed in with us, and we talked about the weather, Kentucky basketball, and juicy rumors we'd heard that were safe enough to pass on to competitors or strangers.

I watched Reno pack the filly's hooves with one of his more common concoctions, a blackish mess of cedar and pine tar, though I didn't dare ask him why he thought she needed it. Filly had run just fine. When I'd shown up at five-thirty, still hunchbacked from another cold night in the Chevy, Reno was sitting outside Flare's stall with a black slab Bible across his knees, his hands running over its leathery cover like it was an animal that needed to be calmed. Danny and Dawg were cleaning stalls and staying well clear of their foreman. The Bible wasn't new to me—Reno'd been known to pray over his horses before a race—but something about this stunt seemed different. He'd set a camp lantern at his feet, where it couldn't do his eyes much good, and he seemed to be opening the Bible swiftly and at random, reading whatever verses he trapped under a stabbing finger. The few words I caught sounded punishing and mean. They fascinated the big horse, though. He peered in right over Reno's elbow, ears pricked forward, with his buddy rooster perched on the peeling wood next to him, the bird's eyes a scornful gold.

I was ready to knock off at nine, hungry and grungy from my share of horse sweat and slobber. The morning gloom had burned off, and I figured the crew would do fine without me. Dawg was covered from neck to knees with a slick of linseed oil from a spill in the feed room, but he didn't seem too flustered about it. He was more sure of himself every day. Danny had gotten the whirlpool working, a thing which made him happy and loud; he stood a horse in it right away. Jenny took off to cadge a few bucks from another barn. I was headed for the public showers across the road when Alice showed up stewing in her own personal vinegars.

She was with Marlou Johnson, another midlevel trainer who'd suffered her share of setbacks. Marlou's way of dealing with the prejudices and skullduggeries of the business was to dress like a regular southern lady—in wool skirts, jackets, blouses with bows, makeup, teased and sprayed hair—and make a story out of that. She was the trainer who looked like a school secretary, or a Girl Scout leader, both of which she'd once been. She complained about how hard barn work was on nylons and fingernails. Journalists loved it, even though her horses seldom did well in the races that mattered. The other trainers dismissed her as "sweet." I knew she wasn't any sweeter in the confines of her girdled heart than Alice was, but she'd gotten a certain number of monkeys off her back. There were clients out there who were happy to leave horses with a Scout leader, assuming they wouldn't get scammed. Marlou made her way.

She broke off her chat with Alice with a puzzled look on her roundish, rouged face. I guessed that Alice had proposed some kind of wolfish deal that didn't sit too well with Marlou, not so early in the day. I decided to use the occasion to tell Alice about my expanded employment.

I got the full treatment.

"What you're telling me is you're about to become the black widow spider of Delvecchio's life, is that it?" She was hanging some bridles from a cleaning hook but still managed to grind a little outrage into her voice.

"Thomas McGhee got me the job. I've got nothing to do with Roy."

"Which never means he's got nothing to do with you. If I had a dollar for every girl who limped out of that man's bed—"

"It's just work," I said. I noticed Marlou biting her lip.

"No," Alice said. "It's never just work. Not to me. But I can see how that makes some sense in your slow-learning head. I believe I'm looking at a bad day here, so let's leave it at that. You swear to work my string first, every day, crack of dawn?"

I nodded out my version of solemn.

She eyeballed me. I could see she'd gotten her hair washed, clean clothes on under the green coveralls, which was more than I'd managed. She squinted above the bowls of her cheeks, though I couldn't for the life of me read any feeling, good or bad, in that squint. If I'd gone too far with her the night before, she wasn't advertising it.

"Do me a favor, Kerry, and change the subject. Tell me a good thing about my horses."

I did a quarter spin on the heels of my boots, pushed the hel-

met off my forehead. "The new one ought to go in blinkers
every time. I think you'll be right about him. He worked like a
charm." Then she dismissed me exactly the way I wanted to be
dismissed—without a smile or a stutter—though I still felt dicey
about the way we were dealing with each other, like I'd missed
whatever message I was supposed to receive.

The bathroom had been remodeled since I'd left. It had
working showers, new sinks, good mirrors, and lights. About
time, I thought, since it would be the busiest spot on the
grounds before long. Grooms, hotwalkers, riders—a lot of folks
lived like nomads for the whole meet, then headed over to
Churchill Downs or up the coast to Maryland and beyond. I
read a sign taped above the paper towel dispenser that advertised a free Easter Sunday dinner sponsored by the track. I
rolled my head from side to side to loosen my neck muscles and
wiped some backstretch grit off my cheeks. With less than forty
honest bucks to my name, I'd be there Easter for the turkey and
gravy and waxed paper cups. It wouldn't be the first time, and
maybe not the last.

I brushed my teeth double time while a hollow-eyed woman
in a stretched blue sweater rinsed her two kids in one of the
showers. The kids squealed and jabbered in Spanish until the
block walls echoed with their energy. I watched the mother dry
both of them with a thin white towel that had probably been
lifted from a motel. I offered her one of mine, but she wouldn't
take it. While their dad worked, those kids would play at the
edges of the parking lots or in the empty field near the equip-
ment sheds. They'd nap on the squeaky bench seat of an over-
driven sedan. The mother was younger than I was, much
younger, and I wondered if the next time I saw her she'd be pat-
ting out tortillas next to a camp stove, trying not to think about
the immigration people or new shoes for the kids.

I peeked into a mirror, then undressed. My objective opinion was that I looked like hell. Not even a long, hot rinse was going to change that. Slim to begin with, I'd lost enough weight to worry about. My hipbones and ribs were downright gaunt. My tits drooped. The palm-sized bruises bleeding yellow and green along my side and left thigh didn't improve the look. If anyone walked in they'd assume I'd been kicked—and kicked good—by a pissed-off horse. Though I didn't know how they'd match that assumption with the pressed-in quality I read in my face. That seemed to come from beyond horses.

A shampoo was better than nothing, however, and before long I was enjoying the pleasures of soap and water, reminding myself that my body still knew simple cravings. I washed my hair twice. I scrubbed fingers and toes. I shaved my legs, which was a damn hard thing to do standing in a shower room with a dull razor. When I finished, I buffed my skin until I was convinced that every inch of it was alive. The sight of clean underwear and completely steamed mirrors made me feel prankish. I even survived rebraiding my hair.

While I was pulling a rumpled shirt over my head, a heart-faced gal with a black wire ponytail barged through the door, toothbrush and toothpaste in hand. She looked like she was about fifteen, neat in her faded jeans and oversized sweatshirt. She wasn't a rider. I could tell that from her tippy-toe walk. Something about the enthusiastic way she swiped a mirror clear, leaning over the white sinks and grinning at herself, gave me the willies, though, so I packed up my ditty bag and slipped out as fast as I could. I thought about her glossy hair and how groups of guys gathered west of the barns to talk or swagger or make bets with their loose change day and night. I knew how a girl like that could make a place at the track. The truth was I'd fallen into that ditch a few times myself, giving fast blow jobs to dusty boys who smelled like molasses and linament, laughing about it, sharing cool beers. I squeezed my bag under my arm and stepped to the muddy fringe of the path, where I spit until my mouth was dry.

I was good at shoving bad memories aside, always had been, so it seemed sensible to head over to the track kitchen and get some eggs and coffee and toast. Maybe I could find room on a heated breakfast plate to make fun of myself and some of my mistakes. But it's funny how we're all targeted for awful moments in our lives, the kind that freeze up the circulation and the soul all at once, how we don't have any control over when those moments occur. I've never been exactly clear on who's in charge of the universe, but I know she's not interested in making things easy for me. Not dull. Not easy.

They led the mare right off the transport van in front of me. There she was, splendid in a red traveling blanket, all four legs double-wrapped in blue, though the white stockings on her forelegs were still partly visible. She was commanding as the males in her family are—I'd seen her sire run, and many of her half brothers. Broad between the eyes, neck fitting perfectly into a powerful chest and shoulders. Even in the starburst glare of the trailer, I recognized that copper-ore coat, the short-coupled stance that advertised pure Quarter Horse-type speed. There weren't many mares who looked like that. I knew it was Sunny.

Then the fear bore down. Eric had sold her. Or Eric was here. Or Eric was using the only bait he had for some kind of terrible lure. A groom stepped ahead of her and tried to coax her down the rubber-lined ramp. She wouldn't move. She looked out over the barns, the knotty traffic of people and dismayed horses, and chose not to budge. I felt myself drifting forward, as though the trampled patch of ground underneath me had become a breakaway ice floe. *Don't rush. Never rush her,* I thought, trying like all hell to transmit my thoughts to the unfamiliar groom. Sunny always liked a view. And it never paid to contradict her.

I floated into a greenish oblong of shade, moving in just the right way to have the mare look at me. Only me. And that's when I saw it, how the poll between her ears was more peaked than domed, the jawline more shallow, how the pucker of the white blaze was all wrong. Her coat faded to a Georgia dust red, and I realized with a crushed-tin feeling that I'd made a terrific error. That was a lovely mare, a well-balanced mare. But she was not my Sunny. I'd made her up.

A doctor, or a friend if I'd had one, would have blamed my mistake on being hungry and tired. But I knew better. I'd gone kin to mourning mothers who grapple ghost babies in their arms. I wanted what I didn't have bad enough to grieve it into the world.

I sagged against a fence that ran near the transport trailer. Track security had plenty of experience with people who drank or bet over their limits. Surely they'd cart me away too, for wishing beyond mine. Unfortunately, even my forlorn, black-jacked moment didn't last. They trotted the mare off the ramp and followed her with a nervous bay, another chestnut, a hammerhead gray. This was a racetrack, after all, even though the beauty of the grounds sometimes made it possible to forget that. This was a Vegas-speed shuffle of humans and horseflesh. Nothing lasted for long around here, except hope.

It was several minutes before I could breathe without feeling the concussion of my heartbeat. I hadn't been honest with myself. I wanted Sunny back more than I could say. She was all I had left of my hard work and striving. The thought of losing her paralyzed me. The idea of seeing Eric paralyzed me. To stop my hands from quivering, I tried to borrow a rule from my mama's book, one that seemed to work for her. Always look the devil in his wide red eye. Give full face to what you fear.

I'd called Eric from a truck stop a few hours after I left him. He'd answered the barn phone because there was no one else left to answer it. He'd become the wrong man to work for.

"I only took what was mine," I told him.

"Kerry." His voice was thin, without marrow.

"Don't say a word. I'm calling to set things straight."

"That wasn't my damn money. Yours either. I'm going to need it back." I couldn't hear anything above the ratchet of diesel engines, not a radio tune or a hungry, stall-banging horse. For one black second I wondered if he'd gone that far—gotten rid of them, every one.

"How's Sunny?"

"Fine," he said, though without any kind of feeling I recognized. "I'm running her whether you're here or not. Sticking to the schedule. She's going to be goddamn Mare of the Year. Are you heading to your mother's?"

I wasn't about to tell him my plans. I didn't answer.

"Go on down there, then. Cool off. We've got a few days left on the big loan, maybe a week."

"I'm out of it," I told him. "You might think about saying you're sorry." I didn't even hang up, just wiped my hands on my jeans and left the gray club of the phone receiver blowing in the highway wind. It seemed the right thing to do at the time.

Now I had to wonder. He probably had money left, maybe enough to pay the vig on the loan. He had the horses, though technically he couldn't sell them without my signature. He also had his new friends, the ones who'd crowded me out of my own barn with their surefire tips, their drugs, their schemes for Sunny, their loan-shark cousins who were advertised as boys who would *always come through*. I knew what that meant. That meant business first. Part of me was sorry I wouldn't be around to see my husband drink down the trouble he'd brewed with those people.

The other part of me was nothing but squeezed-in sorrow. I was bound to Eric Ballard yet, I was, I was. The best feelings I'd ever had about myself had come into focus in that man's dark eyes. I remembered the tight lounge line of his soothing words to me, how he'd slept like a child on our wedding night, how I hadn't been able to sleep at all even after going rigid with love, the kind we were so good at. Eric's body, as strong as it was, seemed barely lived in. No scars. No badly healed bones. I lay there watching over him, and watching over myself too, I guess, thinking of everything we hoped to do together and how we didn't have to do it all at once.

If only I'd taken my own advice.

I needed to call him again. Confess my part in things, even if I didn't use those words. He'd tell me about Sunny's training if I asked, knowing how I liked my good-girl rewards.

It was a lot easier to plan a call to Eric than to do the deed. When I finally found an open phone, I couldn't go near it. A force field welded from embarrassment and hurt surrounded the phone from ground to sky. Calling was a bad idea. Calling was weak. Eric would get to me in some new kidney-pounding way if I called. But sizzly angel images of my good horse hung in front of my face, taunting me. I had to do something for the real horse and the once-real me. To relieve the bright light and the gnawing.

I got the answering machine first. Swore and mewed a little, then looked at my watch and realized Eric had to be in the barn, he just had to, because this was the late-morning time he used to sleep off his uppers or pay the bills, whichever seemed more important at the time. On the second try I got somebody who sounded a lot like Salty, a farrier we sometimes used, but if it was Salty he pretended not to know me. Eric picked up after a long minute.

"It's me. I was thinking about Sun."

He drew a breath that sounded like an unspoken bluff. "I'm glad to hear from you. Have you forgiven me yet?"

I waited.

"All right. I can understand that, honey, I really can. Maybe you'd like to know I've taken some punishment myself. I've been paying it back."

"Are you square with those guys? Did Dean help out?" I went from irritation to dug-in stubbornness. If Eric had settled his debts so quickly, if his father had bailed him out like he said he'd never do again, I'd weep tears of frustration. And relief.

"No. *No.*" There was a bark of harsh laughter away from the phone. "Got my ass *and* my arm in a sling right this minute, no thanks to Daddy Dean. We owe twenty K more with the vig. I don't have it."

"They beat you up?"

"And I'm feeling no pain." There was another hacking cough of amusement. "I'm sending somebody down to your mother's with a peace offering, darling. To make it up to you. Because I've got a plan. Running three horses this weekend, including your precious Sunsquall. Once she's tuned up I'll do the big races here and at Big A. Win the dough. Aim for the Breeders Cup. Meanwhile, I'm trying to get buyers for the two-year-old. And we've got almost a week to get the cash. Me," he giggled, "I've got a plan."

He was as bad as he'd ever been. Words slurring on Percodan or Valium or off-the-cliff fear. It was possible he was lying to get what little help I could offer or just to mess with my messed-up mind. Eric could be a terribly capable man.

"You'll be glad to know they didn't use a pipe. Not on me. They're saving the pipe for Sunny."

"You bastard," I shouted, suddenly grabbing at the phone box like it was his pretty, dream-doped face. "What did you tell them this time? What have you done?"

I heard phone clicks and satellite snaps on the line. Nothing else.

"I'm calling the stewards up there." I gouged my knuckles into the change slot of the phone. "I'll tell them what I know about your so-called friends. I'm calling the commission right now, you creep."

"Kerry, Kerry, Kerry." He sang my name about ten times. "It's cool. The early odds on Sunny are seven to one. They'll go up more if Vargas puts his horse in."

"And you might not win. Remember Stevie? Do—you—remember—Stevie?" I felt like a passenger in a skidding car. Ideas, pleas, sentences broke up in my mind.

"I'll never forget what happened to Stevie. I'm not a god-damn robot. I hate this . . . I hate these guys as much as you do."

"No, you don't." My throat was rigid with disgust. "They belong to you. I can't wait until they pull your license."

His voice went hard and low, like he'd finally found some subterranean level of himself he could control. "You think I fucking care? I'm going to stay in one piece, keep my horses in one piece. That's the bottom line. You could help by sending that money back."

"It's mine."

"It is not." His voice still cool, even more guarded. "Nothing you got from up here belongs just to you." And he hung up.

$\mathcal{W}$hat a solo woman will do to save herself.

I appeared to have a single problem with an on-the-dime so-
lution. Twenty or thirty thousand dollars would buy time for
Eric and what was left of our string, at least in the short run. No
one would threaten Sunny, no one would bust arms to have her
throw a race. I could wire my scoundrel husband the ten grand I
had in the car. Maybe I owed him that much. I surely owed it to
Sunny. It was no use believing I'd made a clean break coming
back here. I hadn't. Nothing about me felt clean.

But the ten thousand was the easy part. The hard part would
be getting the rest. I could ask Roy Delvecchio for money. Roy
would want me on his horses, in his bed, on his arm when he
thought I looked good enough, at his side when an owner
wanted to schmooze with real horse people, the kind who still
got dirty. I'd get some new clothes out of the deal—he'd have to
spot me those—and the chance to spend a bedeviled summer at
the Meadowlands or Aqueduct or Belmont, the scrappy little
hells I'd just left.

I could ask Billy T. for a loan. He'd lend me the money be-

cause he had it and because there was something between us
that hadn't gone away after a stretch of empty time and error.
Which was why I wouldn't go to him.

And Alice? I had no blessed idea what that woman wanted,
ever. Would she help me? Could she? I knew the begging I'd
have to do to make this deal was going to be some kind of surrender. I wasn't sure I wanted to surrender anything to her.

I could drive north, make some kind of stand there.

I could hightail it to another track. Lie to myself about fresh
starts. Again.

I could be a total chickenshit.

I was stuck on that idea, curlicuing the backside like a three-
wheeled wagon, when Dawg swung around a corner with a
sudsy bucket in each hand. "Yo," he said, both to me and to the
hot water that sloshed down his legs. "A man at the place asking
after you. Tricked-up dude. Danny says he's a trainer."

I ran a quick hand across my face checking for stray tears or
snot. "What's he look like? Mustache?"

Dawg shook his head and tripped on past with his buckets.
"Got some white hair, all I saw. Might be he's still there."

Billy T. Always wanting to make things easy, even if they
weren't easy for him. The thought of him on Alice's row, looking over her horses and saying nice things about them, made my
cheeks burn hot. God only knew what Alice would say to him in
return. Or to me.

She made it sound like I'd just missed him and that she didn't
have time to give me the details because her time had already
been wasted. "Tolliver was here," she said from behind her desk
in the tack room. "I was going to leave you that much on a
note."

I knew better than to thank her.

"We're not in the business of sorting out your dates, Kerry.

Reno was reminding me of that." Alice angled her head toward the loft above the stalls where Reno was rooting around for extra sections of alfalfa. I knew he'd never said such a thing.

"Sorry I wasn't around."

"I know it. I know you do everything possible to hide your charms under a bushel basket. Tolliver's nice enough, and I got some fancy words out of him about my Flare horse which cheered me." Alice's eyes shifted, then glimmered like she enjoyed my fidgeting. "Good thing you're cleaned up. I'd say the man is going to ask you out to dinner."

I blushed to my eartips. It was too much. Billy trying to be nice to me, and Alice shearing him off for it exactly when I'd been thinking about them both as human bank accounts, and Reno and his boys working hard on the aisle behind me because that was the first matter at hand, working hard for the horses. That was all I really wanted. I didn't want a dinner date or a quarrel or ugly debts to settle. I wanted to ride and muck and cool down. I wanted what I could manage. I spun away from Alice and threaded my way past Dawg, who was sprinkling the ground with water to keep the dust down. Some fat, streaky sparrows had dropped in behind him to peck for seeds. They fled in front of my hard strides, settled for a second, then fled again. From the black heat of his stall, the rooster flapped and screeched.

Half a minute later Danny caught up with me on the far side of the sales pavilion. A hand pulled at my waist and he was there, breathing hard. "Whoa. Hold on. You run off so fast I almost didn't catch you."

I looked at him, too surprised to ask what the hell he thought he was doing.

"It's my break. And about damn time. I heard the Hell Bitch ride you down, thought maybe I could buy you a cigarette."

I stopped walking. Saw how his sleeves were rolled up to where his arms went white and hairless, and how his skin crinkled around his sandy eyelashes. Wondered how to tell him to get lost. "Don't smoke," I said, gulping in the air I hoped would give me a steadiness I didn't feel. "Though it's about the day to start."

"I know how to handle that," he said. He nudged the flat of his hand near my hip, and there was a flash, just a tiny one, of a small gold stud in his left ear. "Visit my club over here a minute."

"I'm not in the mood."

"Good," he said, "I'm all about moods."

Danny's club was the trunk of whatever expensive car he thought he could get away with leaning against. Just the day before, he told me, it had been a midnight blue Bentley. There'd been a nice Porsche 944 nearby, but it was too low to loiter on. Today's choice was some kind of champagne gold Cadillac with a Virginia vanity plate that read RUNWIN. It looked like it needed sitting on.

"Did you really whomp that girl like I heard?" Danny lit a hand-rolled cigarette and watched the smoke ribbon into the air before he put it to his lips. "Sounds like a real catfight."

Louisa Fett. I'd been lucky enough not to think about her for a whole day. "Yeah. It's not a habit of mine, but I'm sorry to say it happened."

"There's plenty of rough types around." Danny waved his hand up the hill. "I know you hold your own. Have to, especially in that barn."

"Alice is all right. She's fair."

"And piss mad about it as far as I can tell. Reno too. Acting like the world's about to meet its end."

I slid onto the spotless bumper of the Caddy, thinking I'd try to stay put for one polite minute. "You just haven't been in Kentucky long enough. What with tournament basketball and the Derby coming up, the world *is* about to end. That's how people feel around here. A lot crazy."

Danny sucked in some smoke and settled next to me. "It's different in California. I was there for a long while and liked it most of the time. You kind of get in your own space. Made me forget about the uptight life."

"So why'd you leave all the good weather?" I was happy for him to talk about himself.

"Same reasons anybody would. Better job. Little trouble with the girlfriend. Ex cetera. I ain't too exceptional."

I shook my head. "None of us are. But you didn't haul all the way out here to work for Alice."

"No." He shrugged. "The good job was in Florida. I just didn't get there in time. So I do my stretch here like everybody else, wait till something comes up."

"And the books you're always sticking your nose in?" I glanced over to see him pulling his hair out of its curling ponytail. He was a drifter. He'd admitted that. But even drifters had their stories.

"You noticed that, huh? It's just a gig I have, sort of like a lucky rock in my pocket. I used to read war books as a kid, so I took back to it. World War Two, Civil War, some detective mysteries. Passes the time and all that."

"I never had the patience for it," I said.

He shrugged, his streaked hair spreading across his neck. "Looks like you've put yourself together pretty good. You know what you're doing. I'm more or less a scavenger type, pick up one habit here, one there. All kind of bits and pieces. Books come from a long time ago."

"And the fancy tea stuff? That from California?"

He laughed and tossed his cigarette out over the pavement

like it was a tiny baton. "I wouldn't be much good if I didn't have some California craziness in me, would I?"

He talked a little about Santa Anita and Del Mar and Golden Gate, about the spread-out cities and the dull, weedy concrete patches he'd lived on. He told a good story about helping a fellow with some stone-mouthed Quarter Horses at Ruidoso, which led to a few weeks on a wild commune in northern New Mexico. No meat, no clothes. He'd loved his stretch at the Fair Grounds in New Orleans, although the steady Cajun partying had been bad for him and he'd tried to cut back on that. He said he'd never been married, and I didn't see a reason to doubt it. He liked being a roadie. He brought up a short stretch in the army, where he got his GED and cleared up some troubles, mostly with his parents, who he mentioned only once. He'd done some work as a mechanic in the military and still liked to mess with engines now and again, though there was something about horses—he wasn't sure quite what—that he liked better and kept coming back to.

"I'd like to do what you do. Ride them that way, so you really know the suckers top to bottom. I never learned."

"I could teach you fast enough. Down on the lower track." I made the offer before I even thought about it.

He turned to me, elbows on his knees, the white sun blanking out his face. "No ma'am, I'm just talking. It's a missed-out thing I think about. One of a few."

"It's not that hard," I said, scrambling to say the right words because, after the morning I'd had, it somehow seemed important. "I hardly remember when I couldn't ride a little."

"Girls look better anyhow," he joshed. "Just don't tell Rogelio I said so. Vain little prick."

Thinking on Rogelio led us to talk about Flare and his chances to win on this track, which we both thought were pretty good. It was slow, picnic-speed talk. The kind men and women have when they're dawdling between caution and want. I'd been there a few times, although I'd never been able to predict what would happen next, good stuff or bad. Then Danny asked why I wasn't a jockey and how I'd gotten where I was.

"Like you said earlier, I'm not too exceptional. Basically too big for a jock, though the sweatbox would probably keep me on the borderline. I never seriously thought of going that way. Just wanted some horses to ride and got to them the only way I could afford to—working for somebody else. Show horses first, then racehorses. I thought about being a trainer for a while, but that fell through."

"Well, it's not too late yet."

"Hard to say what it's too late for." I pushed some of my own loose hair behind one ear. "I keep an open mind."

Danny stepped away to light another cigarette. When the Cadillac rose against my thighs, I realized how tense I'd held myself.

"I heard things aren't so good with your husband." He watched his smoke again, like it might surprise him in some way.

"That's not the half of it. You ought to be careful about what you hear."

"So I'm asking you, Kerry." His voice was gentle in that unaccented, untraceable way of his. "If you want to talk some about it."

"It's not even a good beer story. That makes me as mad as anything." I stood and wrapped my arms around myself like I ought to hold a few things in. I understood now there were pieces of that life I didn't yet know how to throw away, parts a happier woman would cherish. "I hooked up with the wrong guy. He had some money and we made some good decisions, then we made some bad ones. The whole thing turned to shit, and I'm sorry to say to you that I'm the one who turned tail and took off."

He was quiet for a minute. "Ain't a lot of shame in running. I've done it enough."

"Yeah, well," I said, swallowing, "maybe you're faster than me."

He was behind me, rubbing my arm just above the elbow, before my voice broke. The wretchedness I felt about Eric, the mess I'd made with him, ran smack into the feelings his touch set off, a lightning stalk from breastbone to belly. Just what I'd been afraid of. "Damn," he said. Then said it again. "You oughtn't take it so hard."

I covered my eyes with my wrist, but he was there anyway, so close I could sense his body heat along the canyon of my back. "My husband got a horse killed," I said, turning to him. "There's a reason to take things hard."

Danny narrowed his eyes. "You mean like a insurance scam?"

"Not this one. This was nothing but meanness. It was supposed to scare Eric into getting his act together. Which he did for a while. He paid his installment."

I was the one who found the horse. Stellar Harmony, or Stevie as we called him. I'd been half awake, worrying as usual about money and screwed-up training schedules, so when I heard noise from the barn nearest the farmhouse we rented, I checked. Stevie was down, and I thought it was the colic we always feared, a twisted gut, blocked, the animal dead or squirming. But when I went into the stall to soothe him, he tried to rise on one strong foreleg. His muzzle frothed with pain. There was blood in the straw; I could see its thick streaks and smears. Blood on the cinches of his blanket.

"What'd they do?" Danny spread his hands wide and made a zapping sound between his teeth, a sound that made me go cold. "One of those battery shock deals on the tongue and ass, make it look like colic?"

I kept saying to myself, *Don't mess it up. Don't lose him. Don't.* I did that until I saw the length of dead-gray pipe in the aisle, laid clean and alone like an offering, and Eric coming into the seared yellow square of my frantic vision, and my pleas for medicine, all the medicine we had, and Eric's face, crooked and shamed and ricocheting between me and our crippled, unstoppable colt. And Eric kicking the cheap, brutal pipe, trampling it like he could destroy what it was and what it meant right then and there. Which he couldn't.

"Smashed his cannon bone," I told Danny. "Easy as pie." I thought of Eric filling a syringe with every painkiller he could find. Eric shaking with disbelief. "He looked like some kind of roadkill."

"Heard of something like that out of Chicago once, a mob deal, but most guys these days, they like the insurance."

"They got their money. Only because Eric borrowed it from another shark. Turns out they're all connected. They want tips, races fixed."

"That don't last," Danny said, shaking his head. "I seen it plenty of times. Stewards are sharp. Word gets around."

"The dead horse belonged to us. We buried him on the farm, didn't even call in a vet. Tips are mostly bullshit anyway, so some of them worked out. I left when Eric decided our best horse needed to throw me and look gate sour. He was getting beyond desperate."

"You didn't do it, huh?" Danny scanned me up and down, arms crossed. "Wouldn't pull his crap?"

"I did it." I turned until I faced the shiny, sightless row of cars. "I left after Eric took a few swings at me. He didn't think my stunt was convincing."

"Jesus idiot. They oughta bust his legs next."

"They probably will after our best mare runs this week. He still owes at least thirty grand, short term."

"Damn." Danny whistled. "Got in way over, didn't he? Sounds like a stupid son of a bitch, if you don't mind my saying."

"Forget it. It's the best you could say about either one of us." My voice hung high and girlish.

"Hell, he's a rich boy, right? Not an old-time tracker? Coming down on him'll make a nice message to customers. Like, say, a public service announcement." I heard a gravelly laugh. "But you're out of it."

I floated on his laughter and the confident speed of his words. "Don't know where I am exactly," I said, "which is why I'm in Kentucky."

He laughed some more. "Aw, they'll leave you alone. You're a female. You didn't take the loan. You got good reasons to walk away."

"You're a better talker than my mother. And you don't look a bit like her." I propped myself against the Cadillac again. "Keep at it and I'll stop feeling like I have to bail the bastard out."

"Like you have what he needs." He was facing away from me, the tips of his flat mechanic's fingers wedged into his back pockets. He'd been pacing, working his legs into the words of my tale.

"I've got a little something. Been thinking I ought to give it to him."

Danny pulled up in front of me. He looked genuinely surprised. "You got a soft heart is what you got. If it was me, the man who beat me down wouldn't see a nickel."

"Well, maybe I'll call it my bad-conscience money." I gripped the rim of a waxed taillight and squeezed until my hands buzzed. "My—what do you call it?—penance kind of thing."

Danny licked his lips toward a snarl. He caught himself, though, and wiped his mouth with the back of his hand. I decided he was better looking when he was just short of angry. "You do what you want. That's what I always say to myself. We do what we want. You got a chunk of change, go for it."

"I don't have it all," I said, wondering why I was telling him so much and knowing why at the same time. "What I need is enough to keep that mare safe. She means something to me even when Eric doesn't."

A well-dressed couple came toward us from the direction of the clubhouse. Their walk had a self-conscious hitch to it, and I wondered if they belonged to the Cadillac. Their chins were tilted in our direction, though it was hard to tell more than that because of their dark glasses.

"I could give you some shark names," Danny said, grabbing a hand and pulling me off the car. "I'd hate to do it because you don't need bad trouble like your husband's, but I could get names."

"No, thanks." We steered clear of the couple and their breeze of rose water and sheepskin. "I don't even have to think about that to know it's a lousy idea. Some other way. I just have to get used to begging."

"You really think they'd take down another horse? Instead of your man?" He pinched at my sleeve like he wanted to share secrets. I saw the thin, cool rim of his irises.

"I don't know. I'm afraid of their options, I can tell you that. I got out of there because I wanted to be left alone. Thing is, that might be too much to ask." I broke away with a jokey pat at his chest. Felt its bone and heat. There wasn't anything else I knew how to say.

"You could always double your money with bets," Danny said, easing into an uphill jog because he was late getting back to the barn. "Maybe do better than that. You could get more than the minimum life. It's what we're here for." And while he checked me once more over his shoulder, teeth showing, thighs gathering for speed, we both laughed out loud at that.

CHAPTER   7

i was headed back to the telephones to tell Eric I'd wire him
the ten thousand when I ran into Louisa slithering out of the
track kitchen with her big-bottomed, red-haired friend. I'd seen
her on the track, of course, but it was fairly easy for us to ignore
each other out there. We both knew how to stick to business. I
could tell from the cracked china look in Miss Fett's eyes that I
wasn't going to be let off the hook this time.

"I'm gonna kick your ass," she said. "I'm gonna go so far up
I'll be in your dreams."

"Nothing new there, Louisa." I looked over at the redhead
and almost winked.

"I been to security. They'll ream you out. *And* I'm passing the
word about you to everybody." The skin around her lips was
shiny with anger. "You won't last the week."

"I can already tell you've been at work," I said, letting my
arms go loose at my sides like I was exhausted with disappointment. "Billy was by Piersall's barn looking to take me to dinner."

I regretted the words as soon as I said them. Everything

about Louisa froze except her throat, which started gulping and pulsing like a frog's. The redhead looked confused, like maybe her ears were clogged, but she finally couldn't keep a smirk off her face, which only made a bad moment worse. I wasn't worried about Louisa as much as I was Billy. I suspected I'd just put him in an ugly position.

"You're dead meat, girl," Louisa squeaked. "Watch your back night and day because you are *dead*."

"Stick to your own rat hole, Lou. I'm sorry about the other day. Let's go from there."

She was too mad to answer. She swished her brittle Barbie hair to one side and gave me the finger instead. I responded in kind. Her buddy, who was doing a good imitation of a halfwit riding shotgun on a doomed stagecoach, repeated her friend's warning. "Watch it," she said, rumbling past me, but her words lacked pizzazz, and I guessed she was about ready to cool off on Louisa.

I got no answer at Eric's barn, not after a million times. Nothing at home, either. I fretted for more than an hour, then told myself to stay cool. The races would begin the next day. I couldn't allow the sizzle in the air to get to me. The University of Kentucky had won another game in the college basketball tournament, and that was all the railbirds wanted to talk about. Even Charlie was wearing a Wildcats sweatshirt over his usual green chamois. The chatter about basketball was nothing but a way to ease the racing tension, though. Another colt aiming for the Derby had shipped in the night before. Kentucky bred, French owned, trained by a no-nonsense Texan, he'd have his first workout the next day. Everybody was anxious to get a look at him. The racing media had shown up and were walking off with all the decaffeinated coffee in the secretary's office. The season was new, pockets were full, the lies with the strongest seams still held water. When I cut through Roy's yard, Thomas stopped me and invited me to drop by a card game a friend of his was putting together at the El Dorado. I tried to call Eric again. And again. Then I had no choice but to back off. Sunny would be fine for the night. Like most trackers, Eric would have to wait for another sunrise to change his misfortune.

*t*homas had told me to come by the game early—"when we playing college-boy stakes." This meant I was welcome to join in before things got serious. I could sit at the table and lose my cash right alongside the fellas for an hour, maybe two. That's how it worked. If I wanted an all-night romp, I'd have to ask around among the fresh hands at the track. Even though I wasn't a stranger, the real game was, like Thomas said, for the sergeant-striped motherfuckers.

I had other offers to party. Roy had set me up to share a motel room with some of his crew. The girls from there were going to start with beers at a nearby rockabilly bar, then work their way toward the UK campus, where they hoped to scare the puke out of some Paco Raban–smelling frat boys or get laid or both. Jenny the hotwalker was going dancing somewhere in Frankfort. Danny had hooked up with a guy he knew down at Maple Leaf Farms. Alice said she was having dinner at her place with old friends, a premeet tradition that went back to her father's time. Reno wasn't going anywhere. He had a horse running at one-thirty the next afternoon. I imagined him stalking the cricket-spotted aisle, slipping his callused hands over tight ligament and bone, talking at the only congregation he cared for.

I showed up alone. There was plenty of celebrating going on—horse people never miss an excuse for a good time. I'd considered staying in the motel room so I could feel sorry for myself in the middle of all that wood paneling and burnt orange carpet. But I hadn't been able to seal any kind of deal with Eric. I was too wired to stay still. Even before I twisted through the smoky gap in the door of the room at the El Dorado Motor Court and somebody pressed a wet beer into my hand, I was anxious enough to fall into a hot tub of trouble.

The room belonged to Wiley Dubois, longtime manager of a good public stable based in California. He'd be in town only a couple of days, just long enough to settle in a few horses and the assistant trainer who would be in charge of them. Wiley had a deal with his boss that he got at least one trip to Florida and one to Kentucky each spring, no matter how flimsy the pretenses. His East Coast friends ought to see him now and again, was how he put it, and try to keep his hand out of their pitiful pockets.

Wiley was a short, stocky man with an oversized head that he covered with a black watch cap. He was in his sixties and liked to mention his days as a punk on the waterfront in San Francisco. The scar tissue above his eyes was evidence of some kind of truth to his tales of brawling and breaking heads for the unions. He loved to say that the racing business was as easy as pissing, filled with pussies and country club fags. But he'd never left the biz, not after his first steady job. And he talked tougher than he acted, as though his yarning on about his bad history was a joke we all ought to get. He ran a decent barn. Had the kind of upright, careful authority with horses some people can

develop. Paid for the first run of booze at his card games. That
was what everybody counted on.

The guy who handed me my first sweating bottle of beer was
tall and shaggy, not somebody I recognized. The woman leaning into the closed plastic-lined drapes was familiar, though.
She worked at Calumet and had the gray hairs to prove it.
There were probably a dozen people in the room, some sitting
at a table that had been set up near the door to the bathroom,
some bench-sitting on the edge of the one double bed, some
milling around near the entrance. I heard what sounded like
somebody pawing impatiently through a bathtub of store-
bought ice. I could smell whiskey and flat beer and lime juice,
although the cigar Wiley was sucking on at his corner of the
table was enough to overpower every smell but the acid cut of
human sweat. Thomas was sitting next to Wiley, mouthing an
unlit cigar of his own. I could see the tombstone shape of an un-
opened pack of cards inside his shirt pocket. Gilbert White and
a guy named DaSilva, who I'd met maybe once, were also at the
table. The people on the bed, who managed to look restless and
drunk all at once, were new to me. Part of the early crew like I
was, I supposed. People who hadn't managed to be invited
somewhere they'd actually fit.

"Heeeey." Thomas motioned me over. "Got you a seat if you
got the jack." I could see from the red threads in his eyes he'd
already started drinking. I could also see that he'd cleared me
with Wiley but not the other guys. "I told Kerry she could sit in
a minute like she used to do," he went on, "and y'all got nothing
to say about it."

Wiley worked his cigar up and down between his teeth like it
was an obscene toggle switch, then reached under his chair for a
Ziploc bag of poker chips. I knew he didn't give a sweet damn.
Gilbert White, a heavy black man who helped run the brood-

mare operation at Spendthrift, acted like he hadn't heard a word Thomas said. He stroked at the fuzzy edge of the paper money packed into his brown cowhide wallet and kept his eyes down. DaSilva was the hard case. He opened his mouth in a wet, pantomime laugh and kicked the chair I was supposed to sit in away from the table with his boot. Then he arched one of his inky eyebrows to let me know he would enjoy taking my money. "Girl's dollars as good as mine," he said, and he leaned back in his chair, waiting for Wiley to cut and deal.

Roy had paid me in cash so I had a little more than sixty bucks folded into the back pocket of my jeans, which wasn't enough even for Thomas's college-boy stakes. I wasn't there for a big score, just some distraction, but I'd still have to be careful. Wiley ran his game simple and fast. Seven-card stud, no frills, no bullshit. Dealer could call for five-card if he wanted. One-dollar ante until everybody got their finger muscles warmed up, then it went to five. That's when they'd expect me to leave. Until one or two other guys showed up and everybody had the perfect buzz on, DaSilva was right. My money was just green enough.

I'm a better than average poker player. Picked up most of what I know from my stepdad, who thinks gambling on horses is no better than whizzing into the wind, while playing cards of a night is an almost religious test of character. He also thinks playing cards is fun as all hell. I'd been lucky that way, learning my drinking and bluffing habits from a hillbilly with the devil's sense of humor. I wasn't going to be able to stay at Wiley's table long enough to learn what I really needed to know: how DaSilva masked himself when his cards were good, or how much of a risk taker Gilbert might be. But I knew Thomas and Wiley well enough to work a few hunches, and they knew me, and after forty-five minutes I was up $30, mainly because I'd been dealt some usable cards.

The shaggy-haired guy brought me a second beer, then a third. He was hovering as close as DaSilva would let him. Behind us, talk centered on the best tips for the races the next day and news about a groom from Puerto Rico who'd been written up for intoxication and who'd probably be suspended. The usual stuff. I concentrated on picking my spots to raise and call bets, avoiding patterns, adding to the table talk in a sort of soft, underdog way. I thought I might be able to use being female as an advantage. DaSilva hoped to wipe me out; he made that clear with his sidelong looks and the noisy slap of his cards. It was possible he'd get his wish, but I aimed to make him work for it. He had a goal other than the goal of playing sly, edgy poker, and in my mind that was a weakness. He wanted too much.

There were plenty of times, especially when I shuffled the cards myself, inhaling the waxy breeze of the deck, that I thought about going out to the car and hauling in my $10,000 stake. The boys would let me play on then; they'd have to. Making a commotion like that was a thing I was almost starved for.

After we'd played a little more than an hour, a guy from Overbrook Farms they called Tony showed up to take his seat, and the party crowd in the rest of the room thinned considerably. There were two women on the bed, giggling like they had a few secrets and flirting in a raunchy way with DaSilva when he allowed it. Thomas claimed he was basically even for the night, and I could see he wanted to stay that way until the game got down and dirty. He folded on two hands in a row, left to take a leak, then folded on the next hand as well. Wiley was up a few dollars, Gilbert was down more than a hundred, DaSilva was maybe $25 in the hole. Once Tony got his chips in order, it was clear that they'd wait for one more person—one more man— and I'd be on my way.

I glanced at Thomas as the deal came to me. "Naw, keep it

this time," he said, pulling a handkerchief from his back pocket to wipe at his neck. "Give Tony a chance at you just to be fair."

Tony, who'd fenced himself in behind three perfect silos of chips, wouldn't even look my way. DaSilva leaned toward me instead, crooking a squared-off finger at my ear. "You not showing courage with the money," he hissed, licking my face with his hot breath. "Need a man to show you. To make you happy." Unlike his women friends, who were mixing him some kind of drink with lemonade and ice, I didn't believe DaSilva was as drunk as he acted. He'd waited a long time to say the words I'd read on his face before the game even started, how he could do more for me in a bed than I could ever do for myself anytime, anywhere. I tried not to react, but the beer had lubricated my cornered mood. I didn't say anything—I hadn't forgotten all of my stepdad's advice—but my jaw shifted and so did the width of my eyes. DaSilva knew I'd heard him.

I called for a hand of seven-card, high-low.

Wiley didn't go for the idea at first. He liked his poker and his scotch served up the same—straight. But he didn't laugh in my face or shove away from the table. He just rolled his beefy shoulders and carefully anted up a white chip like I was a five-'n'-dime cashier asking for exact change. Thomas flipped his chip into the pot with a laugh, saying something to the women on the bed about how evil I was to be going for a hardworking man's money in such a way.

"We work hard, too," said one of the women.

"And your day ain't over yet, is it?" Wiley offered, clamping his teeth on the cigar that had smoldered out long before. DaSilva cussed and threw a wadded-up bill onto the table. Tony cut the cards. I dealt.

With three cards dealt—one up, two down—DaSilva showed the ten of hearts, Thomas a queen. Wiley and I both had threes, while Tony looked gloomy over a king. Gilbert hung a six. Since the holders of the best and worst hands would eventually split the pot, unless somebody could conjure up both, the early action was heavy. When the fourth card went out, Tony pulled in an ace to go with his king, so he threw in for ten bucks. Wiley called and raised him another ten. Before I sent out the fifth cards, the pot was well over $200. Still nickel-and-dime stuff by my stepdad's standards, where pickup trucks and bass boats were the only bets worth commenting on, but it was the first sign of any real gambling the whole night.

I had a problem. I was holding a pair of threes, one up, and three spades, but I was likely to run out of money. High-low games inspire a lot of unsubtle betting, and while I needed to stay in to see if my flush came together, or a second pair appeared to go with the first, the money I had my hands on right that minute might not see me through. DaSilva was already pushing the envelope; he had a handsome queen of diamonds to go with the ten. His mouth was so droopy and relaxed I knew he was stoked. It would give him a lot of satisfaction to break me before the cards flew home. I pushed everyone's fifth cards across the table, guessing how the next round of bets would fall. Gilbert would fold, and everybody else would hang on for the wild ride. Except for me. I didn't have the $50 I calculated it would take me just to see my seventh card.

Thomas was a lousy cardplayer over the long haul because his idea of being unpredictable was to bluff in all the usual places. He was playing for the low hand; that was obvious to everybody at the table. He had nothing face up, but for once a junk hand and the stubborn failure to quit might win him some money. Especially if he could get some of us to fold. He yodeled like a screech owl when he called Wiley's $20 bet, but somewhere after the noise, while he was sprawled in his chair gargling a sip of whiskey, he let me know he'd stake me to the end. He didn't exactly wink and he didn't exactly laser his eyes onto DaSilva, but I knew what he meant. If I had the cards, I was to go after the guy.

My fifth card was a seven and the sixth was the ace of clubs, which gave me two pair with no chance at a flush or a straight. Mediocre goods. Wiley got another garbage card, though I couldn't discount a miracle straight underneath. His hand might be better than mine; my guess, however, was that he was going low alongside Thomas. DaSilva got the seven of diamonds up. Possible flush. Possible straight. Definite two pair considering the way he cupped his hands near his chips and kept his eyes within that perimeter.

I'd been right to think DaSilva wanted to level me. Wiley put up twenty to see his last card, and DaSilva called the bet and raised him twenty-five. Thomas made the call with bills from his shirt pocket. Tony folded with a string of teenage swearwords. I reached across the table for the blue-and-white box the cards had come in and scribbled an IOU inside the curved flap. DaSilva told me to go to hell.

"Her money's good. She's cool with my boss," Thomas said.

"Your boss fucks them all, that don't count." DaSilva looked at me like I was pure weasel shit. "You broke. You out."

"I said I'm covering." Thomas came up in his chair, all the slack good feeling gone from his face.

"Man's right, Tommy." Wiley splayed forward, elbows wide across chips and money and ash. "I ain't broke that rule in years."

"Damn." Thomas took a cat's-paw swing at the table.

"It's okay," I said to Wiley, not ready to give DaSilva the satisfaction of my closed door expression. "I'm out."

"Hell with that," slurred a voice behind me. "How much you need? You need twenty? Mimi, you got twenty?"

It was the sloppy women on the bed. They weren't ready to see me gone. They were especially not ready to see DaSilva's fine ideas about himself feathered in cash.

"We're really doing this because we like him," said the one called Mimi as she wobbled over to take an unfocused look at the mess on the table. Her heavy black purse swung like a sledgehammer past my ear. "He ain't paying us enough attention." So Mimi, whose hair gleamed somewhere between purple and liver bay and whose silver-studded belt dug into my shoulder, popped some pearly snaps on her chambray shirt and fished the damp, talcumed tube of a $50 bill out of her bosom.

Gilbert and Wiley set to laughing like hell, tears swimming off the edges of their eyes. It was just one of those things. Tony, who'd been sulking by burning through a pipeline of cigarettes, grinned and lit up a fresh one for Mimi, who put it right between her glossy lips. DaSilva cursed in two or three languages and called us all bitches in no uncertain terms. Wiley okayed the loan since it was coming from outside. I matched his bet and spun out the last four cards.

A five of spades for Wiley. King of clubs for Thomas. Jack of spades for DaSilva, who was trying to hold his face together while Mimi's partner pelted him with packaged condoms from across the room. A nine of clubs for me. I figured I was done, and I was right. Wiley and Thomas went low, and Thomas won out. DaSilva busted my two pair with three jacks, and I was in the hole for most of the money I'd borrowed. Mimi waved me off when I told her where to find me and how I'd be good for it come payday. "Sorry, honey. No damn way. I got more where that came from, as you know." She jiggled the ledge of her breasts. "You made it worth it anyhow. He's a dickhead, a total asshole prick. I just wish he weren't so damn cute." Then she went back to stretch out on Wiley's bed with her buddy, a twelve-pack of beer on the floor nearby, HBO on the television. "He's got to leave sooner or later," Mimi's friend said, yawning and yanking her jeans out of her crotch. "We're here waiting."

I thanked Wiley and tried to get away before I said anything stupid. Thomas let me go without backslapping me too much; he still had to play cards with DaSilva for a good portion of the night. Wiley allowed as how I ought to get one more drink before I took off, then they all went back to it—their huddle of jestering and machismo. But I wasn't able to get out the door before the shaggy guy who'd been supplying me with beers stepped in front of me.

"That was a righteous try," he said. "Let me grab you a drink."

"Got horses to run in the morning," I said. "I'm wrung out, thank you."

"Can't ask you to hang loose another minute?" He had a narrow, forlorn face to go with his long hair and patchy beard. I took him for an easygoing stoner.

"No. Thanks again."

"But I know you from New York. That Breeders Cup party last year at Belmont with the band. Your husband was singing and—"

On came a backlit memory. Rollicking. Dizzy. I was in the black, off-the-shoulder dress I'd wanted so much, with the man I wanted to believe in. I saw the red-curtained bandstand ... Eric's wide, bleached cuffs ... his sorrowful crooner's mouth. He'd put on quite a show that night. Drunk and charming and nearly aristocratic. Owner of a filly who'd won four good races and who'd go off as the second favorite in the Cup's

Distaff race the next day. Unfortunately, Sunny suffered a fracture and had to be pulled up. It was the beginning of our end.

"Nope," I said, "you got the wrong me. I've never been there." I fullbacked my way into the sharp night air. Being a good stoner and probably a normal, kind man, the shaggy guy didn't try to follow.

Thick, low clouds had herded the weak light of the quarter moon to a strip of sky just above the horizon. The beacons of Bluegrass International Airport dueled to the west. It looked bound to rain, maybe hard. I was thinking about how much I wanted to let loose and beat DaSilva, how I should have hauled my big money in there and gotten that short-term-victory jolt, when somebody rapped on the passenger side window. The shaggy guy gone bold, I thought. He wanted to make me mad.

"Give me a ride?" The face bobbing above a bulky army field jacket clarified itself through the smudged glass. Danny.

I leaned across and opened the door. "You stuck?"

"Not too bad." He gave me a hitchhiker's Cheshire cat grin. "I'm just lazy about walking back and saw you leaving."

"Hope you did better than me." I revved the car into reverse. "Lost my magic poker touch."

"They playing cards in there? Damn. My buddies couldn't never get that organized." He looked over his shoulder at the trim brick face of the motel. "Guy I know from Maple Leaf is only in there because he struck it rich at Turfway. Rooms is hard to get. Then he hustles us out in favor of the ladies."

"Spending all the money he won?"

"Hell, yes." He laughed. "Kept two girls all by his lonesome."

I swung through the back entrance of the track, headlights barely cutting into the canopied dark. Danny asked me why my luck was bad.

"Weak cards. You know how it goes. The sorry part is I hardly cared about losing. I wanted to beat those guys, but it wasn't about money."

"Didn't care?" He twisted in my direction, and I could taste the dusty resin of marijuana rising from his clothes. "What about that horse you want to bail out? Thought you was getting money for that."

He had me there. The afternoon had stalled on me. The evening had dragged me down. I was letting myself slide back into the unsoaked stain that had become my life after Stevie's killing.

"Come on, Kerry. We got to work this out. I'll make up some tea if you can stand that."

I felt drained. Cards. Grinning man faces. No food. "I don't know. It's hardly—"

"Stay a minute. Hell, stay all night. I got room, and boss man was supposed to rig up a space heater. It'll be cold sleeping in this car. And I don't mean nothing by the invitation that isn't honest."

"I've got a place to go to, Danny." I spoke slowly, maybe a little sadly. "But the tea could be all right."

I parked as close to Alice's shed as I could. The barns were quiet except for the occasional stir of hooves in straw. The main lights were off in Alice's aisle, but I could see movement near the bunk room across the yard and splinters of bright light around the door of the tack room. There were eyes all over. You couldn't get near the horses without being watched.

Danny unlocked his door, then left to get water for the kettle and to peek at his horses. Even though there were watchmen around, he wanted to see for himself. It was like checking sleeping children, he said, a habit you never got rid of.

"I'm thinking ginseng for you, little lady. For strength and easing and all that shit." Danny closed the door as he returned, hung his coat on a nail. "Your aura is looking clouded up, as we say in California."

"You planning to uncloud it?" The way he was being all careful with me made my head feel light.

"Until I get out of bed to tend that horse that's running tomorrow, it's proper to do whatever."

I didn't have a response to that.

"I've smoked the limit tonight." Danny stretched his arms above his head to work off a yawn. "That's a damn fact. I need my tea."

While the water boiled on the dented hot plate and the pale root steeped in the simple black cups, we talked about horses. The claimer Danny had going tomorrow was the one Alice had entered at the secretary's request. He was an all right horse, and they'd approved him to run in blinkers, but he would be jumping up in class and running for a $20,000 tag. He didn't appear to have much of a chance.

"The distance is good for him," I said. "He's pretty fit."

"But look up in that sky where that rain is and tell me how he'll do in the slop. The track'll be a mess."

"I haven't worked him in mud. Is he supposed to be a quitter?"

"Aw, he's just a regular nag that's easy to be with." Danny handed me a cup with both hands. There was no way to make the exchange without brushing fingers. "Not like the ones who kick you when your back is turned. I've had that mean bastard kind. I'd like to see him treated fair."

"Bad weather will make the whole day a gamble." I was on the bed. Danny sat near my feet on the roll of his sleeping bag.

"I got a few ideas about that. Picked up the good word on the fourth race tomorrow. Somebody who knows somebody."

"You planning to bet money?" I noticed how his unshaved jaw made him look more hard bitten and used.

"I can't sit here and say I have a foolproof system, 'cause I don't. I used to. Worked up my own blend of speed figures and everything. But I buried it deep after a couple of bad afternoons in New Orleans. This is a solid piece of info about a horse been working over at the Horse Park."

"How much?" I was just talking to keep him going, enjoying the earthy syrups of the tea, the way Danny hunkered over his own steaming cup. I didn't want to think about my own money.

"Maybe I ought to ask how much you're good for?" He slid over to lean against the bed frame, near my knees. "I'm ready to put three hundred dollars where it counts."

I blew a low whistle across the top of his head. "Hope the odds are right."

"They are. And I'm not laying out until the last second. Got a friend to seagull the horse's trainer right to the fifty-dollar window, just to make sure the story's straight."

"You good at this?" I asked.

"When I need to be." His hair shadowed his eyes as he looked up at me. "This won't go down unless it's right."

I set my empty cup on the cold floor and shook myself awake. "Eric could have used more sense like yours."

"Ain't much doubt about that from what you say." I felt Danny's knuckles above my ankle, slow and warm. "I guess what I'm trying to ask is, do you want in?"

Did I? Did I believe I could double or triple the money I had? Did I think I could buy myself out from under Eric without help, that I could balance the scales between us with luck? The answers were the usual. Yes and no. If I lost my stake, I'd have nothing left but a slow car and a few scraps of crusty clothing. Eric and Sunny would be beyond me. But if I won, I could buy a certain kind of freedom. The same impatience I'd felt at the card game rang and jangled in my head. I wanted to break clean from the gate toward the next stretch of my life. On my own. Unbeholding. There was no good reason—not in the breath and night of that barn—not to be bold about it now.

"Why not?" I released the words like tiny rising balloons.

"No lie." Danny's hand was squeezing my thigh before either of us knew it was there. "You make a decision like a bow shot, I know that's so." He jumped to his feet and reached for my teacup. "I guess you can spot me in the morning."

"No." I stood too. "I'll get the money now."

He shrugged, turned to refill his cup, then turned back to me like there was something he'd forgotten. I knew what it was. He'd wanted more of me before we got to the money part—more story, more skin, more time to dress up the transaction. And his chance was gone.

I slipped into the yard, accompanied only by my sparking thoughts and the slow red fade of the taillights on a security van. Reno must be somewhere nearby. I could feel his hard eyes locked on my back just as they'd been locked on the dry black cover of that Bible. He wouldn't trust us—me and Danny—because that was his business. People who twined up with each other didn't always pay the right kind of attention to their horses. Reno would be scouting me, had probably been doing it since day one. I toyed with the possibility that losing the bet would drop me so low I'd never recover. I'd be a certified bread-line mucker forever. But maybe the only routes to respect were always gambles. Maybe. I dug through my car like a terrier. When I came back into the yard, I kept the plastic-wrapped block of bills out in front of me like a church candle. It would worry Reno to see that—he'd know I was passing off money and he wouldn't know why—but at least it wouldn't be a secret. That was the most I could give him.

I stopped, however, when I saw a shape skip from the wall near Danny's door toward the far end of the yard and scramble over a closed gate. A few seconds later a dog barked down the road. My heart jolted, then steadied. The person was too small to be Reno, much too small to be Danny taking off for a piss. I rapped at the base of Danny's door with the side of my foot, balancing the money on my open palms. I didn't like the fact I hadn't been alone.

Danny looked at me with a kind of half-speed sympathy before he took the cash. Then he tried to steer me back into his room. He'd lit some incense—I could smell it—and some kind of shallow bowl lamp. I noticed he'd changed shirts.

"There's ten thousand, give or take. I'd only hope to triple it. And you need to swear you won't talk to me about it tomorrow. I don't need the details."

He pushed his wavy hair behind one small white ear, and I could tell I'd stunned, then irritated him. He hadn't expected so much money. "Well, hell, Kerry. You make it sound like this can't be a bit of fun."

"It can't yet. Not for me."

"You need to come on in here and relax some more." He shackled my wrist with a strong hand, reached over to rub my neck. "Forget all this about your husband."

"I can't. It's . . . it's not the time yet. Even if I want it to be."

His face shivered with impatience. He started to protest, then stopped to look at the weird shapes thrown onto the wall by his flickering lamp. His breathing was deep and rough in his chest. "Christ in heaven, you're damn hard to prepare for, but I'll do right by the money. My source is good."

"As good as they come, I'm sure." I suddenly felt hot eyed. If he won, Danny, too, would expect his share. Of me.

He stared from the other side of the beat-up doorjamb, waited.

"I saw somebody leaving the barn just now. I need to check with Reno."

"Boss man is right in there at Alice Piersall's desk patrolling with his evil eye. I saw him. He don't need to be checked with." Danny spoke louder than he needed to, loud enough to be over-heard. "What you saw was Maria Dolores, works down the hill. She's looking for my friend from Maple Leaf."

"And he's not here," I said, automatically.

"No, he's not. And you are. I ought to make you stay until there's a smile on your face."

I made myself look up at him, his glowing earring, the simple bridge of his nose. He moved and somehow drew me closer without touching me. Then we were kissing, and I could feel how his body was wider and heavier than I'd thought, how he was channeling a greed for touch I hadn't felt in a long time. I broke away, mouth numb, my head frightened and nearly empty.

"You could stay, but you won't," Danny whispered. "You think about that long and hard." Then he slowly closed the high, gray-painted door, leaving me to stare at blurring shadows and the thrashing afterimages of flames.

CHAPTER 9

*t*hat night I slept in the room Roy set up for me. It was in a motel on New Circle Road—a battered pink rectangle, bug free and cheap. The room was a wreck because there were at least two other girls living there, maybe more. Scattered blouses, ratty hairbrushes, leaking bottles of perfume. The towels were all wet and snaky on the bathroom floor, and the carpet was crunchy with chips and flakes I couldn't identify. The only person there was a girl with a widow's peak and a smear of black eyeliner who said her name was Simone. She was watching an old black-and-white movie with the sound turned down. She said I could shower if I wanted, and I could have the other bed since the sheets were clean and she didn't think anybody else would be back for the night.

What I wanted to do was turn the ruckus in my head down to the level of that silent TV. Instead, I lay on the bed in socks and unbuttoned jeans and a bra while Simone did the same six feet away. She didn't offer gossip about her horses or her connections, which was fine with me, though she did ask for a package of cheese crackers when I made a visit to the snack machines outside.

A mattress, a pillow, a wide place to sleep. I should have curled up like a whipped sled dog. But I didn't. I watched Simone watch a woman who looked like Barbara Stanwyck get in trouble with some men in wide-shouldered suits. I watched her chew the crackers and drum her fingers on her belly and never get up to go to the bathroom. Every once in a while she held what looked like a folded washcloth against one side of her head. When I finally mentioned Roy, she half faced me with a cloth mashed into her spiky hair. "Fuck that," she said in a drowsy voice.

A few minutes later, I undressed and closed my eyes. The sky behind my lids was lead gray and stark. It would be hours before I slept. I thought of Barbara Stanwyck wearing her fang-collared gown with the rope of perfect pearls. I wanted to take care of myself like that. With style. With eye flashes and certainty. With a knack for action instead of worry. Between restless shoves at my pillow I considered the idea of mailing the necklace I'd taken from Eric to my mama in Florida for safekeeping. Eric could have whatever the tote board brought us, but he didn't need every damn thing. I worked with that idea until I found the kind of sleep that let me hear one of my roommates pound the door because she couldn't find her key. I smelled her when she finally tumbled onto the bed in a hot spritz of tequila and sex. It didn't take long for her to spread out like I wasn't there at all.

CHAPTER 10

i'm as superstitious as I need to be. So I don't mind admitting that the accident put the shivers on me.

It had rained, and rained hard. When I got to the barns in my anorak and waterproof pants, with a double set of goggles around my neck, the tractors had already floated the track once, squeezing the water to the surface, where it could begin to drain off. Alice decided not to work about half of her horses; she planned to use the morning to ship in some more from the farm. Since two of my rides were racing that afternoon and Roy had also decided to hold back most of his horses, I was able to hustle up only three mounts, none of which would go until after eight-thirty, when the track would be floated again. Jenny spotted me a couple of bucks, and we went down to the kitchen for doughnuts. It was dark and mucky. The drizzle took the clatter out of the early morning, but there was still plenty of bustle at the kitchen because nothing had changed the fact that it was opening day.

I used the wait in line to pick up a late ride on the lower track from a consignment agent I knew. Jenny wanted to have breakfast with some friends; she allowed as how the dancing the night before had gone real good and she had some gossip she wanted to catch up on. I stuffed my doughnuts in a pocket and told her I'd been boring. Played cards, gone home. There was no reason to say more than that.

I drifted by Alice's shed, where I could see Danny hard at work on the horse that would run that afternoon. A vet would come by later to check for soundness and give the animal the Lasix that was legal to use in Kentucky. The farrier would probably drop in to take a last look at the horse's shoes; he might want to change them for plates with a better grip. I knew Danny would spend most of his time walking the horse out and grooming it to a high gloss. He was real picky that way. We'd talked the night before about the best way to tie off a mud tail, and I wondered if he'd take my advice. Seeing him stoop and bend in the bucket-colored light, realizing with an acid twinge in my stomach that he had all of my hateful, hopeful money, made me wonder what I truly wanted from him. He seemed a fairly regular guy, easygoing, capable of keeping himself happy. I'd liked kissing him—that was the damn straight truth. What I didn't like was how I was using him now, how I was mostly defining people by what they could do for me.

I went on up to Roy's barn to eat. Thomas usually kept some instant coffee in a large communal thermos, and there'd be a chair to sit in somewhere, a dry spot. When I saw Thomas, his eyes were still leaky from whiskey and smoke, but he was at full tilt. The night at cards—no matter how good or bad it had gone—was a closed book. He had on his rubber Wellingtons, a shiny black jacket with DELVECCHIO RACING STABLES printed in bright yellow across the back, and a Jim Beam Stakes hat. Roy had three horses running that afternoon and another dozen he hoped to get out on the sopping track for some work.

Thomas said Roy wanted me up on the twitchy General Assembly colt no later than eight-twenty. He also took the time to tell me that Wiley had walked off with everybody's money once again. "That fucker Gilbert did all right too, which is enough to send a man back to churchgoing." He rubbed his stubbled jaw with his fingers. Cold rain dripped from his hat brim. "DaSilva didn't even finish up. You might like to know that." I thought of DaSilva being led to his fate by big-boobed Mimi and her friend. I hoped he was still pinned flat like a bug somewhere, sucked dry and late for work.

Roy flagged me down soon after and repeated Thomas's instructions. He reminded me we were trying to teach the General Assembly colt tactical speed; I was to move him right along after two furlongs. "If the inside's cuppy, stay off it," he said. "And for Christsakes keep Pete away from you." Pete was the assistant clocker who identified horses as they came to the gate. Roy wanted to avoid posting an official workout time if he could. Like all trainers he planned to advertise the colt's fitness when he was good and ready. I'd always thought Roy was at his best in the morning, pinpointing his horses, organizing their training schedules same as a good pool player organized his shots. He seemed almost relaxed in his water-streaked jeans, a pair of mud-slathered python boots, one of those waxed cotton coats the Euro trainers favored. By eleven he'd be draped in a silk-blend suit, looking as slick as a commodities broker, which is maybe what he really wanted to be. His eyes would be jerking back and forth in their deep sockets, searching for a manicured hand to shake or a cluster of potential enemies to analyze. Now, with horses on his mind and a steady spring shower leaking into his collar, he was almost tolerable. I tried not to think about the young girl loitering under the spilling eaves in front of me and what she and her pink, pouty mouth meant.

I ate my doughnuts on a retaining wall in front of a horse named Dormezvous. He was an oddly dappled brown with a narrow chest and lop ears. He wore a cribbing collar, which meant he had the bad habit of chewing on wood and bloating his belly with air. He rubbed his bony eye sockets hard against my hands as I scratched him and talked about my barns in New York and the way I liked to arrange things on a rainy day when I was in charge. I told him I liked dogs better than cats, route horses better than sprinters, my Mexican food with plenty of spice. I told him I'd had mixed luck with people. He seemed to enjoy the conversation.

Roy's colt worked well, partly because the track was so uncrowded. I had to sit down on him big time past the half-mile pole, but when I asked him to shift into high gear, he did. It would take practice to get him to lay off the pace where he'd catch dirt in the eye and have to tolerate the rumps of other horses in front of him, but he tended to be fractious in the gate, Roy said, and had a habit of breaking poorly. He needed to learn to save his speed and stalk the field by degrees.

It was full light when I got to Alice's horse, and even though there was some wind whipping through the glassy sheets of rain, the barn seemed more alive and expectant. I could see the creamy knuckles of blossoms on the dogwood trees, and the refreshed tint of the grass. Alice wanted me to breeze a rabbit-eared roan mare that Rogelio usually worked just to keep her sharp, a task so basic she sent me to the gate without a pony or a groom. There still wasn't much of a crowd up there. Charlie was sipping coffee and conferring with another outrider about the need for what they called dogs, or traffic cones, to keep horses from working too close to the rail. They both thought they could do without them. The water was draining off real well. I watched Mark Holmes pony the champion mare Red

Light Rising through the gate; his wife, Peg, the mare's usual exercise rider, was aboard. Eric and I had always wanted to run Sunny against that fast, leggy bay. Seeing Mark slumped in a western saddle on his shaggy pinto while Peg rose knock kneed in the stirrups to stretch her muscles reminded me how far I was from that possibility.

What happened next is the kind of thing that happens at tracks although none of us gets used to it, or cares to talk about it much. I was trotting the roan on the outside, getting her warm and realizing that she was a hard mouthed witch who'd make me prove my hand. As Charlie told it later, it was a two-year-old that got loose, dumped its rider near the far end of the grandstand, and went for a tornado spin. If the young fool hadn't been outfitted with a full set of blinkers, which cut off its peripheral vision, maybe things wouldn't have happened the way they did. We'd never know.

The horse tore up the stretch at a good gallop. He was lucky there; he didn't sideswipe anybody hugging the rail. But he caught sight of a pair of stable mates pulling up past the finish line and went after them. By then, Charlie had seen him.

Charlie had his job because he was funny and bossy and able to treat everybody pretty much the same. He was also good at the dangerous parts. Somebody later said they were like bird dogs on point, him and his sorrel mare both. He dropped his coffee to the ground, slapped the sorrel awake with a pop of the reins across her shoulder, and was at full speed in about four butt-pumping strides. They were going to cut the runaway off before he hurt himself or somebody who mattered.

The way I heard it, Charlie came alongside that two-year-old and tried to grab his whipping reins. He missed, had to pull up to pass the other horses, then tried to herd the runaway right into the rail. All he got for his trouble was a busted hand. The first I knew of it were warning shouts from back at the gate. I could hear them because I was barely cantering, and the wind whistle through my helmet wasn't very loud. I was lucky. I looked over my shoulder and saw the loose horse running head high and terrified, being bumped by Charlie's game mare, all of them feathered in a thick beige spray of water and mud. I was lucky because Charlie saw me and eased off just enough to make sure the horse didn't bolt across the track in my direction. If the two-year-old thought this was a race, Charlie would work it that way until the animal tuckered out. He'd ride parallel as well as he could, a shield for the rest of us. The outrider posted near the chute on the backstretch was already on her way to help him out.

But horses are panicky and herd bound, and thoroughbreds are given to running right up to the edge of control. When they splashed by me, I got the impression the runaway was letting up, but I couldn't keep a close eye on him since my own mount was causing me trouble. She sensed the confusion and wanted to join in. I nearly had her settled when I got a bad feeling. Mark and Peg Holmes were on the far end of the turn, pressed against the outside rail because they'd seen what was coming. There were two riders along the inside, however, who had not. They'd been hand-galloping, concentrating on working eyeball to eyeball and neck to neck. If they saw the outrider waving in the distance, they didn't make much of her signal. Then the two-year-old broke hard in front of Charlie, just keeping his footing on the turn. And Charlie's voice, which had been ground down to a croak from all the hollering, went dead.

The runaway split the pair at top speed. The exercise riders had seen him by then but knew better than to make a sudden move. All three horses bolted as one for a stride, but it was the inside horse who took the bump. A couple thousand pounds of muscle and leaping bone—wham. I felt the collision in my own chilled marrow. The inside horse hit the barrier, stumbled as its hindquarters collapsed and slid, then scrambled back into stride. Its rider took the blow right across the leg.

A few strides later the runaway faltered, his foreleg finally caught in the dangling reins. He went down in an ugly, splattering fall.

The first thing I noticed was the silence. No more bellowing shouts, no stuttering hoofbeats. I couldn't even sort out the wet hiss of traffic on Versailles Road. And everything had gone small again to my eyes—the bright yellow poncho of the outrider, Peg Holmes's red crash helmet, the bobbing figures crossing the perfect green infield to help out. For one long, elastic moment we were there as we'd always been, a scattered group on plain, lean horses, all of us strung along a backstretch that rippled and scalloped the light like it was a quietly flooding river.

I wrestled my mare to a halt. The track would close once the ambulance pulled in. And I could tell they'd need the ambulance. Charlie had grabbed the bridle of the bay who'd banged the rail; its rider sagged left and cartwheeled off into the mud. The other outrider had hold of the runaway, who was up again but clearly favoring a leg. I figured the smart thing to do was turn around, get the roan back to Alice's barn before I got in any trouble. I'd do no good as a gawker.

The Holmeses passed me before I managed to turn the mare. Red Light Rising was prancing and swinging herself at a wide, anxious angle away from Mark and his long-suffering pinto pony. I could hear that good animal working the metal snaffle with her front teeth, just chomping it. I could see the wild desire to run spiraling in her eyes. But she wasn't going to run. Not today. Peg and Mark looked grim and more than half spooked as they trotted by. There was too much you couldn't control in this world, too damn much. Peg's hands were marbled white and red from the tension of holding back the mare. It wasn't until I looked down, mainly to avoid acknowledging the luck we'd just seen play itself out, that I realized my numb hands were exactly the same.

I had the roan relaxed to a walk and could see the white gooseneck of the equine ambulance floating toward the gate when I heard a voice calling after me and saw Billy T. ducking under the inside rail to wade onto the track in my direction.

"Ho, there. Ho. Just stay." He seemed to be hailing my horse instead of me. "You all right? We couldn't tell a damn thing from over there."

Billy was huffing from his run across the infield, his cheeks pink with exertion. He was wearing a dun-colored trench coat I'd always liked, and since his hair was dry, I figured he'd lost a hat somewhere along the way. It took me a minute to realize that he must have a good reason for being out there.

"They're not yours?" I said, choking up a little with the fright I'd put on delay. "Not those horses?"

"No." He spoke gently, talking to the mare as much as to me while he reached for her bridle. "One is Preston's, I think. And the runaway belongs to I don't know who. Betsy was up on Preston's horse, though—Betsy Shires. She's done some work for me."

"Well, go on and help, then." I tried to lather an impatience I didn't feel onto my words. "We're all right. Charlie saw to that."

"Yeah." Billy looked down the stretch where track officials and volunteers were milling about in the slop. They had Betsy sitting partway up, though it looked like she might be unconscious from the pain. "Charlie did what he could. He kept it off that Red Light mare."

"He did. That would have been worse trouble, if I'm allowed to say that."

"Sure," Billy said. "Say whatever you need to. None of us likes when this happens."

He began to lead the mare along, his rubber boots sucking in and out of the deep mud, head bowed with effort while we both thought about what I'd meant. The runaway was a nobody horse. We hadn't recognized his saddle blanket or colored blinkers. Red Light Rising was a champion, a rare achievement of breeding and heart. If she'd been hurt, we would have called it a damn shame tragedy and imagined all the pure running that mare would have done if her luck had held. We were like that on the track—sentimental and given to dressing good stories up as legends—and we usually worked up the lives of our horses better than we did our own.

"You don't have to pony me," I said. "This one's steady."

"If I don't get you past the ambulance and truck, somebody else will have to. I saw how Alice sent you up here without any help."

"Didn't think I'd need any. Not with this old gal."

"Well, it gives me the chance I've wanted to talk to you." He looked over his shoulder at me, eyebrows straight with seriousness. "Seeing as how you've decided to put my balls in the deep fryer with Louisa."

I had a strong urge to cover my entire face with my smeared goggles.

"You have a way of making people real mad, Kerry."

"I'm sorry. I was way out of line on that."

"No kidding." He tightened up on the mare as the ambulance nosed past. The ghost white vehicle, driven by a state vet with a look of mechanical concentration on his face, rolled ahead so slowly it barely splashed its clean fenders. Sometimes they would put a horse down right on the track. I'd seen it happen. We all had. The idea that that ignorant runaway might soon be like my poor Stevie rolled in my belly like a cold rock.

"I *was* going to ask you to dinner," Billy said. "That part's true. You're just a little hard to catch."

"Some things never change," I said with attitude. "I had the idea to take *you* out to Del Frisco's if you could find the time, but I'm plumb out of money."

Billy straightened up inside the trench coat. His face shimmied from confusion to suspicion. "Don't tell me Delvecchio's not paying you on time. He's tried that stunt before with his girls."

"No," I said. "It was cards. I lost most of it at cards."

"Damn it, Kerry." He clucked at the mare and walked on. "Did you bring any good habits back here with you?"

"Fighting, gambling, bad love. That's about it for me right now. Maybe I ought to write some country radio songs."

He shook his head, and I watched his thick, wet hair brush against his turned-up collar. He knew better than to take me too seriously. I was like a punk sister or, worse yet, a damn predictable ex-girlfriend. Yet he kept putting up with me. And because I couldn't strangle old feelings about him, I kept being bitchy.

"Here comes Charlie," I said, glancing behind us. "We're good."

"Maybe so." Billy released the slick bridle and rubbed his stiff fingers down his leg. "So I can hope for that dinner? You practically owe me."

"I do," I said. "I owe you a lot. But I don't know if we should see each other. Not out of business clothes."

The roan hip-hopped into a trot, no doubt feeling my own

nerves. I tried to work her into a standstill. Billy watched me
with his hands jammed deep in his pockets, all the smile gone
from his strong-angled face. "Should I ask what you're afraid
of?"

"No. Don't." I focused on containing the roan. "I think we
both know the answer to that. I'm the Mistake Girl around here,
every minute facing my bad choices. I'm aiming for recovery,
from lots of things."

"Dinner?" Billy never raised his eyes but the word was not to
be refused.

"Okay," I said, cracking, giving in to the first good feeling of
the day. "I'd be honored. Let's do it tonight."

He stepped clear of the roan, who immediately broke into a
jog. I felt strangely abandoned, even though he was the one
planted in the shimmering mud. I wished I had the guts to tell
him how fine he was. I wished I'd been steady enough to hang
on to him when I had the chance. But I hadn't. I'd let Eric wa-
terfall over me instead. Another mistake. I weeded around that
regret until Charlie drew alongside us, hard lipped with anger
because he hadn't prevented trouble and had dislocated his
thumb to boot. He cussed over the top of Billy's head and told
us both what a bad business it was, how that runaway had killed
himself by being stupid. "Can't remember the last time a morning went so bad," he grumbled. "Have to be two years ago when
that young one got turned wrong way and ran head on into
O'Rourke's horse. I was gone at the damn dentist's." None of us
had an easy thing to say after that, so we worked our way closer
to the chiseled limestone of the grandstand just as we were,
heads hanging, miserable, knowing the meet would open in a
few hours, the track fresh and clear, the crowd cheering,
whether any of us were ready for it or not.

. . .

Word of the trouble spread like a grease fire on the backside, and Dawg was at the gate to meet me with a lead shank. Alice had sent him uphill on the double. I could tell by the way he was craning his head atop his skinny neck that he was worried about the mare and every step she took.

"She's fine, but we didn't get any work in." I dropped the reins and let Dawg hook her up. "Alice coming? She say anything?"

Dawg checked the mare closely for scrapes or bumps. He didn't appear to hear me.

"Nobody got close to us, Dawg. What do you think you see?"

"Nothing. Just wanting to be careful. I don't like the mess I made of them run-down bandages neither. Look like shit."

I squeezed my legs to urge the mare into a walk. "Is Alice coming?" I asked again. The gate area was mashed with trainers collecting their horses. Even the reporters had left the dry comfort of the office to take a gander.

"Sent me outta there like a pit bull was behind us both. We didn't know nothing but that a accident was happening." Dawg shrugged. "She didn't say nothing else to me."

I noticed that Dawg had traded in his Georgia hat for a driving cap of navy blue wool. It was covered with small pearls of rain. He'd also shaved some kind of design onto the back of his skull. I could only imagine how Reno would react to that.

"Her horse that goes today be the first I ever seen in a race," Dawg said. "I mean one I really know. Danny says maybe I can walk that horse up here this afternoon. Think she'll go for that?"

I hesitated. "Reno likes his grooms to take their own horses to the paddock, but you never can tell. Hell, it's your first race day. Why don't you just talk to Alice?"

"She's a little hard, but I'm planning on it." Dawg stretched
one arm deep into the sleeve of a black nylon jacket, then the
other. "I tried to dress good, knowing how she is and all. Shaved
a letter in my hair too, for luck, you know, thinking she might
be for the commitment."

I could see it now, the tail and dip of a capital *P* just above the
cords of his dark neck. Dawg would be good in the saddling
area, I thought, with his concentration and slow, graceful stride.
He'd be proud to handle his boss's horse. There'd be touts
watching the animals for signs of lameness or the sweats, children under umbrellas with their parents, the spicy smell of
onions and chili from the concessions, rain dripping from the
oaks. Dawg would help Alice tie down the claimer's slick, gray-
ish tongue. They'd buckle on the new blinkers, tighten the
white elastic girth. Then Dawg would have the claimer's halter
and lead shank to keep, and his rain sheet. Win, lose, or trail,
Dawg would be the first one to the horse when it was over,
while the jock was still breathing hard and swearing about one
decision or another. It would be Dawg who would treat the animal right no matter what happened in the race; he'd wipe the
muck from eyelids and nostrils while everybody else stared at
the golden lights of the tote board.

I dismounted before we got to the barn. I didn't want to lay
eyes on Danny. Didn't want to babble into some kind of gloomy
story about the accident to Alice. She'd learn the details soon
enough. Patchen Preston was an old-line breeder and trainer,
one of the few men in Kentucky Alice would admit she respected. She'd hear about his horse and Betsy Shires before she
wanted to.

I ducked into the ladies' room to clean up. It was crowded.
The air was clammy with the smells of animal salt, pipe rust,
and mud. I wormed my way in front of a sink to wipe my face

with a bandanna from my pocket. It was just like the faces of the two or three other women I could see, cold smacked and pinched, framed by sopping hair. We all knew what the judgment was, why our eyes flickered at one another in the mirror. Yet we couldn't help doing the girl thing, fussing with our snot-glazed faces and calculating how we looked to all the man eyes out in the barns. We still wanted to be pretty. But there wasn't any way to get around the facts. Blemishes were harder to cover on the backside. We looked like who we were. Masks were thinner here, bones more scraped against.

I thought again about Billy, how I'd always felt good around him even on days I must have looked like a walking shock of corn. Billy. He'd brought out a smooth-sanded version of me, a person I liked. A person who thought she was ready to take on Eric Ballard's cut-glass, cutthroat world. She'd been wrong about that.

I was trying to suck some water out of a faucet when I saw the *Daily Racing Form*. It had been tossed into a corner because it was too thick to stuff into the trash chute with the tissues and brown paper towels. I picked it up. No way I was going to look at the local races or even begin to second-guess what Danny was doing with the money, but there might be something about Sunny in the Belmont clips, and if there was, I wanted to see it.

I soon found what I needed. Or dreaded. A tiny paragraph reminding *Form* readers that Sunsquall, the *torrid pace mare*, would be *running in good company* the next day. Despite her long layoff, she *worked sharp* and her *connections were confident*, which meant Eric was talking too much as usual. *Seems a solid threat* was their conclusion. *A threat.* Every letter in those words pumped air bubbles into my blood. *Threat.* As far as I was concerned there were too many of those around. Far too many. I dropped the *Form* in the sink and marched myself out into the rain on locked legs. The skin on my neck buzzed and prickled. I'd come back to my garden spot. Gotten honest work. Tried not to make the wrong people mad.

Yet. I thought about Betsy Shires laid out like a scarecrow, faceless in the mud, drenched. I thought about the whitewalled eyes of that doomed runaway horse. If Danny lost the bet, I'd have nothing left but desperation. Helmeted, hunched against a seeping chill, I ranged up and down the barn aisles, looking at horses tucked in the back corner of their stalls. Most of the grooms had shut themselves away with coffee and cold knuckles. I was the soldier on lost patrol, searching for a checkpoint she might not be allowed to find.

CHAPTER 11

*W*hen there was nothing more to be done at the track, I called my mama. I guess I hoped talking to her would help fill the blanks I kept finding in my own thoughts. The motel room was empty, though I could tell at least one of my roommates had been back. There was a snarl of mongrel brown hair in the sink, and the washcloth I tried to use was smeared with what I hoped was pinkish lip gloss. I slipped into dry underwear, then picked up the phone. The receiver looked like it had been set down on a book of burning matches, but it worked.

Mama was home. She'd already had her shell walk on the beach and done her critical rundown of the horoscopes in the local papers. Since her move to Florida, Mama cherished late mornings with her coffee and cigarettes out in what she called her sunroom. She worked almost full-time as a nurse for some kind of private hospice, pulling about four shifts a week. The job gave her money to fritter away, she said, and kept her from getting plumb sick of the sight of her husband, Cliff.

"Kerry, honey, what in hell have you done with Eric?" Mama never stumbled much in conversation. "He's been calling like he thinks I'm hiding you down here, and it's got so I let the answer machine pick up for me every time."

There was a low mumble behind her. My stepdaddy, Cliff. Wedging in his opinion. "Cliff wants to know if he needs to go up to New York and tan your husband's hide. He also says howdy."

Just hearing her made me see what a mistake I'd made. I'd been bullied, teased, harped on, and comforted by that sandpaper voice all my life. Mama would have taken me in and worked her two-story Florida condo into a patch of true home. I could have slept on the custom fold-out couch she was so proud of and watched her fry up ham for breakfast and plotted a dozen revenges on Eric's mean ass with her help. I could have bought her the red wine she likes and mixed up a pitcher of sangria for a tray in the sunroom. Mama would have taken care of me and let my bad decisions wander like stray cats. But while I was imagining that—weeks of slow, unaccountable seaside mornings—I heard what Mama was actually saying.

"What's that again?" I made myself listen.

"I said I didn't recognize him and I didn't let him set foot in this house, though he acted nice enough. Said he was an old friend who'd heard you were living down here. Now, what's going on? I'm thinking I need to be worried."

There was another grumble in the background. "Cliff says I ought to say what he looked like so you can identify him."

"Identify who, Mama? I'm not getting this straight."

"The man looking for you, honey. It was Cliff got me all suspicious about it like he always does, from his police training. He thought it might have something to do with the phone calls."

I caught my breath. What had Eric said? *I'm sending somebody for you, darling.* Only he didn't know exactly where I was. Not yet.

"Did he say he was from Eric?"

"No," Mama chuffed through a drag on her cigarette. "He wasn't dumb enough to tell me that to my face. And he wasn't no Yankee. Sounded mostly Kentucky to me, though it can be hard to tell that off a young person these days. You all always want to sound like somebody else."

"He didn't leave a name, did he?" I couldn't think of any friends I'd seen lately who'd look for me in Melbourne, Florida, though Eric certainly knew Mama's address well enough.

"Clyde or Clive, something like that. He laughed when he said it, like it was a secret you'd know. Skinny, good suntan . . . what's that"—she covered the phone for a second—"well, of course he had dark hair, I was getting to that. Your stepdaddy still thinks he has to remind me of every little thing even though he didn't see the boy. I remember there was something about his face that didn't set right with me, but I'll be damned if I can say what it was."

"Don't talk to him. Don't say anything about me."

"I didn't," Mama snapped. "And I can't. 'Cause I don't know a blessed thing. Where are you? You want for Cliff to come get you, something like that?"

I told her I was riding at the home track, and she knew well enough what that meant. "I left Eric," I said. "Not quite a week ago."

There was a pause. I imagined Mama's fingers pulling at her earlobe the way they did when she was thinking. "Not much surprise there, I'm sorry to say. You find somebody else?"

I cringed at the quick way she peeled off the layers of my life. "That's not what I care about."

"I bet it was money that ruined you on him, and not another girl. A Pisces like that is not a fit for you."

I bit hard into my lip.

"Kerry? You ought to come down here. Things is good for us right now. We'd like having you." Her words were steady and polite, her way of saying she cared for me but knew how to keep her hopes level. "I know you can get work you like up there. Maybe you'll want to go back New York way when you feel better. It's not my business. But I'm a little more like your late Memaw every day—must be from the old ladies I look after, since I *am not* getting old myself." She laughed. "Being with family might be best. You won't have to think out everything yourself."

"Thank you, Mama." My fingers felt swollen and rubbery around the phone. "I'm holding up for now."

"Stubborn as ever." She almost said it like it was a question.

"I guess."

"I never did allow as how that was a bad way to be. Still don't. Cliff and me love you. I'll do you up a star chart today, see what I find. You make sure and call us back."

She didn't actually say good-bye. She always left that for me like it was a word that didn't need to be spoken since it hovered over us in the air. She'd been that way since my daddy's death, which was mostly my whole life, as he'd been killed in a cement-hauling accident before I turned five.

Cliff got on the phone right after. It was his job to hang up and maybe smooth any feathers that had been ruffled by Mama or me. His voice wasn't deep, but it carried well. You could tell just by hearing him say good morning that he was a mountain boy with a temper and the confidence to go with it.

"Your mama says to call Aunt Fernie in Frankfort when you need to. She forgot to add that in. She also said she's holding on to that package you sent. It's in the linen closet." My stepdad was concerned. I could hear it in his voice so clearly that I barely gave a thought to the safe arrival of the necklace. Cliff had never

liked Eric. "How worried should I be, Speed?" he asked, using
the nickname he'd given me when I got hooked on galloping
horses. "Still got the gun I gave you?"

Cliff had been an MP in the army straight out of high school
and a county deputy after that, until his drinking messed with
his career. Now he was doing security work for small busi-
nesses. He'd hated me going to New York since he despised
Yankee cities and everything about them by reputation. He'd
taught me to shoot when I was young because it was a thing he
said I ought to know how to do, like tilling a garden or changing
spark plugs in my car. He'd given me the gun after I got married. I assumed it was still in the kitchen cabinet of the house we
rented from Eric's parents.

"No. But nothing's happening like that. I'm the one mad.
Not Eric."

"Then who's hanging around my door, asking after you?
What makes you think that boy won't get ugly?" He was not a
man to let a matter drop.

"I don't know."

"Do me a favor, honey." I could see him bowed over the
phone, his bottle brown eyes still with concentration. "Go see
Harmon out in Paris and get you another one. You got money,
don't you?"

"What hasn't been stolen at cards."

Cliff laughed, reminding me again why Mama had stuck with
him when things were bad and why she cared enough to drag
his butt to Florida to straighten him out. He'd been a high-
spirit troublemaker as a young man, which is exactly what made
him a good cop, he said. He also tried not to take himself too seriously. That was the bad devil got brewed into bourbon and
beer, he said, the taste that made every word you said one you
couldn't take back without a fight. He believed he was over that

now. Florida was a suck-ass, crowded alligator swamp, but it had its good points. When he trusted himself again—and it had been nearly ten years—he told me he'd beg Mama to retire back into the Kentucky hills, where the air got cold enough to sparkle and there were hoot owls to answer in the night.

"Go back to the table, then, Speed. Don't get afeared of that."

"I'm not. Though I might care for something more than saltines to eat every night."

He hesitated. I could hear his breathing. "You need some money help? I don't have to pass that on to your mama."

"I'm making my way. If I sound down low, it's because a horse spun out at the track this morning and I hate to see an animal hurt. It's pretty this time of year, though. Which counts for a lot."

"Don't I know it." He sighed. "Ain't no other reason us ignorant hillbillies love it up there that I can think of. The Lord always did make it pretty where there wasn't good jobs."

"Yes sir." That was my sign-off. The way I let him know I'd given all I could.

"Reckon so, honey. We love you. You tell Harmon to give you a goddamn good deal when you see him, all right? Tell him I said so."

I hung up and sat on the edge of the bed, the surface of my skin running hot and itchy, my throat clogging like an old pipe, until the sad-eyed girl who did motel housekeeping knocked on the room's hollow door and asked to come in.

CHAPTER   1 2

*B*utton-up jeans. A light turtleneck. My polo boots, which
were about the best thing I still owned. I got all dressed up but
had nowhere to go. Or only one place. I looked out onto the jig-
saw puzzle of billboards and warehouse docks I could see from
the motel, at the wind-smeared gray clouds, and I knew I had to
get back to the track even if it was only to listen to the races on
the buzzy speakers of my car radio.

Traffic was backed up half a mile on Versailles Road, sign of a
good crowd, though nothing like it would be on the coming
weekend. Waiting bumper to bumper with the Oldsmobiles
and striped conversion vans, I noticed a jet parked at the end of
the airport runway, gold Arabic writing on its side. Charlie
Hamner was right. We'd finally told so many tall tales about our
fine bluegrass country it had gotten attractive to the rest of the
world.

I expected to stay in the car, maybe watch the huge Ford tractors parade to and from the equipment sheds trailing their har-
rows, maybe put my feet on the dashboard and doze. The radio
said the track was rated sloppy, and the announcer ran down the

scratches and overweights for each race. He also said they'd probably get an upgrade to muddy by race three or four because the rain had pretty much stopped. And so it had. I decided to walk for a bit. It would make me happy—or as close to happy as I could come—to see horses headed to the paddock with their arched necks and checkerboard rumps. I'd like hearing the echoes from the grandstand. All I had to do was stay clear of Alice's barn, which was easy if I kept to the far edge of the backside where most of the consigned two-year-olds were stabled. I didn't want to jinx Danny.

I didn't recognize him at first, probably because I wasn't making human faces come into focus. I was wandering along the newer, more open shed rows on the ridge, admiring the stock. I never tired of looking at horses, their rippled strength and eagerness. I made sure I knew whose barn I was passing, sorting the monograms and stable colors through my memory, but I wasn't paying attention to the massive transport trailers parked along the road. I didn't care who or what they carried. I still felt crisp from my mistake about Sunny.

He saw me. And like he always had, he raised hell, falling off a trailer's side ramp like a dropped string puppet. He spun into the gravel to my right, waited for me to shoot him a give-a-shit look. Which I did. Then he held his face steady, on the edge of goofy, until I knew him. His hair was different, burr cut, rinsed so dark it was almost maroon colored. He wore a couple of wide ear cuffs. More muscles than I remembered. But it was definitely Kevin. Kevin Anthony Brown. The boy I had once called a best friend.

I didn't even think about it. Just charged him, and he charged me, and we went into one of those dancing bear hugs that can last forever. I hadn't laid eyes on him for three years; it had been a lot longer than that since we'd really hung out. But we'd always cut each other a lot of slack, a whole lot, and there'd never been a bad moment between us that I could remember. He held me hard enough to squeeze water out of my eyes, and I thought, *This is it, this is what I've been waiting to grab hold of.*

"Shocking." Kevin leaned away from me. "You look totally thin."

I didn't say anything. Running with Kevin had always meant he did most of the talking.

"I can't believe how lucky I am to find you. You're not supposed to be here." He arched away from me again, still gripping my elbows. I thought I smelled chocolate and smoke in his words.

"I'm not?" The last time he'd seen me I'd been right here, or close by anyway, breaking horses for Billy T.

"Don't tell me you're back living with that church dress aunt. Please. Or I'll have to rescue you right this minute."

He was a regular yearbook of gestures. Hand on his forehead, hand on his swivel hips, mouth spurred into a frown. I couldn't keep up, but then that had been our goal way back when, to live lives that no one we knew could follow.

"I'm just riding," I told him. "Last I heard you were on the show circuit."

"We're dropping off some nags from Aiken." He flipped his fingers toward the truck. "I'm whoring with this outfit for money. They'll deliver me to Warrenton so I can hook back up with Hughes."

I knew Doral Hughes from the old days. A trainer of Grand Prix and Olympic jumpers, famous for the prices he set and the parties he liked to throw. Kevin had publicly mocked the lapels on Hughes's imported riding jackets until they became friends.

"Motherfucker." There was a shudder along the trailer's aluminum side as a voice growled loud enough to interrupt us. It was followed by the panicky scramble of hooves. "Pretty boy," the voice picked up again, "get your ass in here."

"Duty calls." Kevin gave me a politician's smile. "Can you wait? These jerkoffs are going to watch some races before we roll on. I'd like to whisper in your ear."

"Got nothing special to do."

"Good. Great." He hugged me again like a child would, every joint loose. "We'll blast from the past."

He leaped into the truck with the grace of a cat, and I remembered again how easy it was to underestimate him. He could really dig his heels in when he cared about something. He was also lazy, loud, too fond of drugs and attention. He'd barely managed to graduate from high school, though I knew he was plenty smart. When we were young he claimed that his only goal was to have lots of unexpected fun, that boring Lexington and boring Kentucky were his to stir crazy. I wondered if he still claimed such things. He looked good, handsome in a moody, costumed way. I wondered what his gig with Hughes was all about and whether the graphic design classes he'd once talked about had come to anything. I doubted they had.

He was a natural with horses, which was another thing somebody glancing at him wouldn't guess at. I watched him unload four road-weary animals with the concentration and strength the job demanded. There were two guys helping him, a tall, sleepy boy with country shag hair and a bulldoggish older man whose neck joined his chin with no interruption. The older guy was the driver, and he was plenty short on patience and common sense. But Kevin got the help he needed from grooms there to meet the horses. The job was done with nothing worse than a lot of grunting and spitting.

Kevin's eyes slanted with fun. "My love, I am now yours forever. Let us get the fuck out."

That was easy enough to do. We loped down to the Chevy, leaving Kevin's partners to find the mutuel windows on their own. The sky was a low washboard of white sliding above a light, tasteless wind. Kevin said he didn't want to eat, or to get near anything having to do with equines. He wanted to drive. First stop was to be this dive bar over on Euclid Street near the UK campus.

Just seeing him fumble with the door handle, jiggling his hips and bending at the knees like he did, brought the scraggly red lines of road maps back to me. We were the same age and had met on the fringes of the horse show circuit when I was day-dreaming about the Hermès saddles and warm-blood junior jumpers I'd never be able to afford. Kevin, who grew up near Georgetown, was on the circuit mainly for the parties and because his parents didn't care where he spent his time. We schemed with the other kids we liked—Marcia and Chris and Wheezie—the rich kids and the tagalongs. Kevin and I developed reputations as good, fast braiders until we were spending our summer weekends as far away as Tennessee and Michigan. The deal was we'd have our client's horses and ponies ready to go by 8 A.M., all of them. We'd wait for people to leave the show grounds for the night, get high, put on our aprons, step up on stools with our combs and thread, and braid manes and tails until our fingers wouldn't uncurl. Fifteen bucks for a pony. Twenty-five for a horse with a French-braided tail. Kevin took breaks for cigarettes, candy, and speed. I stuck mostly to dope, or Vivarin. We'd talk and laugh like crazy people through our dry mouths while the horses leaned against our knees and slept. It was good money, plenty for me to chip in on expenses at my aunt's place. Mama didn't much like me rollicking all over hell and gone, but she was in Florida by then and had to admit that her life there, with Cliff still hunting for sobriety and a steady good mood, didn't offer much for me. That summer with Kevin was my slingshot time. I'd hurled myself out into the world and waited to see what I would hit.

Once I got us into downtown Lexington, Kevin started with his stories of scalping tickets at Rupp Arena and the one time he'd tried to snatch an old lady's purse. They were stories I'd heard versions of before. It was only early afternoon, but I could see that by the time we got to the bar Kevin would be strung tighter than barbed wire. I'd gotten him out of trouble in such places before—watering holes crawling with college boys who liked to practice being surly—and he'd bailed me out a time or two as well. When I angled us east on Euclid, Kevin started telling the one about the football player who'd tried to seduce him when he was just sixteen. His voice skittered with glee. I considered asking him what kind of pills he was on.

"Pull over here. Here." He took an exaggerated swipe at the wheel. "Down that alley, then turn, then turn again. You re-member, don't you?" He gave me a mournful, round-mouthed look. "Oh, no. You couldn't. I didn't do it with you."

I eased the Citation onto a gravel apron next to a short stretch of droopy hurricane fence. "Where are we going? I thought Star Lounge was a ways yet."

"It is. We're just going to get stoned first. In a sentimental spot." He blinked like he'd tasted a bad recollection. "Maybe I forgot to mention that."

Kevin dug around in a small tapestry weave bag that he pulled from the pocket of his leather jacket. It was warm in the car, and dry and quiet. There were some buildings backed up to the alley, all of them the bright orange brick of Lexington's old neighborhoods. Kevin fished out a beautiful inlaid wood pipe, filled the bowl, lit up, and toked. It wasn't until he passed the pipe to me and I placed my lips over the damp ring he had left on the stem that I realized he'd done something to his eyes. He had long lashes for a man, black, curled, and his caramel irises always seemed to go coppery when he was mad. I didn't care much for what he was currently doing to his hair, but I was flat out amazed that he'd gone as far as getting tattoos under his eyes, which is what the lines under his lower lashes seemed to be. Permanent eyeliner. The first word that came to mind was *minx*.

"You finally noticed," he said, fluttering his lids like a junior miss. "You always said they were my best feature."

I snorted. The pot hadn't had time to get to me yet, though it hardly mattered. Kevin was getting to me plenty. "They still are. If we're not counting what's in your purse."

"And we aren't." He leaned over and emptied his bag on my lap. A matchbox, rubbers, an antique tin for the weed, a slick leather thong, crumbs, what looked like a tube of lipstick. "There. I had it done in Washington. Tell me it's lovely, and I'll tell you about your best feature."

I took a deep drag on the pipe and held my breath until everything seemed to be leaving me, even the weight of my clothes.

"Have to be your tits," Kevin continued. "I never got further than that."

We burst into honks of laughter, both of us. We'd always told each other everything we knew about sex. But the one time we'd gone at each other, well, we'd been braiding for hours, Kevin had been sipping on beer, and he'd coaxed me out of a stall for a break. I needed to be careful because the Welsh pony I was working on was famous for rubbing his braids loose as soon as he could. But I left the stall anyway, and movie-swooned into Kevin's arms because I was tired. Then, suddenly, it wasn't this Rhett-and-Scarlett joke anymore. We were nuzzling and kissing and working out how screwing right there between temporary, tarp-roofed stalls would be our kind of thing. We'd do it till the guard dogs barked. Neither of us was a virgin, though we halfway acted like it, feeling each other up with a lot of friction, then sagging into a crooked embrace. I pushed my apron down, he rolled my shirt up. I wasn't wearing a bra, so when he put his hands on my tits and started stroking them in silence, I realized we were changing ourselves—the frantic, clingy friendship we had—in a way that didn't include words.

I don't know which of us groaned first. Kevin was working his fingers under the snappy band of my panties, and I was tongue-flicking his ear when it happened. We both sounded out, wanting to encourage each other, I guess, even though we were plenty curious and horny. But something was wrong about it. The pitch. The way we both *oooohed* at once. He snickered, then I swallowed a hiccup of laughter. Five seconds later we slid to the sawdust and trampled grass holding our bellies. I tucked my shirt in, and we howled some more. Kevin later told me it was more than a month before he could finish it off with another girl. He couldn't keep it up. Foreplay had gotten too damn funny.

"Most men would say my legs are good, Kevin. The real suave ones."

"Then they're wrong, *chérie*. Tell them I said that. You got showgirl legs under those awful boy jeans you wear." He reached over and pinched at my thigh. "But for me it will always be your face. You have one, you know. A rare good face."

I started to make a crack about bone structure and how he'd make a better woman than I did on that score. But Kevin had zigzagged on me again. I could feel it in the swirly heat of the car. He was trying to tell me something. It scared me to think about why he wanted to get serious. The skin was pale and tight around his long, straight nose. He stared at the dashboard. I wondered if he was on the verge of trouble, real trouble, with Hughes or someone else.

"Girl," he said, making a quick grab for the matches in my lap, "I'm changing tunes. Feeling too old to grab-ass any Sigma Chis today." He filled his lungs with a hit. "Let's drive to Paris." Paris. The little town I'd once lived near. Except for trailering horses to a farm off the Paris Pike for Billy T., I hadn't stopped there in more than three years. Kevin had always loved the town, mainly because it wasn't his own. It was just like him to think a trip up there would be fun.

"No excuses. Give me the keys. I won't have you driving on a cloud of Iranian sensimilla or whatever this good shit is. You are useless when you're stoned." He zipped the keys out of the ignition. "I'm used to it. I drive big fucking trucks on drugs all the time."

We switched places. I buckled my seat belt while Kevin applied some outrageous fuchsia lipstick to his lips. Then he stomped the brake pedal and lurched us out of the alley. I sank back in my seat, my entire head feeling like some kind of velvety skullcap. It occurred to me I might be winning—or losing—a lot of money at that very instant, but it wasn't a thought I could hold on to.

He wanted to go out Russell Cave Road because there was a big house he had to drive by, one he'd once imagined buying and living in. "Fantasy is what I eat," he said. "What this reformed redneck still lives on, don't you know." He sang the words like they were lyrics to an anthem. I kept one eye on the box churches and shotgun shacks we passed. I hadn't really aimed for a spot in the countryside since I'd snuck up on Three Pines Farm. If we turned on Ferguson Road, we'd roll right by Mama and Cliff's last house. I wondered if I ought to ask for that.

Kevin chattered on about himself, some girlfriend who had a daddy in Congress and some kick-ass tattoos on her butt, nothing so subtle as the lines under his eyes, you understand. He mentioned something about a boyfriend, then Hughes and a desk drawer full of rainbow-colored foreign money, but what he said was so garbled in his mouth or my shooting star mind that I couldn't quite sort it out. Kevin had never been one for keeping his stories straight, so when he mentioned men to me I couldn't tell if he wanted me to assume they were his lovers or not. He knew it wouldn't shock me. And I knew he was capable of accepting any offer that was made. In that way we were maybe not so different.

We spun by some of the more prominent estates. Domino Stud. Spendthrift. The dope made me more of a rocking chair romantic than I wanted to be, so I got a lump in my throat passing under the gnarled, spreading oaks and catching sight of a few mares with foals grazing in the wet fields. Kevin loved the homes we could see from the road, and he remembered every detail of the ones he'd toured with the Garden Club. He practically drove us into the ditch twice while he gawked. He said he could never decide whether he preferred brick or limestone as a façade. Had the same problem in Virginia, where the Federal style sometimes took his fancy above the Colonial.

"I've got to marry up the way you did. I'd like to have a nice place to live." He leaned back and pressed at the steering wheel like it was a barbell.

"So do it." It was not a topic I wanted to go on about.

"Hughes's already married. Bitch spends most of her time in Antigua wrinkling her skin."

"Sorry you missed your chance."

Kevin swung his head slowly in my direction, then blew me

an obscene lipsticked kiss. "How is Eric, by the way? I forgot to ask."

He knew Eric a little. I'd made sure they hooked up at a Christmas party once. But he hadn't come to the wedding, a fact that had relieved me at the time.

"I guess you're glad the bad guys haven't cut on his face. Or do you still care?"

It was a mean thing to say. "Of course I care." Then I stopped, tried to reel in a snagged, fluttering thought. "How did you know he'd been hurt? Have you seen him?"

"No." Kevin smacked both hands against his cheeks, letting the car veer. "No. No. No. It was the talk of Aiken, is all. Awful vulture gossip. They said it was crack dealers."

"It wasn't," I snapped. Defending my husband wasn't a dead reflex.

"I also hear expensive things about that Sun Chief mare y'all showcase. Like maybe she's more recovered from her injury than a person might think. Stakes ready."

"I couldn't say. She was fine when I left, but she needs a couple of prep races. Conservatively."

"And you miss her. And you're not together with Eric, right? Should I be unhappy about that part?"

I flattened a hand on the creaky black leather of his jacket. "Probably."

"Then I'm sorry to hear it."

He turned down Ferguson, and we were past the house Mama and Cliff had rented before I was ready to see it. It was a story-and-a-half clapboard cottage on about two acres that had been carved out of a large estate by some independent coot who'd worked his way up from tenant farmer. A good place for us. I'd had an attic bedroom I loved. Cliff had a woodstove and room to garden. There was a fishing boat on blocks in the yard now, I saw, and lean-tos for chickens or dogs. Mama's green rose trellis was still standing and her bushes had been cut back for winter like they ought to be. I wanted to feel a whole patchwork of feelings about the place right then and there, but I couldn't. The feelings weren't where I could find them.

"I'm positively in love with this," Kevin said. "We do breakfast in the little place near the crossroads, healthy corned beef hash for me, gravy biscuits for you and your tremendous munchies. Then we go to that pawnshop and paw through the scuzzy jewelry. You wouldn't believe the rings I've gotten that way. Incredible tacky stuff."

"Cliff wants me to buy a gun." I read the real estate signs at the entrance of a Greenwich Road farm. The acreage was being broken up into residential lots.

"Old Deputy Dawg? What's that all about?"

"He thinks I ought to have one for when Eric gets crazy, I guess. Or just in case. I had one in New York."

"I bet you did," he said, putting on a gangster sneer. "Haven't you heard it's all sweetness and light and hair-sprayed bangs down here, honey? Y'all is just fine."

It was a Kevin twist, cut down everybody, get mad about hypocrites or money you didn't have, then do a ballet spin and laugh about it. For a long time I'd admired him and how he slung around all these raw reactions we weren't supposed to have. He was so unchained. But I could also see how he was a pain in the ass. The eyeliner, the congressman's daughter—they came from playing to a younger, wrecking-ball crowd.

Paris was a proud old town that started to modernize itself toward ugliness in the 1960s, stopped when it realized quaint was the way to go, then began to die on the vine anyway. Mama had always blamed the decline on the rich folks who lived outside town but didn't support it. But she'd done her buying in

Lexington, or at the discount places off the interstate near Georgetown once the Toyota plant got built, just like everybody else.

"Damn, that diner place is shut up. I was looking forward to making those bigots wait on me." Kevin nipped at his caked lips like he was trying to smear his teeth with pink. Then he whipped into an empty parking place on what looked like an empty street. "Pawnshop on the corner is the place for me. We'll get you a blue steel Navy Colt. A swell army man dick to go with your new independence."

"I don't think so." Cliff's friend Harmon worked at another place farther in town, though that didn't make much difference. I didn't need a gun. I wasn't going to get one.

"How 'bout some sparkly trinkets and baubles to cheer up your pretty face?" Kevin had refilled the pipe and was fortifying himself.

"You really want to do that here? In daylight? Before lunch?" I made a neck-stretching scan of the sidewalk.

"Cops here aren't often up to hassling a white boy. You ought to remember that." He opened the door and crawled out, a scuttle of knees and elbows. "Just keep the window rolled up if you're staying. No reason to tempt good citizens." He stood and pulled his jacket smooth over his waist, shrugged himself into a slow workingman's amble he'd borrowed from some memory. He shoved open the bar-covered door of the pawnshop with one hand and was out of my sight. I settled in my bucket seat, hoping it wasn't really mildew I smelled under the fog of marijuana. I declared to myself that I wouldn't try any more drugs for a while, that a day which had started like this one ought to be a day in which nothing else was allowed to happen.

I looked at the slice of Paris I could see through the windshield. Faded plastic flowers in a flower box in front of an old home chopped into apartments. Cigarette butts fanning out from the entrances to shops. New street awnings. Obsessively polished brass mail slots. It was a town like most towns, going two directions at once, neither of them toward perfection. The door to the pawnshop flashed like a signal mirror, then went black along the edges, and I saw Kevin slip out. He crab-stepped around the corner without even peeking my way.

No presents for me. Kevin hadn't even been inside long enough to ask about the antique officers' swords or weirdo ninja junk those places hang behind the register. He'd once been ridiculous about giving me gifts. Fluffy blue teddy bears, cross-stitched pillows—perfumy girlie junk which let us both laugh about how Kentucky boyfriends treated girlfriends and how we would never get wrapped up in all that. I was allowed to buy him only cassette tapes he preapproved. That was a big rule.

Three minutes later he was back in my dreamy frame of vision, looking as stoned as he was with his eyes crimped against the afternoon light. For a woozy moment something about him put me in mind of the card player DaSilva. I shook my head to see if it might really rattle. Kevin knocked on the driver's side window even though the door wasn't locked. Then he mouthed a long, wagging sentence at me. I popped the door.

"And the winner is—"

"Your congressman?" I guessed.

"Gong. Big gong, Miss Kerry. I was trying to ask about your birthstone. I was remembering it was that watered-down scum green one, but then I couldn't be sure."

"I'll say diamond." I reclamped my seat belt, realizing that I liked having Kevin back, that I almost loved it, even though his games were more persistent than a puppy's.

"Nothing exceptional in that establishment. Plenty of guns,

though. And boring neck chains the asshole owner claimed were eighteen-karat gold as though a man of my taste wouldn't know better." He turned on the car, sniffled.

"Maybe he caught sight of your eyes. That might have thrown him."

"Ah, all those guys ever do is watch where your hands go. Mr. Stud Gone to Fat never even looked at my face. If you'd come in two minutes after me, asking for a weapon and batting your Patsy Clines, we might have had some real fun. Pairs make them nervous. You and me, we could be the backwater Bonnie and Clyde."

We serpentined out of town, Kevin too worked up about something to stop at traffic lights. Until Paris Pike, we didn't talk.

"Where'd you go after?" I asked.

"Huh." He glanced at me with his eyebrows bunched together like something had gone wrong and it was all my fault. "Oh, that. Smokes. I went looking real fast for cigarettes. Couldn't find those either, Bonnie."

I smiled with lips I could barely feel. After a few neon moments of silence, I looked hard at the fluty pipe we'd left in the ashtray. The dry, cinder taste of my mouth and the way the tarnished sun hung behind the blurred, grasping trees made me turn away.

"What are you doing for Doral Hughes?"

He didn't seem to hear me at first, so I repeated the question.

"Hughes? Oh, him. I move horses mostly, or help him select his prospects. He says he likes my instincts. We're supposed to go to Germany this summer to sort through some warmbloods, then down to Rio, if I get my way." Kevin's voice was flat and scratchy, as though he was trying to keep the volume down even for himself.

"And that's the whole job?"

"If you're saying I'm not ambitious, go ahead. I've heard that all my life. Hughes pays me what I need, and we have our certain kind of fun. You might say I keep him out of worse trouble." The way he said it, half laughing while he kept his back stiff, warned me off the topic. I tried to remember what I'd heard about Hughes beyond the usual: that he was rich, that he'd drugged some green jumpers before he sold them to wealthy amateurs who thought they were better riders than they were, that he overcharged his clients. I knew exactly what Kevin would say about those things. He'd say Hughes was no worse than the next guy.

"We should have stayed together and worked up our own angle on the horse business." Kevin let the car drift for a second, then pressed the small square of the accelerator and slung us around a narrow, dipping turn. "That's the only change I'd give up something to make."

I raised my chin and let fresher air pour down my throat. I wanted to agree with him. We had skills. We knew how to be tolerant. Still, Kevin and I wouldn't make it very far together; he had to see that. We brought out the wrong shadows in each other.

It was harder to say good-bye than I'd expected. I suddenly wanted to go back on the road with him, talk all night in a bar, memorize a phone number that would always reconnect us. The irritations I'd felt dissolved into a thick, anxious sadness that flopped under my lungs. He pretended we'd see each other soon. I was to drive up for Hughes's Easter bash, or we could hook up for the Derby. He'd probably be in New York sometime, too, if I decided to pick up those pieces. He asked me a few grinning, rapid-fire questions about people we used to hang out with, as though either of us cared. Finally, he gave me some goggle-eyed kisses—Parisian kisses, he called them—on my cheeks. "Do us both a gigantic favor and find a nice old man with deep pockets who can still get it up. Be happy and have the money too. I'll come visit, play in the hot tub with your kids." He pulled a sad face but his eyes were still skipping like stones. "Right now I'm about to crawl into the sleeper of that horseshit truck and take a nap." He mounted the ramp one crooked step at a time, like a wrung-out gunslinger, all for my benefit.

*t*he races weren't quite over, but there was a solemn feel to the backside. For all but the eight or nine horses in the last contest, the day was done and gone. I heard the patter of rain on the dogwoods before I felt it, not as cold as it had been that morning, but insistent, like it had a job to do. I dug into the backseat of the Chevy for my anorak and a drier pair of gloves. I could definitely smell the mildew then, filling the car as if the stuff I kept there hadn't been lived in for a long time. Dropping my forehead to the beige upholstery, I made a bullet fist and drove it into the foam seat cushion time and time again. It didn't make me feel much better.

Things looked battened down at Alice's barn, almost abandoned. Jenny the hotwalker came out of the last stall on the near end, a stitched lead line looped over her shoulder. I made a beeline for her, suddenly dreading the sight of Danny and what he might tell me. Jenny waited by the stall. I hadn't noticed how pigeon toed she was or how her chin was splotched with old acne scars until then.

"The new colts ship in?" I leaned into the stall to check the horse standing there in a gray plaid blanket. It soothed me to look at him and inhale his dry, dandered scent.

"Yeah, we got three of them. I'm thinking of coming on as a groom. Missus Piersall could use me."

"Are they all babies?"

Jenny nodded carefully, as though it was a fact she'd chewed on. "Rough broke is what them guys said, but this one is sweet as pie. It'd be a good job."

"Sure," I said with most of the enthusiasm she expected. "There's plenty to learn from Alice and Reno."

"They pay on time?"

"Yes." The horse shuffled in his straw, dropped his head. "You won't get cheated here."

Jenny dragged a hand across her forehead. "Cheating don't worry me like straight bad treatment does. Missus Piersall looks like she don't stand for bad treatment." She walked to the end of the barn, hitching her bald corduroys up over her butt. The rest of the new horses were on the other side of the shed and needed tending to.

"You might ask Reno to get you a bulb for this fixture," I said, looking at the dying yellow light in the stall. Jenny went on like she hadn't heard me.

"Got business here?"

The voice seemed to breathe right onto the short hairs of my neck. It was Reno, his face as rigid as I'd ever seen it.

"Huh? Sure." I yanked on the sleeves of my anorak and stood straight. The horse in the stall moved close enough to nudge me between the shoulder blades.

Reno glared.

"These new ones, the horses," I fibbed, "I came to see if I could ride them. If Alice needed them worked tomorrow."

A muscle twitched high on the slab of Reno's cheek. He

didn't believe me. Had he seen me the night before, with the money and with Danny too? Was he hot over that? If he was, then I could tell him to go to hell and stay there. I hadn't broken any of his rules. Quick as I thought those things, I steadied my gaze and tried to draw some anger of my own from the glowing coals of his eyes. But he didn't stand still long enough to suffer that. He stepped around me and went out into the slanting needles of rain. No coat, no hat. His blue shirt spotting and staining with water.

I knew Reno wanted me on guard. I also knew I hadn't done anything to him, or to Alice, so I figured to shake the moment off. Except that Reno was about as easy to shake as a trailing redbone hound.

I visited Flare and his scoundrel rooster, who was tearing and picking at invisible critters on his splotchy breast. Flare liked to be admired with talk, so I put together some low, flattering sentences for him. I looked in on the filly and a bay mare who'd been recovering from some mild soreness in one leg. Peeked in the claimer's stall, which was freshly bedded but oddly empty. I hoped he hadn't broken down. It seemed like Jenny would have mentioned if he had; injury wasn't the kind of news that kept. Breathing through my mouth, I made my way closer to Danny's bunk room door. Before I could see if it was locked, Alice hailed me from across the yard, where she was talking to a couple of people made anonymous by their army green rain gear. She was draped in an emergency orange poncho that looked like a giant tattered kite.

"I was hoping you'd show up," she said, gliding in beside me and clamping my biceps with a hard, bare hand. "I wanted to talk over what happened this morning and maybe get your ideas on the green horses I just brought in. Danny's got the afternoon off to spend all his money, but maybe you could whip us up some of that tea he does. You watched him pretty close that time, didn't you?"

For the second time in five minutes a warning buzz started in the tiny bones of my ear. Alice was sounding me out about Danny, letting me know she was keeping her eye on me. I shrugged off her hand and dug into my pocket for a bandanna.

"I don't believe I saw much more about it than you did. Maybe I can get the hot pot in the tack room going if you've got some Lipton's."

"So you didn't absorb that Chinese magic, huh?" She angled her face to peer under the brim of my hood. Her words were softer than I expected, though I knew very well what she was asking.

"Afraid not. And it's Japanese, not Chinese, if you really want to know."

She drew her chins back. "I'm interested enough to maybe let that boy teach me how he gets that good flavor some day. But I'll put up with the piss water you make if I have to. At least it'll be warm."

We stepped into the tack room, and I filled the pot with distilled water from a plastic jug. Alice settled into one of her folding chairs. She nosed around in her overstuffed workout book, mumbling out loud, then cleared her throat to brag about one of the homebreds she'd just brought into the barn. She thought he had the package—conformation, bone, in-line breeding. She couldn't wait to get him under saddle.

"How many rides you think you can stand?" She flipped back through the ragged pages of her book while she asked.

"I'd like to get to where I'm making two hundred a week one way or another. And a place to stay. If you're asking me to be honest."

"I'm asking if you want your card filled. That's what I'm asking."

It was a generous offer, made with a throaty, grudging voice but made just the same. Alice was giving me a chance to lay roots and save paychecks, and this time it looked like there wouldn't be any strings attached. She hadn't said anything about living at her farm.

"Sounds like a damn decent shot. What did I do right? Did that claimer bust the tote board this afternoon, or what?"

She sank down until her neck disappeared into her broad chest. "That's the thing about you, Kerry. You mostly act like the dumbest-shit woman I know, but there's no slipping some things past you." She wagged her head, exasperated. I stayed confused.

"That claimer you've been working raced fine. A helluva sight better than anybody expected, given the sloppy track and the fact we drew the seven hole in a sprint against our betters. He finished fourth, two and a half back. I put Donna Carter on him, and she said he was driving, she got good response even though he had no love for the mud. He just wanted to get out of it. So we got a piece of the purse, and he came out on all fours just so I can give him up to a claim. At twenty thousand. Which is more than he's worth."

"Who snatched him?" I had a bad feeling about the answer to that question.

"Your friend Roy Delvecchio, and I'm wondering why. He's got no room in his barn for cart horses like that. He paid too much. I only ran the poor creature because Phil Kronce asked me to."

"Did you see Roy?"

"Hell, no. Reno got the slip and handled the whole thing

with that snippy assistant of Roy's. Made Reno almost as mad as it made me—except I've been feeling too tired to get it up like I ought to." She paused, looked wearily at the hissing hot pot, and went on. "Reno's halfway acting like it's your fault, like you set Roy onto the horse with a tip about the blinkers or something like that. I'm not quite the one to believe that bullshit. Delvecchio needs a better reason. The man shelled out twenty thou for the horse when he could have gotten him for fifteen the next time he runs. I don't believe he'd waste good money even if he was pillow-talking with you."

"That's not happening."

"I did try to suggest to Reno that there was only room in your bed for so many men."

My face went stiff and I felt my veins fill with heat. I stood to give some force to my denial. "There's nothing—"

"I know, I know." Alice waved me off. "That was out of line. I'm just practicing a little local paranoia. Indulge me. Will you ride for this barn, or not?"

"And give up Roy's horses?"

She looked at me with a childish furrow in her forehead, like there was something about me she couldn't quite put in place. "I'm trying to set you on some sort of straight course here. That would be part of the deal."

"I'd like to give him notice, mostly for Thomas McGhee's sake." As hesitant as I was, I knew I was better off with Alice since there was no way I was going to ship north with Roy's outfit when that time came. Alice could give me a sort of home.

"Through the weekend is fine. You'll get most of what I got, except two or three mounts go to Rogelio. I got a feeling he's going to do good here and catch plenty of race rides. He shot through a gap in the fifth race that nearly impressed even me."

We were quiet while I poured boiling water into two mismatched mugs that were dusty with chaff. The tea bags were stuffed into a cracked plastic cup along with some artificial sweetener and a bent spoon.

"Roy's not always predictable. I doubt he was spending his own money on that claimer." I plopped the tea bags into the mugs. "Maybe he just did it to bug us."

"You mean to bug *me*. Who he never even acknowledges. I heard he's got a turf horse he wants to run against Flare in the Elkhorn Stakes, but why shit on me now? All it does is peeve me. Niall's horse, the Arab one, will be in that race, and I can guarantee you at least two good horses from New York will come down for the purse. It'll be a free-for-all. He can't control that." Alice rubbed at her eyes like they hurt. "Maybe you're right. It's male menopause, and Delvecchio's misfired his tiny nuts."

We had a laugh over that, the idea of Roy losing control of the hormones he was so proud of. Then Alice went on to tell me how she'd talked to Mark Holmes. Red Light Rising was fine, but Betsy Shires wasn't—she'd gone straight into surgery over at the university—and Preston's horse might have a chipped knee. The colt who'd caused the trouble had been put down. His ankle had shattered, and it hadn't made anybody feel good to watch the ambulance roll past the barns carrying its doomed, sedated cargo. His two-bit trainer—a gypsy who did most of his running in Ohio and Illinois—looked ruined, his blubbering lips so gray, Alice said, she'd been afraid he'd have a heart attack right then and there. She told me this in a matter-of-fact way while she slurped her tea. She'd put down horses in her day, but I knew it never got easy. And if it was one you'd raised, well, I'd been told it wasn't like losing an actual child, though there were moments it felt bad enough.

I was working toward a short speech where I thanked Alice for having some confidence about my future when a scrawny rebel yell grated down the shed row. I sat bolt upright, spilling tea across my knuckles. I knew exactly what that sound meant. Alice rubbed at her eyes again.

"That's the whistle blow for me to get out of here," she said. "I'll let Reno take care of any celebrating."

I stayed glued to my seat on the tack trunk.

"Yep." She rustled her poncho back into shape. "Don't forget our deal now. You are mine."

I tried to smile at what I hoped was a wisecrack, but nothing came of the effort. I felt frozen except for the dome of muscle between my lungs and innards. It flickered like a busted wing.

There was another yell, then Alice lumbered into the aisle, and all I could hear was excitable voices and a few snorts from the alerted horses. I knew Danny was back, probably with Dawg, and he was in high spirits. I just couldn't make myself go on from there.

When I finally looked out the door, my leg muscles as cramped as my breathing, I saw Jenny, Danny, and Dawg clotted together under the overhang of the dripping roof. Dawg was dressed as I'd seen him that morning, though the wool cap now rested backward on his head. Danny's hair was down, hanging in wet buckwheat-colored hanks. He was wearing a neon poncho exactly like Alice's except that he had twisted it sideways and pushed the material behind his shoulders like it was some kind of superhero cape. His nose and cheeks were red, and the front of his dark green T-shirt was bibbed with rain or sweat. When he saw me, he raised both arms straight over his head and opened his mouth as wide as it would go. I saw a chain of teeth. Dawg clamped his hands over the top of his head and grinned.

"He shoots," Danny hollered. "He scores."

Jenny shook her head in wonder and went back to her post

around the corner. She'd told me earlier that she'd given up playing the ponies when she gave up hard liquor.

"How about a victory kiss?" Danny boogied toward me with his hips in a sloppy disco grind. "I done you right this time."

I stood still while he rolled in and planted a hot one over half of my mouth. I tasted beer and cheap dope. "I ain't really told anybody else all of it," he said in a happy whisper. "I got what you want right here," and he patted the small of his back. "More than thirty-five thousand. It was a hellacious day."

I started to kiss him back but settled for a peck near his ear. He didn't seem to notice the difference. He signaled Dawg to join us, and I watched the boy swoop in, all bright eyes and smile.

"We done good," he said. "Real good."

I'd locked it up—the possibility of winning. Locked it up so tight I didn't know which way to move. They wanted an audience, so I tried to grab hold and listen to their war stories. Dawg went on for a while about how much he liked taking the claimer to the saddling area for the second race, where everything seemed so important and tense, and how what he called a red horse had reared and flipped on its back right next to him and Miz Piersall, a near miss he decided to read as the kickoff for a run of good luck. Then he told me how he won his first $100 using a tip from Danny. "I didn't even touch my money after a point," he said. " 'Cause I still had that horse to cool before them other folks took him away, and D-man here, he had the gold finger on my behalf."

Danny dropped his head modestly. "We went along real nice. It ain't always that way, but today the lady sat with us. I missed the daily double for you, darling." He gave me a crooked grin. "But I boxed an exacta on the four race and boom."

Dawg scooted back in mock fear. "The man scary at the fifty-dollar window. Spooky."

"I should've come," I said, troubled by the blankness I felt knowing I could send Eric enough money to get him through his next payment. Troubled that I didn't feel relieved.

"Naw, huh-uh." Dawg slapped hands with Danny for about the tenth time. "This was working mens."

Danny slid under my arm and cut me off from his partner. "That would have been fine. I wish you had. We'd probably been luckier yet." He turned to Dawg, who'd taken a wad of bills out of his front pocket. "I'm gonna remind you like you asked, Raymond. You take that pile on back to your mama or your sister, whoever it was you talked about. Take it right on home after you clean them last stalls."

"Uh-huh," the boy said. "Just thinking what a set of car speakers would cost."

"Don't think," Danny said. "It'll ruin you. Clamp your sorry brain to a shovel right now. I got a little more business."

"Uh-huh."

"Uh-huh is right." Danny faked a roundhouse punch in Dawg's direction. "You keep the boss off our tails and we'll try it again sometime. Clean the stalls. That's the deal." Danny turned back to me, his eyes crimped by new lines at their corners. He looked a little like a trail's end cowboy. "Come on in here," he said. "We got some talking to do."

It was strange to be back in his room. The refrigerator was covered with a mess of dishes, forks, and puddled candle wax. In the foggy light of the afternoon I could see the unused window fan and two or three stacks of curling paperbacks, more than I'd noticed before. The bed was oddly neat, I thought, with the gold batik sheets tucked under the mattress with military precision. Some habits never die, I thought. Either that or Danny was addicted to the few rituals that made sense in his head. His teacups were nowhere in sight. His sleeping bag was folded in a rectangle at the foot of the bed. And there was a white plastic trash can I hadn't noticed before. It was crowded with crumpled paper towels and scraps of colored tape.

Danny weaseled out of his poncho and wet shirt and dropped them both on the floor. I watched while he pulled a thick pad of money from his damp waistband—some of it rewrapped in the original plastic—and dropped it on an empty plate on top of the fridge. I'd never seen him shirtless before. He had high, narrow chest muscles and small beige nipples, but there was a fullness to his belly that told of the kind of older man he'd be—bulky, hard to knock down. I also admitted what I hadn't wanted to admit the first time I laid eyes on him: the way his soaked Levi's drew up around his thighs made him look good and well hung.

As though the money sitting smack on that plate had cleared the air between us, Danny seemed to read my mind.

"I'm getting out of this wet stuff," he said. "You can watch or not watch."

I flushed a little. He unbuttoned the jeans, then pried his feet out of his black sneakers, taking time to comment on my polo boots, which he hadn't seen before. "You got the looks to wear those, you know. The right kind of legs. I'll never figure out why so many women wear stuff they look bad in. I don't mind a girl who's what you call fat so long as she don't pretend she's not. I never have gotten that." He moved close enough to snatch a pair of dry jeans from his bag near the end of the bed. His own legs were thick with muscle and covered with light golden hair. What I could see of his butt looked nice and strong. "You got a opinion?"

"Not really." I watched him step hastily into his pants. "I wear what riders wear. My mama always said I had a limited sense of style."

"I bet she never said you weren't pretty." He gave me his best

Danny-boy grin, tilting one eyebrow. "I know that for a fact." And he let his words drift between us while he combed out his hair and tied it back with a length of dark string.

"Are we talking business?" I asked.

"Yep." His face was squared away and serious now, the way I hoped mine had looked all along. He brought the money over and sat next to me on the bed. He was still shirtless, and I inhaled the sharp, nervous smells the day had wrung from him. I could also see that the plate he set carefully on my knees had last been used for toast or something else that left behind a buttery sheen and a rind of black crumbs.

"All that gambling tuckers a man out." He fell back on the mattress with a husky sigh. "You might want to count that out loud, or just thank me, either one."

The sheaf of bills was as wide across as my palm, some of it crisp, some of it dirty. It smelled like paper money always did, inky and secretive.

"Well, come on. I either bought you out from under your bad husband or I bought you a giant truckload of fun. One of those facts ought to lighten you up some."

I reminded him that Eric needed more than I could give him, words I was sorry I couldn't say without shaking.

"He *said* he needed thirty. The truth probably ain't that bad. Or it's a lot worse. I know guys who had to be down fifty K to the bookies before they got hurt. Tell yourself he's lying. Give yourself a break, maybe don't send him a dollar."

My face twitched at the suggestion. It was a tempting idea. Still, I couldn't get past the fact that I owed Eric something. Money was what he would get. "I'd like to even my scores," I said.

"No," he said. "You want to get back something that's already out of your life, which is a backwards kind of understanding in my eye. You ought never to look over your shoulder like that. But it's your deal, so I go with the flow. This is a occasion for celebrating."

"What are you celebrating?" I slid close to the edge of the sinking mattress, where I could watch his rising white chest and the brassy tufts of hair under his arms. They were more real than my multiplied money. Or my conscience.

"Making it through another day. Having cash in my pocket. Walking out ahead."

"Thank you."

"Damn right," he said. "You got good manners. But I know you're here to do better than that."

He pulled me back to lie next to him, the tops of our heads brushing against the cold block wall. At first I just wouldn't think about it. Kevin's dope was still marinating in my brain, and all of my movements seemed silky and wavy. My tongue felt like it needed to peel. Danny was the one who took the plate of money off my lap, who worked my hair out of its braid with me hardly noticing a thing. He ran his hand under the stretched hem of my turtleneck and began making tight, warm circles on my stomach that soon matched the quick pulse I felt in my neck. I rolled toward him with my eyes closed, thinking I should kiss him, which would be what he wanted, but he rolled me back. "Not yet," he whispered. "You take it easy." So I lay flat and tried to find the closet in my mind that would let me do this the right way.

Danny nuzzled and stroked my hair out across the sheets. He slipped his warm fingers up around my nipples like he was almost afraid of them, then said he hoped it was all right if he went slow. He'd had some beer and liquor earlier, and some lousy weed, and he needed to work through that. He asked me to swing around on the bed, then he knelt on the floor and took off my boots one at a time while he admired them again, touching the tooled leather with his callused fingers. He wanted to know where I'd gotten them, and I told him, smiling while I did because he acted so casual with his hard-on tunneling up to the waistband of his jeans. He peeled off my socks and went to massage the arches of my feet, but I couldn't take much of that. It made my body vibrate too fast, so I asked him to climb back on the bed. I got my own shirt off, and by the time I'd wriggled half out of my jeans Danny understood he was going to need to do a few things my way. His blue eyes fanned gray, and the short, pale muscles in his shoulders bunched for just a second, but he had himself stripped bare before I did. We tried to slide together on the narrow bed.

"Damn, who kicked you?" He asked me that between kisses at my collarbone and tits.

"Just a horse." I'd told him about Eric hitting me, but he didn't make the connection. If everything went the way I wanted, there were plenty of connections Danny wouldn't make. He'd like me, he'd like me in bed, and that would be it. End of story.

He eased me flat onto the mattress, then hunched and concentrated. Traced the curve of my calf with a fingertip, nipped wetly at the insides of my thighs. Paused. Went down on me with humming and lust. What truly got me going was the struggling and working of his whole body, the uncomplicated heat we made. I rolled him over, put my mouth on him as long as he could stand it. By the time I climbed onto him and settled into the rhythm of his hands, we were both long past planning. I was all muscle and light. Danny gathered and held, gathered and held. After a blood-spun time I shuddered, feeling like the inside of me was shedding an old skin. I dove deep—*Don't think about it, don't think, it's never the same*—and it was done. Over.

"Shit. What they say is true. You rider types is strong and tight." We collapsed side by side. His chest rose and fell between his panted words.

It was a line I'd heard before, as good a way to fence in feeling as any. "Like that's a surprise to you after all the tracks you've been on."

"Naw. You're right." His reddened face and ears got redder. "I did know. But you might have to go in a new category."

"Sure," I said. "Feel free."

"Don't be telling me you haven't done that business with some nice grooms."

"Trainers," I said, wickedly. "Mostly trainers. That's where the payoff is."

"Plenty of payoff right here, missy," and he pointed to his polished prick and the money both. I grinned at his joke while I fought the sudden urge to like him less because it was over. We'd gotten past the mystery we might have hoped for. I wondered when getting past things would stop being my goal. I found my turtleneck and put it back on against the seeping damp.

"I'm not one to talk much," Danny said as he scrounged around for his own shirt. "But I hope you didn't do that because you felt like you had to."

"No," I said, giving again what he asked for. "I did it because I wanted to. I like to get laid. And you're cute."

"So shut up about it, right?"

"Right."

"Will you stay?" His blue eyes were wider now, and still. Our bodies had sealed back together in some places, slick and warm.

"Sure." An easy word to let loose. "Okay."

"I'd like to sleep some of this off with you here," he murmured.

I could handle that. I even wanted it. To be held. To sleep the way a woman ought to sleep after work and worry and love. I'd gotten what I wanted, after all. A debt settled. Some security for Sunny. Once I made the decision, I could barely keep my eyelids from lowering.

Danny ran a careful hand down my thigh, then slipped out of bed. It wasn't even dark yet. He needed to take a leak, he said. He'd do that and swallow some medicine for this cold he thought might be coming on, and he'd be back. He put on his jeans while I made a yawning wisecrack about his full ass. He said something complicated about the cold medicine being from his friend Maria Dolores, the woman from last night I'd almost met. He told me again he'd be right back, that he could bring some food, but I was burrowing into the tangled, salted sheets, finding relief there, feeling tired down to my soles. He pulled the sleeping bag up over my shoulders, right to my chin, before he squeezed out the door. I knew he'd be back. And he was. Some time had passed, I'd been dozing, but he came to the bed naked and fast. Then it was like a fire had been stoked inside me, a furnace fire. We were pounding and hard. He drove into me without whispering about it, and I liked that. It was our way of saying there was nothing to forgive. Nothing to hold back. When we finished, I remembered I'd missed my dinner with Billy T., but I was too smooth-melted to regret it much. Danny wrapped around me and fell asleep. After some stray thinking about how Eric would react to his windfall, I slept too.

It wasn't until hours had passed that I sat up thirsty and off kilter. My hair was a crackling rat's nest. My eyes were pasted shut, breath stale. It was still before dawn, before the horses needed tending, but I knew soon enough what had happened. I could smell it surely in the bolted, silent dark. Danny was gone from that room for good.

CHAPTER 14

*O*f course he hightailed it with the money. It didn't take half a second to figure that out. His duffel had been packed the night before, only I'd been too blind to see it. He left his sheets and his sleeping bag with me underneath them stinking of foolishness.

I catapulted off the bed with one thought in mind. It would take me two minutes to get to where Maple Leaf Farms stabled its horses. I'd bang tubs and yowl until somebody there told me which Maple Leaf scumbag was the friend of Danny's he'd talked about at the El Dorado. I'd track that friend, corner him, pull out his fingernails with my teeth if I had to. I'd find out where my sweet-talking, ear-blowing, fuck-stealing thief had gone. Then I'd follow him.

That idea lasted about as long as it took for my bare feet to go cold on the grainy cement floor. I wanted it. I wanted to squeeze Danny's gulping, conniving throat until it was as crushed as my pride. But the gypsy tracker in me knew I didn't have a chance. All I had to imagine was what *I'd* do in Danny's place. I wouldn't tell anybody where I was going. I'd drive somewhere fast, a place far from horses, and I'd keep a short-term lid on the cash. I'd fade into the gray roads and meals of everywhere America. Crowing all the way.

I can't begin to say all that soured inside me. I cared that the money was gone, and I cared even more about the way I'd lost it. Tricked and conned and pissed on. But once I gagged the panic out of my head, I had to ask myself what I'd thought I was doing. I'd been willing to roll the dice. If Danny had lost the bets, I'd be just as wiped out as I was now. Why did I think I deserved more than ruin?

I considered that while I wiped Danny off my thighs with his incense-smoked sheets. Then I dressed and opened the bunk room door. There was enough light to make out the yard, but the aisle was still dark. I could hear horses filching from their stuffed hay nets in the stalls. And from across the gate I heard a woman baby-talking to an invisible creature, a lover or a cat.

I stayed in the doorway and tried to breathe slowly, all the way down to my toenails. Danny, it seemed, had been a compassionate asshole and had left me my polo boots along with my girlie twist of underwear and my anorak. I wished right then that he had taken everything, and I forced myself to keep my hands out of my jacket pockets even though they ached with cold because I knew it would be like him to leave a little money behind as a hedge against his guilt. Or not his guilt. Danny wouldn't suffer that. You weren't allowed to feel guilt on the backside unless you stupidly ruined a horse. No, he'd leave the money the same way a man who thought he was on a pure luck streak would leave a cocktail waitress a big tip.

I heard the swoosh-whump of hay being shoved out of the loft. Reno was starting his chores and Danny's chores too, probably not troubling his head about where his groom was when he

needed him. To Reno we were all failures, screwups to be toler-
ated because a racing stable needed horses and he had only one
back and two hands and his horses needed more than that. He
expected nothing of us beyond drinking, fighting, robbery, and
an incomplete attitude toward our jobs. We always talked about
how our lives would get better, how they'd change. If, when. If,
when. Reno believed we'd never get any better, and neither
would he. We were seed hulls, dry scattered crusts. All of us.

Work seemed like a way to stay numb. Around the corner I
found Jenny squeezed into two sweatshirts and a greasy pair of
pigskin gloves. She was filling more hay nets. I asked if I could
help her water the horses. She said sure. She wasn't awake
enough to care why I was doing Danny's job. When she got
awake, she still wouldn't care. I was halfway through watering
when Dawg showed up. He took over the buckets and the tubs.
Reno was in the feed room measuring vitamins and pellets, and
I asked him if he wanted me to fix up some mash. He said yes
without acknowledging who I was. "Chart's where it's always
been at," he said, gesturing to the posted grid that laid out exactly what each horse ate each day. "Then go tell me if that gray
horse looks good or not."

The gray horse was one of Danny's, but I knew damn well
Reno had already checked on it, probably twice. He left nothing
to chance. The horse stood along the back wall of its stall with
one hip cocked and its head hanging lower than its half-moon
withers. Hadn't touched its water or hay, although it was sniffing restlessly through the straw bedding for something to take
in its square teeth. Its blanket looked tight around the chest so I
adjusted that, checked its bandages, made it step forward until
there was weight on the cocked leg in case that was a problem. I
scooped up a single pyramid of dark manure which wasn't fresh

but which looked normal enough. There was a faint yellowish discharge from one lash-rimmed eye, nothing from the nostrils; the skin temperature at the muzzle and between the legs felt close to right. I ran my hands all around the horse's angular face and neatly trimmed ears, feeling for something. I didn't know what. Then I opened my jacket wide and let it smell my armpits and between my sore breasts. Horses liked that. They wanted to know who you were, what about you didn't change. I felt the long, hot streams of breath go right through to my skin and remembered how many nights I'd dreamed of sleeping in a stall like this one. Chilly black air, soft bedding, the warm blood, bones so much longer than my own. I thought about all the good mornings I'd found short, stiff horsehair on my clothes, my palms. How my whole body was oiled with the oils of horse sweat and leather. I thought about the storybooks I'd read as a kid. The field ponies I'd cried to when I was a little girl alone. Caring for horses was all about basic comforts and needs—for them and for me. I could find a reason to go on in that, couldn't I? In the giving and taking of comfort?

The gray's head went up stronger on its shoulders as it looked for one more caress. I ran my hands over his smooth neck, trying not to think where else those skin-running hands had been. He was another horse I didn't know, one in a great, crowded world, yet there was something between us. Even after my fool's night, I was still capable of blunt animal feeling. That was a rope to cling to.

Dawg was the one who asked first. *Where's Danny? Why you lettin' him lie back with a hangover head while you work?* I told him Danny was gone, that was all I knew, and I hoped he'd shut up about it until we were done with the horses. He could tell I wasn't joking. His lips moved a little like he wanted to say something in Danny's defense, probably something funny, but he stopped short of sounding out the words. I asked him if the lame mare Danny had been doctoring took extra oil in her mash. He thought she did. And some honey too. Danny, Dawg said, was a big believer in honey.

It was Jenny who cut through the bullshit. She waited until we had nothing left to do but clean stalls before she came over and told me she'd heard about what I said to Dawg.

"Yeah, Danny's split," I said. "But I hope you all don't think it's a problem for me." I could tell by the way her eyes darted left under their freckled lids that that was exactly what she thought. Jenny had been committing herself more and more to Alice's barn. She wanted that decision to be a good one. "It's a problem for this barn, one that'll take Alice about two minutes to fix. I won't miss him one way or another."

"Did Maria leave too? Little lady, curled black hair? I know she hated the head man at her barn." Jenny was hooking up one of the jumpy new colts when she said this. I couldn't see her face to tell if she was just yakking, or trying to say I was an easy mark who ought to pay more attention.

"Never met her." I thought about the figure who'd rabbit-run over the fence when I brought Danny my money. Right before he'd tried to foxtrot me to bed. I tried to remember what Danny had said about her.

"Don't guess you did," Jenny said. "Way I heard it was they both came over from some place in California. They weren't married or nothing, but you know how it is."

"That's right." I felt prongs in my throat. "I know how it is."

It was Dawg who nagged me into telling the truth. He kept drifting by while we groomed, asking to borrow brushes and picks, stuff he could get from his own boxes if he looked hard enough. Said he didn't know why Danny would leave a good job so quick, why he hadn't said something the day before. He seemed to believe that gambling together had made them some kind of friends. "He didn't have all that much. Nine hundred dollars might be what he had. Can't hardly get a car for that, and that's how he was talking. Wanting a car for this and that. V-8 engine and shit."

A bitterness I could taste snaked onto my tongue. "He had plenty of money, Dawg. If you stop your stupid mouth long enough to think about it, you'll figure it out."

Dawg's hands went slack on the scraper he was holding. "You can't say he stoled from you. You have to talk to Mr. Reno. You can't say D-man did like that."

"Close enough. There's nothing anybody can do about it now."

But Dawg tried. And I could have whipped his narrow butt for it. He went to Reno, then to Jenny, then back to Reno. Reno didn't breathe a word in my direction except to say I had six rides that morning. He didn't gloat. He remained the same as always—watchful and hazardous—which was worse. Jenny found the note. She felt like somebody ought to look through Danny's stuff so his leftovers could be rightfully scavenged.

"I reckon this is for you, Kerry." She handed me a book with a piece of paper stuck through its middle. "I always thought your name was spelled the regular way, like in that movie."

It was one of Danny's paperbacks. She told me she'd found it under the edge of the bed. She said she hadn't read what was written on the pink farrier's receipt that was folded inside, but I knew she had. And what she'd read made her ashamed to stand next to me.

Dear Kerry—*he'd gotten that part right*—you will not like what you find out this morning but I had reasons. I dont think you need money to waste on your husband your all right. I like working at the barn Maria D. has other ideas. She is stuborn. Like you are I know your mad. I am sorry.

GOOD LUCK   Easy come Easy go

He'd drawn the *u* in *Luck* in the shape of a horseshoe.

There was $500 stuck in the pages of the book.

Jenny had walked off a ways with her shoulders jammed up near her ears like I was giving off vibes she didn't want to hear. I tore up Danny's note and stuffed it and the money in the pocket of my anorak. "I'd eat it if I could." Jenny looked back at me through her stringy brown bangs. There was a dry, scaly fold between her eyebrows. I lowered my voice, suffering the humiliation that wet my words. "I said I'd eat it if I could, but I'd probably puke it up in five seconds. Danny's gone. I'm the biggest idiot in Kentucky."

Jenny shrugged. She didn't seem to want to get involved. She'd told me once that she had a hard time with most people.

"The prick left me a little money. I'll pay you to clean out his room so you can move in yourself."

Her mouth twitched with interest. I knew she'd been sleeping on somebody's trailer floor. "Prick," she said, and the word came more easily to her than it had to me. "They're all pricks. Don't have to tell me that." And she laughed. "Or pay me, neither."

We worked together like meshed gears after that. Right alongside Reno and Dawg. I rode half of my horses before Alice even got to the barn, taking my instructions from Reno, who laid out his sentences like they were high voltage cables. But he let me do my job. Track conditions were near perfect. Clear and bright, light wind from the south. I brought my fourth ride past the finish line in fifty flat, and Alice was there to see it. Charlie was at the gate on my way out, looking lordly and showing his bandaged thumb to whoever asked to see it. He was also offering tips on the day's seventh race, a $50,000 added for fillies and mares. I didn't respond when he asked me how much he ought to lay out on Sunny in her Belmont run that afternoon. Sunny. Threatened. The last thing I could bear to think about. My white-faced silence got him going.

"Well, don't talk then, Miss Lady K. We all know you're not no fun. Heard it straight from Louisa Fett."

I tried to sit my horse like a stone general, but Charlie knew he had me. I was half surprised I had any soft insides left that could feel a stab.

"Aw, I'm messing with you, getting that goat." Charlie scratched at his sideburns, his bad thumb saluting at a funny angle. "Louisa talks too much about nothing. You get on down there and bring that red filly of Alice's back up here for me to watch. You're good for each other, and good for me." Pete, the assistant clocker, who was leaning near the single hinge of the gate, chuckled at that. He liked to hear Charlie sing on about horses. It was trackside symphony. I did what I'd been doing all morning: steered my ride carefully and carried my head on my shoulders as if it was a cracking eggshell.

Alice left the grandstand—I could see her bright pink vest floating through a knot of gossips—but it never occurred to me she'd follow me back to the barn. It was a terrible time to talk, and we had terrible things to talk about, so of course she cornered me. I hadn't even gotten my saddle off her colt before she let fly.

"I used to have a rule in this barn," she said loudly. "No fucking. And it wasn't a problem. Now I seem to have a problem."

Jenny had the Lord Avie mare ready for me to tack up, but

she looked afraid to bring the animal closer. "You don't have a problem with me."

"That's not what I hear."

"What you might've heard is Danny is gone, which is no new thing around here. You need another groom."

"I'm told he stole something. I've already called security about it. I'm also told you had your pretty little ass where it shouldn't be."

"Whatever little bird is whistling at you," I said, "is telling tales."

That should have been the end of it. Jenny had my girth cinched and was fixing to lift the mare's forelegs to smooth the skin so it didn't gall. Rogelio had legged up onto Flare. We were supposed to run together to tune Flare for the Elkhorn. But Alice grabbed the mare by both rings of the bit and looked at me with eyes peeled white with anger. "Get in the office and get in there now." Her whisper was so rough and choked it carried better than her speaking voice. I could see Reno was holding back the big horse to see what would happen. "Move," Alice said. "You're not getting out of this."

I ripped my helmet off and asked Jenny to keep the mare ready. It looked like whatever dams I'd built that bad, cold morning were about to be flooded out.

"You want to tell me anything before I ask the steward to write up you and Danny both?"

I didn't answer. I didn't even set foot in the office but stood outside while Alice began her version of pacing, which was more like rocking her wide body from one side of the room to the other than anything else. She was saving up some hot breath for a lecture.

"I should put together a pamphlet that features you and pass it out to the sweet high school girls in this county. It would list all the mistakes you shouldn't make in your life and how you made them. All the ways you can throw it away. Maybe I could do a filmstrip."

I still didn't say anything. I could see how she thought I'd betrayed her version of good behavior even though she had no idea what I was up against with Eric's debts. Still, I felt a bar of heat glow across my forehead as though a bare wire coil had been turned on inside my skull. She was digging deep, and I wasn't in the mood for it.

"You make me as close to philosophical as I'll ever get, Kerry. It's always been easy for me to see people like horses. Breed for certain traits and you'll get those certain traits, and so on. Most people are the product of shoddy breeding. They get no smarts, no stamina, no focus—or not enough to matter. They're boring or they're damn messes. What we get around here"—she swept her hands in front of her like they were plow blades—"are the damnedest messes.

"Then somebody like you comes along and ruins my theory. You're a little like Seattle Slew or Flare the way I take care of him. Those colts came from nowhere, what they got can't be bred for. Except you keep pulling up lame every which way. It took me some time to see that, but now I've got it plain as day. It's a flaw of character, the kind you trigger yourself. You won't ever get anywhere. You got no heart."

I looked at her wet, preaching mouth and the motion of her chopping hands. But I saw the haggard flicker in her eyes too, the things she was afraid to preach about.

"I got work to do," I said, trying to tamp down the truth of what she'd said. "Roy cooks my liver if I'm late."

"Are you listening to me?"

"I am. You're telling me I'm a baby. And a bad apple to the

core, which I've just about proved today. But you haven't said I can't ride horses."

"Reno wants me to let you go." Alice's lips foamed at one corner. "He's asked several times. Swears you and Danny were out to make money off me. That you spiked me on that claimer with Delvecchio."

"I'd never do that to you, Alice." I set all my weight in the heels of my boots and said what I believed. "I got no reason to help Roy take horses. I'd never *have* a reason. I made a big mistake with Danny—if that's what you want me to say, I'll say it—but it didn't cost anybody but me."

"Damn, don't you see?" Alice took a step toward me. "It wasn't just a mistake with that boy. I warned you off. I told you." She took a bellows breath. "I ever talk to you about the black horse my daddy kept, the one that killed a groom? Couldn't anybody handle him but Daddy's man Edward. Horse had to be drawn from the stall with a pruning hook, he'd stomp anybody who'd go in with him. But he could run right, and since we had a home barn, his rank reputation wasn't always known. Daddy ran him in Chicago and New Hampshire, let him get claimed whenever he needed a ball of cash. But that black horse always came back to our barn in two, three days because nobody but Edward could work with him. Nobody could keep him. Daddy would shell out a few hundred dollars to be polite, nowhere near what he was worth, and that horse was home again. Did that until the devil got so old we had to put him down with the shotgun right behind the barn. What I want to know is what you got to offer besides your smart talk and your pussy that makes you worth the trouble of taking back."

Orange light surged behind my closed lids. Alice couldn't stand that I'd been in bed with Danny. It lit some fuse. And she lit mine. "It's not the first time, Alice. Probably won't be the last." I spoke through set teeth, lost the temper I'd been trying to keep. "Sometimes my fun has a way of turning on me."

"Not sometimes," she shouted. "Every time. Every damn time. Danny fucks and robs you. That cardboard cutout husband fucked and robbed you. Roy Delvecchio. Billy Tolliver. Mason—"

"And what about you?" I shouted back. "What do you want to do with your paycheck and your bedroom and your advice that's so different?"

It would have been kinder to kick her in the face. Or swing a two-by-four at her head. Her skin went from red to lard white, and her throat swelled like her tongue had doubled over inside.

"I'll finish up." I was surprised by the plunging meteors in my chest. My words burned as deep inside me as they did in Alice Piersall's eyes. "I'll ride the horses the way I always do. You can fire me when I get back."

I got up on the mare Jenny was still holding. The mare was a little walleyed from the shouting, but I ran a steady hand along her arched neck, hoping to soothe. Reno was there, watching Dawg circle Flare on a lead with Rogelio in the saddle. He stood as stiff as a queen's guard. They'd all heard most of it. They knew it was over for me. I'd come to this place to be low and plain, to learn how to fit in again, and I'd run through the only two people I'd tried to be connected to. Done it in a few fast hours. I was in the Land of Make Do and Make Believe, and I'd somehow still messed up.

𝑛othing to do but run. Dash like a winter rabbit. Bust cover like a quail. I would go to the motel and pick up the stuff I had in the room there. Drop by both barns and get the money I was owed. Say an honest, face-to-face good-bye to Thomas. By the time Sunny cleared the shady far turn in her race at Belmont, I'd be driving through Tennessee on my way to a Danny kind of life without horses or history.

While I repacked the rear of the Citation I thought maybe I'd found the kind of windy emptiness I'd been after all along. My hands were slow and steady. My brain seemed capable of only one task at a time. So I checked the gauges in the car, checked the oil, checked the tires, but it took me a minute to figure out why the engine sounded as woolly and padded as it did. Lucky for me I was still my mama's daughter—quick to worry and get all snoopy about it. I eyeballed the tailpipe. The baking potato jammed into it peeked back at me like a shy turd.

Louisa Fett, that clever girl, had paid me a visit. Because my head was tundra clear and because her idea of revenge was so pitiful—as if I wasn't worth more trouble than a store-bought potato—I shifted into the kind of overdrive that leaves the scenery blurry. I'd seen Louisa on the track that morning butt-warming horses for Billy and a trainer by the name of Arnie Cole. I knew where she'd be now. Before I left town, I'd give her my kind of farewell.

She drove a little Ford Ranger pickup that was easy to locate because the airbrushed frame that held her license plate was stenciled with her name in purple letters. The truck was parked in Billy T.'s reserved spot, which was something I might have expected. I started carving into the paint of the truck door without being sneaky about it, so I guess one of Billy's grooms saw me. Maybe even recognized me. I was still shading in my artwork when Billy showed up and took the keys out of my hand.

He seemed taller with the midmorning sun behind him. Or maybe my childish try at getting even had shrunk me. But I refused to be embarrassed that he'd caught me acting like an idiot. You had to be worth a damn to be embarrassed about the things you did.

I pointed at the side of Louisa's truck. "It started out as a giant dildo, but then I figured she wouldn't recognize it so I changed the shape some." Billy's eyes were milky with care. "What do you think? Think if I spell it out, she'll learn to read?"

"I think you're in a heap of trouble. You're lucky Louisa's not around. You're lucky Scott called me and not security."

"That's where you're wrong, Billy. Seeing Louisa or one of the puffballs from DeLong's office would be the best thing that's happened to me today."

His nose wrinkled as though there was a smoky smell in the air. "I've got horses running. I've got owners down here right now. You want to tell me what the hell is driving you crazy this time?"

"Maybe I'm just hungry," I said, feeling split in two by my own pettiness. "We haven't had our dinner together yet."

"No, we haven't. You didn't show up. I'm not even going to ask where you were because it won't help me understand why you're acting like a delinquent. This"—and he waved at the scratches I'd dug into the truck—"this is so far below what I expect of you, I—"

"Louisa's riding my horses. I'm jealous."

I got him with that one. I could hear the air hissing right out of his chest.

"Oh, come on, Kerry. You can't expect me to . . . you never used to care about things like that."

"Maybe I should have."

"I think maybe you should be mad at the person you really need to be mad at. Louisa doesn't have a thing to do with this."

I told him about the potato. He pulled a hand over his lean face, then rubbed the back of his neck to get at the tension there. "You said you'd leave her alone."

"Well, I can't. And anyway you could call it my final mean act. I'm getting out of here for good."

He looked genuinely surprised to hear that. Bothered. So I told him about tripling my money with Danny and losing it all, and I told him about my desperado idea to buy some safety for Eric and the horses I'd abandoned up north. I told him about the lead pipe and Stevie. About the guilt. I left out the part about being in bed with Danny. He'd guess that on his own.

"And now you're chasing the lying-eye jerk . . ." Billy stopped, trapped me with a hard stare. "No, that's not how you'd work it, is it? You're not leaving to find that man. You're just quitting." He closed his eyes. "If you needed money, you could have asked me. A job, somewhere to live. I'd have helped with that."

He meant every damn word, but I could see from his straight back and the way his fingers brushed at his gold tie clip that he was also thinking about the owners who were waiting for him. He was so perfectly responsible. "Would you have loaned me thirty grand to bail out Eric?" It was the saltiest, most testing thing I could say. And the most unfair.

"No." He barely hesitated. "I wouldn't have. Especially since he probably owes twice that much. I wouldn't give Eric Ballard a tin dime even if it would make you happy to be around me. I guess that's where I draw the line."

"Maybe I drew the line sooner, Billy."

"Maybe you did."

Track patrons walked past us in that quick, fluid way people have when their sap is rising. It was a grand day to race. Men with programs rolled in their certain fists and women in pastel skirts and jackets—they all peered into Billy's yard. They could tell winners were stabled there. There was a polish to the place, an anxious gleam.

"I really am leaving. You're right. I thought I could raise a new flag here, be a good girl and start over, but I can't. Eric's a mess and I left him and that's made me some kind of mess too. I seem destined to serve my time in a shit storm. Everybody stand clear."

He looked at me in a way that pried open the pain in my ribs. "God damn. I thought about it, you know. I thought about buying Sunsquall back, just flat out buying her and getting her down here just so I could see you ride her. I've never seen a woman happier than you were in those days. That's the first thing that came into my head when I saw you again. Hell, maybe even before that, because I saw you grow up with that filly. She made you glow. Just like Ballard's money did. And I've got the damn money now, I've got plenty, and I wanted you to know that so much." His voice struggled like it was trapped in wet sand. "But I stopped myself."

"Why?" I couldn't swallow.

"Because I decided Kerry Connelly didn't need another bastard deciding what she should do."

"Even a top-line bastard?"

"Even that."

After a silent breath or two took me back to the speechless pleasures we'd once shared, he lifted a hand toward my face and cupped it just short of my cheek. I felt the warm life there. The organized tenderness. I leaned in to fill his palm, then the whole curve of his arm. I buried my face in his sun-basted jacket, just buried it.

"I guess I know how to be a disappointment," I muffled.

"No, not always. Don't stamp yourself that way. You've got too much good in you." His chin lifted as though he was trying to locate something on a faraway hill. "I've been thinking about Chantal and everything I didn't tell you about that. She's a drinker. Or she was before she left me, and I'd be surprised if this new man has found her to be much different. I learned a lot from Chantal. And I learned it the hard, ugly way. I'd like more than anything to fix things up perfect for you right now. Get you started with your horse, training, riding, whatever you want. I can hardly say how much I'd like that." He held on to me like his words might jar me loose. "And the damn fool part is you might let me do it. For once. But I'd be wrong to play the fixer, Kerry. I couldn't fix Chantal. I can't fix you."

I pressed in below his neck until the words faded to slow breathing. "You think I shouldn't try you?" Half joking, half not. Afraid of how so many gates were suddenly swinging shut.

He was quiet for a long time. "I think you could, but I'm not supposed to say even as much as that. This isn't easy for me, don't think it is. If I hadn't sold Sunsquall, I'd have . . ." He stopped again. "You've got to refigure. Stand alone for a minute. Find that part of you I've always known. You're right not to follow that man who took your money, but maybe you should leave here if it feels best. Just make sure you understand what you're leaving for."

"I need to get out of trouble."

"Eric and your own self are most of your trouble. He's likely to make new problems for you. His judgment is shit." He couldn't help saying it. His face colored until he looked like he'd been slapped. "I'm sorry. I'll straighten this out with Louisa if I can."

I chewed my tongue flat to keep from adding on the wrong thing. Billy deserved his kind of finish. He turned from me after a damp kiss to my forehead, slowly reassembling himself as the best man he was. He smoothed the panels of his dark blue jacket, smoothed the boyish fall of his hair. I could see how devoted he was to his work and the steel-eyed, careful decisions that defined it. I could see how well he knew himself. What he'd learned about the chance game of love. He walked within his body as though he didn't need to protect his brittle frame, or his feelings. He carried himself. Away. Away. And unlike me, he didn't seem to worry about the puzzle collapse of the sky.

CHAPTER 1 6

i beat it up to Roy's barn and asked his assistant to cut me a
check for what I was owed. Billy was right. I needed to clear
town to clear my mind. Roy's assistant gave me a razor-thin
look, one he'd heisted from some of the sueded snotnoses who
ran at Saratoga. He said he might be able to settle with me in
cash, if there was enough in the box. I said that would be even
better. He asked me how much I owed on the motel room. I
said I had no idea, Roy never said anything about it to me. I was
running on raw nerve from my talk with Billy, and it made me
fidgety. Stand alone, Billy said. In some ways—the impulsive,
rumbling ways—I was close to hard-ass perfect on that. Too
perfect. My hands balled up and knocked together at the level
of my belt. Roy's assistant took a step backward.

"Be cool," he said, showing himself for the wimp he was.

"I am cool." I felt what was left of me evaporate into an ugly
stare. "I just didn't know you and Roy were running a company
store."

He looked all manner of ways then: peeved, embarrassed, flat
footed. I repeated that cash would be fine. As he left to open the

portable safe they kept in the tack room, I wondered why Roy selected assistants who were so much like vice presidents. All it got him were slim, dog-eared boys who'd never take charge.

When he came back with four $10 bills, I looked at them with a greasy feeling in my belly. Made myself keep looking. The stern, soulless face of a dead president, the endless squiggles etched in moss green—those were supposed to get me to Florida. Where I would squash my racetracker self like it was a palmetto bug. Start selling piña coladas or plastic sandals. Whatever pointless girls did.

"You want me to tell Roy you're quits, right?" The assistant had a clipboard in his hands now, and a sport coat over his catalogue oxford shirt. They seemed to make him feel better.

"That's the way to do it. I'll say good-bye to Thomas myself."

"Thomas is at the clubhouse with Mr. Delvecchio. I'd be happy to—"

"Don't worry about it." I rapped knuckles again to see if he would jump. "I won't hang around and cost you your ass."

Just then Mr. Delvecchio eased into the yard as gracefully as a docking yacht. He was trailed by two tailored older men and three frosty-haired women who were dressed in gold buttons and wide, sharp pleats. Behind them came a dumpling-faced teenage boy in coat and tie who was herding a toddling little girl with her hair divvied up by white satin ribbons. Roy didn't hesitate a millisecond when he saw me. He shot his starched cuffs, stretched his tanned neck, then introduced his assistant to the two men although it was clear they'd met before. And he stood grinning like a mayor as the assistant shook hands with each of the pointy-nosed women. The boy was left out of it since it was his job to keep the little girl away from the horses and washtubs and scissors.

"I'd like you all to meet Kerry Connelly, one of the finest rid-

ers we've ever had." Roy's teeth shone. "She's got a part of the
Sun Chief mare that's running at Belmont today. We're lucky to
have her down here at the moment."

The shorter of the two men clasped my hand between his
and named the people in his party. His skin was as smooth as a
Sunday glove. He had a horse running today too, he said, a
feisty two-year-old they'd purchased with Roy at Fasig-Tipton
the year before. He was gracious and well spoken; they all
were—nodding, smiling, making eye contact with me as though
a glance was as good as a secret handshake among people who
mattered. The short man said he knew a little about Sunny, and
he named two other mares that would be in the race so I'd understand he was authentically in the game. I understood plenty.
It was Roy and the women he hoped to impress with his com-
mand of the proper bullshit. A trivia king in the sport of kings.
What he didn't know was I'd ridden his $300,000 horse once,
and the animal was scared bug eyed of anything running on his
left. The jock who'd take him out in today's maiden special
weight had had better luck, but I noticed Roy didn't mention
my experience. I told the man I'd seen his colt run, that he ran a
lot like his famous sire, and that I hoped I'd have a chance to leg
up on him before long.

"You hear that, don't you, Roy?" The man arched his back
until he seemed to feel taller. "You give this little lady a chance
at my boy when she asks. She looks like she'd be good for any
horse down here."

Roy grinned and rebuttoned his suit jacket. The women giggled and swayed in their itchy cloud of perfume. One of them
opened her small, coral-bright mouth to speak to me but
stopped, probably because she had no idea what to say.

"Good luck to y'all," I said, cutting loose like a good mucker.
"I'll be watching that colt." They thanked me, every one, and

collected themselves again as a fleet. The little girl ran among their legs in her poofed-out dress, ribbons straggling. She was the only one not concerned about getting her feet dirty. The boy lurched along behind, bored, too gangly yet to join the rumba of power and money. I watched him and thought how my husband once followed his father like that, learning to imitate all the wrong habits of competitive men—until I realized I'd conducted the entire conversation with my four $10 bills crushed like grocery coupons in my left hand.

Roy was back beside me before I had the money properly folded and stashed.

"You direct a good parade," I said. "Hope that colt pulls it off for you." He didn't bother to respond to my sarcasm. He knew the colt didn't have a chance. It was his business to persuade folks that losing extravagantly was a purer kind of glory.

"I need you a minute," he said. "Come in here." He shouldered me into one of his feed rooms and closed the door behind us. His visitors were just on the other side of the shed row frothing over their sleek thoroughbred. But even that wasn't enough to keep Roy from working his angles.

"Timmy tell you I quit?" Timmy was the assistant.

"He said something to that effect in my ear." It wasn't quite dark in the room. What light there was collected like powder on Roy's shoulders, the top of his skull. When he moved closer to me, he appeared to float, as though he hadn't lifted his tasseled loafers from the floor. "You know what you're doing?"

"I'm going to Florida to be with family."

He snorted. I could hear his arms rustling in the sleeves of his fine jacket. "I heard a little bit about Florida from your friend Kevin Brown. Your mother sounds off the wire to me. Kooky. What makes you think you'll do better down there? I said I'd set you up in Jersey or Long Island, whichever, provided your dopehead husband doesn't show his face. You said you were committed to the fat lady."

Kevin? Roy knew Kevin? I had to repeat that to myself a few times before I got it. Just thinking about them in the same sentence gave me a poleaxed feeling.

"Did Piersall pitch a fit about that tag horse of hers I snatched? I had a little fun taking him away."

"I don't believe Alice cares what you do, Roy. She's used to having horses claimed. She's tough."

He leaned in until I could see part of his face in a dusty spear of light. His top lip rolled under as he chewed on one end of his mustache. "Not tough enough to win with the only good horse she's ever had. She doesn't have the knack."

"You think you can beat Flare in the Elkhorn? Why don't I wish you luck?"

"I can beat any horse she and that Zulu foreman of hers touch. Better yet, I know the right people. I can take that gelding right out of her barn."

I thought back on Alice's moodiness. Her worries about Roy. It made sense. It would be just like him to put the moves on an owner like Mrs. Stronheim. But Kevin, old pal of mine, where did he fit in? I drew myself up straight. "I had it out with Alice," I said. "I'm gone from there. Got stuff to do. Places to drive. Did Kevin bring you a horse up from Aiken, or what?"

"I spoke to the prissy piece of shit when he was here yesterday looking for *you*." Roy's voice went lower, down toward the notes that had thrilled and frightened me as a girl. "He probably didn't mention it, did he? How he's everybody's errand boy. He makes deals for Doral Hughes, and a few other people. This time he was tricking for your husband. Asked how long you'd be hanging around. I told him I didn't know. I put him off. So you can see we have a few things to talk about."

I didn't believe him. What he said didn't ring true, except maybe the part about Kevin doing scut work for other people. He'd been the one on my mama's doorstep in Florida, hadn't he? He'd been in Eric's pocket all along. It looked like I was leaving the track just in time. At least that's what I tried to tell myself before Roy clamped my collarbones in his hands.

"Brown gave me this bullshit about Eric coming after you for some jewelry or something you stole from his mother. He said they were keeping the cops out of it. Said he'd been asked to find you and he had." Roy eased himself against me from the knees up, slowly. He knew I'd feel him beneath his tiny monogrammed belt buckle and that I wouldn't like it. He also knew I'd be too frozen to do anything about it. "Know what I think?" he said. "I think you're into somebody else's stash. Drugs or money. You come down here to have your little life without a husband or anybody else in charge. But you forgot how it works. Nobody does a damn thing in this business without connections. You can't *be* unconnected." His hands dropped and became cold crescents under my tits. All that he was doing—the talking, the rubbing, the hoarse lullaby of truths—carried me right to the place I'd been heading since I left New York, the isolation ward for blown-out loners. He was right. I was a torn rag flapping in the wind.

"Ballard, or whoever he owes, will get to you before long. Brown says your husband will be here in a day or two with that horse you trained. Got it in his head to risk her in the Elkhorn. He'll want his stuff. I might can help with that." He breathed under my earlobe. "I'm not asking for much in return. I don't even need you to leave Piersall. Just watch that big gelding for me, handle him if you can. And tell me if she's giving sob stories to the old lady who owns him. I'm in with the lady's kids. I'm close to a deal with them, so I don't feel like getting burned by that lard bitch's crazy shell games. Maybe if you do right I'll come up with a bonus. Ballard will flame out. That Sunny mare would fit fine in this barn. Maybe you'd like to train her again."

There it was. The spit-candied bribe. The perfect one. I listened to it, cradled it like a found treasure while Roy mouthed on, copping me like I was still one of his collected girls. He thought I was so pitiful I'd believe in him. That I'd spy for him. That I was a thick-skulled tracker who'd do anything—*anything*—for a saddle and a second chance. I hadn't given him—or anybody else—much reason to think otherwise.

Except I knew different. I knew I had spine.

Roy said he wanted to give me something.

I wouldn't take it.

Eric was coming after me.

I wouldn't run.

Sunny was in a fix.

I'd get her out of trouble. The simple way. Billy had just given me an idea about how to do that.

Roy waited for my response. I could almost taste his toxic eagerness as he exhaled. I was about to tell him to shove his offer—*No way, find another patsy to dry-hump*—when one last wicked idea came to me. In all his ego and aftershave, Roy had forgotten one thing. I'd been weaned on cards and thoroughbreds. I knew the bloody scent of raw want. The shyster in front of me had made the mistake of telling me exactly what he wanted.

He wanted Twilight Flare.

"Stop it," I said, my chafed skin shrinking back toward a shape I could nearly call my own.

"Sure. Yeah." Roy stepped back and hitched at his trousers until they fell into their proper drape. "You never were much for fooling around, were you? Which reminds me. You don't help me with that Flare horse, I'll make sure the fat one hears about Ballard's jewelry, maybe tell her you sweetened me on the claimer, that you suggested I pick him up. I can make things rough."

I let those words claw at me for half a second. Then I thought of Danny and what he'd taken from me. What Roy had tried to take again. No more. I was standing firm and could make things go rough too, if I needed to.

"I'm not fishing for anything dirty here," Roy continued. "You understand? The steward's a friend of mine, so don't go chasing up that tree. I'm only asking for the word on that horse. Just so you know the score."

The score was the same as always: Roy, 100; me, 0. Or that's what he thought. I thought of the blonde girl with the bitten mouth I'd seen at the barn the day before. Her name was Carla. Sultry, half aware of what she could do to men, she was not aware enough of what a man like Roy would do to her. I made an extra note to separate the bastard from his Carlas if I could.

"I'll think about it." I coughed some moisture back into my mouth.

"You'll do it," Roy said, flatly. "No offense, but I know you."

"Eric wants money from me. Lots of it."

"Do me right, darling, I'll get that mare for you and more. Eric Ballard is a amateur pile of chicken puke. I can take him."

"Alice has kicked me off the team."

He grunted, amused. "You can fix it. That will be the easy part."

I didn't give him the satisfaction of slipping back onto the aisle alone. I was stunned cross-eyed by the flash of unbroken sunlight and all that he'd told me, all I'd understood, but I'd be damned if I'd sneak out of the hay like I had in the old days. This was suddenly a new season, maybe my last. I followed right on Roy's elevated, clicking heels so Timmy would see me, and Thomas, who was there now, and all of the grooms and clients who had their eyes open. It didn't bother Roy, so I swore it wouldn't bother me, not brushing the clinging leaves and stems from my jeans, not any of it.

i found Red Flora, the jockey agent, at the concession stands that faced the saddling paddock. It was sometime between the fifth and sixth race, and Red was paying for a tall cup of coffee and a bowl of bubbling hot Kentucky burgoo. Like a lot of men with his job, Red was single minded. Right that minute his badgering mind was on food.

I cut to the front of the short line of customers and offered to put a lid on the coffee for him. "Kerry?" He blinked his pale eyes rapidly like he was washing them clear of sand. "Kerry Connelly. Just let me get my papers out from under my arm here and I'll sign you right up." It was an awful old joke between us, how Red was going to make my name as a girl jock better than Krone or Smith. Ten years before he might have actually meant it.

"You see the Rogelio kid ride in the third race? Bailey cut him right off, just wiped his ass, but he came home hard. Old Tyler, the valet, told me they had words in the locker room. Fighting words. That's music to my ears." Red represented Rogelio, and every good ride the boy made gave Red another story to shill. If Rogelio stood up to the top riders, the stories would get even better. Trainers might pick Rogelio as their jock for reasons other than the five-pound apprentice allowance he qualified for. His career would be on its way.

Red jammed a plastic spoon into his steaming burgoo and began to shovel it into his mouth. His pig bristle eyebrows worked up and down, and somewhere in his sinuses he kept up a low, appreciative hum. When the bowl was scraped clean, he reached for his coffee, sipped it, and handed it back to me, then launched into a memory of his mother's Negro cook, who'd made the best burgoo in Lexington when Lexington was an old-time city you could still count on. This led to a longer, faster story about a stud horse he called Ahab who had an undescended testicle. It took me a while to realize that the thread connecting the stories had something to do with a pet rabbit that found its way into the cook's Sunday burgoo. I interrupted Red—I needed some serious information from him—and gave him back his coffee. The hungry crowd that had swirled around us in a spiral of torn mutuel tickets and smart-aleck chatter dwindled because it was three minutes to post time, the last chance to belly up for a bet.

"They aren't running simulcasts, are they?"

"No, not until tomorrow. Tenth race from Oaklawn." He went after the sour black coffee just as he'd gone after the burgoo. Somewhere between slurps he figured out what I was after. The question I was afraid to ask.

"Ah, third race, Belmont. Allowance for fillies and mares. You want to know if I've been on the phone." Red was always on the phone, that was his business. He beat the bushes up and down the coast getting rides for his clients.

I shrugged. But even he could see there wasn't anything casual about it.

"I haven't seen nothing factual, you understand. Haven't talked to Royce." Royce Webster called the local races for radio and was wired in to tracks all over the country for news and updates. "What I think I heard was your mare scratched. Last minute. The pace was slow. Without a stretch duel that Vargas mare came home easy."

Scratched? I felt the blood sieve away from my skin. The news confirmed Roy's story that Sunny was on her way here. I locked the door on my fury at Eric's rash actions, then asked Red if anybody had whispered a reason for the withdrawal.

"Not that I heard. Weather was good. Maybe she's going out to Jersey, someplace like that to get her rust off where so many won't see her. Can't you call up yonder and ask?"

"No."

Red looked for a napkin to wipe the stew grease from around his lips. I pulled one from a chunky dispenser on the counter. "Well, damn, honey. You look cut off." He frowned at me with smeared lips. "But don't worry. It'll get better. Always does."

I stared at him until he drew his plastic schedule binder across his chest like it was a shield. His hair had been naturally red once, a long while ago. His white shirt collar was frayed toward the back. His nose was wet and desperate, just like the rabbits he remembered. Rogelio wouldn't stick with him for long. They never did.

"I can't believe you said that, Red. That it always gets better. I've got reasons to disagree. Appreciate the news, though."

"Maybe we're both getting old," he said, not offended. The bell rang in the ceiling above us and the crowd gave off a throaty, rasping cheer. One of the things I loved about this track was the lack of loudspeakers and announcers. If you wanted to see horses run, you actually had to watch. Red let the shout fade, then added his own words to it. "Maybe we remember what we want to remember. Maybe I'm right." I waved as I turned toward the steps that would drop me into the hidden machinery of the backside. Red was the man who'd forever be known for not signing Stevie Cauthen, the most blessed rider to ever stain his diapers on bluegrass. That's what I remembered.

The next worthwhile person I saw was Jenny. She was on the road near Tom Olsen's barn, walking in fits and starts, her raw-boned hands rammed deep in the pockets of her hooded sweat-shirt. There was a mud-bellied Jack Russell terrier on her trail. She was searching for somebody. It seemed to bother her to run into me.

"She sent me to hunt for Dunn, that farrier who rides around with that stripedy mastiff dog in his lap. That's what I'm doing." Jenny avoided my eye and barred her lips shut one over the other. Running errands for Alice only partly suited her.

"Who's this?" I pointed to the terrier.

"Got no idea. You know how it is around here, all of them following the wrong people." She avoided looking at the dog too, as though seeing it there would seal some responsibility she didn't want. "I need to get along."

I stopped her with a touch to her shoulder. "How is it at the barn?" I asked. "I'm trying to get up the nerve to go back there. Act like a grown-up."

"Well, they're fighting over you, if you want to know. Or Alice is. Mr. Reno don't use any words that I can hear, but I know it's a fight. Like to drive me and Dawg crazy after all that's happened. You and Danny sure know how to shit in your nest."

I admitted to that.

"I don't think I'll get in the middle, if you don't mind. It's best I tend to my business. Might want to keep this job awhile." She drew in her waving elbows, and her short neck, like she expected me to come at her with some hard words. I was sorry to see that. Jenny and me were supposed to be on the same side; we were practically the same kind of woman if you sifted through the details. But she didn't trust me.

"I'll take care of it. Just thought I might be able to apologize . . . to you . . . to everybody, I guess."

"Do what you need to. I like working with you, Kerry, but I don't have no demands." She pushed her knuckly fists so far down in her pockets I thought a seam would tear. Her face looked heavier below the cheekbones, more alive. "I'm in this for my own self."

"Rule number one."

"That's right." She talked at the dog now, toeing it with a work boot.

"You think I should go back?"

"I don't think at all. She wants you. You're good on the horses. I think y'all can work it out. This place is crazy for change, though, I know that. I can't keep up with it."

"Sometimes it's better at the farms," I told her, trying a smile. "Working with the babies. Quieter."

"Then I'll try to get on at one of them places," she said. "When I have the chance."

We stood together along a gray river of gravel and silt. Some pinhead had left a hose running. A lean, yellow-flanked bay high-stepped by with a groom on either side. "You think it's true," Jenny asked, "that the skinny-waisted ones like that, the females, ain't as good?"

"Some people swear on it," I answered. "Not enough lung room or something. Me, I think there's always a chance you can outrun your looks. Luck plays into it. And parts we can't see with our eyes."

"I go by how I like a horse in the stalls," she said. "It's just the way I am."

She took off to look for the farrier, the dog right behind her with its pink wafer tongue nipped between its teeth. Stopped briefly to tell me I should come play softball someday, if I had the time. She said she liked to play and the other people she knew were good people. She didn't mean to say I wasn't so good—I sent that telegram to my own head—but I could tell by the way she dropped the words my way, like they were mismatched scraps of paper, that Jenny hadn't decided yet just what sort of person I was.

I stood alone. Somewhere up the hill, the elegant oval of the paddock was filled with entries for the next race. I knew the scene, how it was laid out like a rich man's tapestry: kite colors and quick hooves; Sunday hats and murmuring; brooding, unsure people and their horses. I imagined the fine-boned legs prancing among the oaks, hooves toeing the rubber brick, manes spiking in the light breeze. I had to believe Sunny was all right, that Eric had pulled her from her prep race because he was being pressured to find her a money spot. I hoped I could get her out of his hands before he ruined her. She deserved to be in the paddock among those saddled entries, but not so soon. I recalled her ratcheted breathing and the blowing heat of her nostrils so vividly that I reached into the empty air to comfort her with fingertips and words. There. A portrait of what I'd allowed myself to care about more than anything. Without it, what was I? Nothing but legs and a busted clench I wanted to call a heart.

CHAPTER 18

i stayed near the barns as night fell. Unfinished business, unfinished feelings—those were the wagon trains I followed, looking for the end of some trail.

The evening tasted of rain-watered pollen and the lemon sour of mowed grass. Grooms slouched against posts, folding towels, talking to one another in their worn-out, dusky way. I saw two spattered vets look into the gold-frosted hills to the west as they waited to give a trainer bad news. Somebody somewhere whistled a lone lullaby tune. The meet was well under way. Most of the folks who would succeed this spring had begun to make their mark, and the results were the same they'd always been. The Haves beating the Have-nots. The Have-nots beating themselves.

Answers. Questions. They fueled me for a few throttled minutes. I had a solid idea about how to rescue Sunny, but the elation burned off after a short time, leaving me with the jittered fatigue I felt after a hard five-furlong burst. I'd need luck, strength. I thought of Alice and how I owed her an apology. I let

myself be drawn to her barn by what I hoped was the magnet of
humility.

It wasn't dark there yet. The fingertips of an orange sunset
clung to the wide angle of the shed roof. But Alice's banged-up
brown Suburban wasn't in its parking spot, which was odd. The
aisle was empty except for a chair, one upended bale of glossy
straw, and a lamp—Reno's camp lantern—which hadn't been
turned on. One of the stalls was closed too, both halves of its
white board door hooked shut. Empty. Another horse had been
claimed or sold or sent back to the farm because it couldn't run.

I didn't expect the dog. What I expected was to cast my Paul
Bunyan shadow across the tine marks on that aisle until Reno
sniffed me out, and I could talk to him about Alice. But I never
figured on the dog. It came from nowhere, snarling, spitting,
growling from deep inside its squat body. A mutt with no collar
and with empty slivers for eyes. It was on me fast. I tried to stare
it down but was only able to freeze it for a second, which was
long enough for me to regret I wasn't wearing a jacket or anything to protect my bare forearms. It charged, then veered like a
wolf might, testing the range of my feet. I kicked, missed the first
time, then caught it as it circled with its knobby head sunk into
its shoulders. The snarls pitched higher as my boot dented a pink
flank. I shouted a few words that made no sense, even to me.
Then the dog ran at my left side in a shallow swoop and bit me.

Reno appeared at the far end of the aisle. He had a rake in his
hands and was swinging the butt end in long, sweeping arcs in
front of his feet. He looked like he was skimming leaves from the
surface of an invisible pool. I'd swatted the dog off the juicy muscle of my calf and gone to one knee hoping to drive a fist into the
hinges of its wrecked-looking jaws. It was an old dog, I could see
that now. Old and mean. Reno wasn't going to call it off.

When it lunged at me again, I punched it back with a quick blow to the chest. It scrambled to its bowlegs and came again. Reno caught it at the knees with the handle of the rake and swept it into the side of the barn. Then he knocked it hard across its visible spine. The dog yelped from a foamy mouth. And the rooster, that infernal bird, began to screech from the hot oven of its stall.

"Shut up," Reno shouted, and the rooster stopped. He pinwheeled the rake in his hands until its black teeth blurred. The dog cowered. "Damn thing get you next time like it should."

"Got me this time," I said.

He waited a moment to see if I would complain about being bitten. "I take my measures," he said. "Get the hell out."

"I'm looking for Alice."

"You ain't. You looking to check on that big horse but I won't let you. She's not around. If you knew an honest thing, you'd know that. I told her to get rid of you. She won't."

"Where is she?" I got to my feet, careful not to rub at my calf or even check to see if it was bleeding. My knuckles ached from the punch at the dog.

"Babylon here. Babylon coming round." Reno stared out over the boxcar barns. What he said sounded like a piece to a song. "That horse is my animal," he said. "I keep care of him like I should. He don't need no whores around."

So that was the story. Reno had a sermon about my behavior with Danny in his windpipe, and it wanted out. I told him what happened between me and his groom was none of his business.

"Danny nothing," he shushed. "He nothing now and never was. Him and his other whore is gone, dead for all I care. You don't know what you dealing with now. I do."

His words chipped like rocks at my sore ribs.

"Alice Piersall thinks she knows you, thinks you like her, only she can't see the black clots in your veins like I can because she blinded by love and by what's happening at her farm. You already lie to her once. I tell her she's wrong to keep you, she blocks her ears to be deaf."

I shook my head. Did Reno know Roy had asked me to spy? Did he think I could, or would, hurt Alice? I thought about the stories of his gambling nightlife, realized that Reno would prowl any way he had to prowl if he thought it would help his barn. He spun away from me, and I saw the dark arrow of sweat cutting through the back of his shirt. He stepped in front of Flare's stall. The dog had disappeared.

"I thought to call Mr. Eric Ballard myself on the phone and tell him you down here and need to be stopped. Call right up to New York. But I hear somebody's already spent the quarter. Your husband, he coming to take his pound of flesh. I can tell you that."

I took in some air. "Guess I'll have to take my medicine."

"Guess you will. That Delvecchio man takes our claim horse like it cheap wine or a extra woman to him. Now he wants another horse. That more of your medicine?" Reno's hands tentacled into the empty space around him. I realized he didn't have his Bible. And somewhere he'd dropped the rake. "What she loves lies withered and sick on its pallet and you talking to her enemies like it's no matter."

"I never said a word about that claimer, Reno. Roy's jerking your chain if he says I did."

"Horse is gone." He blossomed his fingers to prove his hand was emptier than a conjurer's. "Then there's another." He meant Twilight Flare. Meant the big gelding was ripe for the taking, like it was my fault.

"Story to tell you," he said, and I could see the centers of light grow dimmer in his midnight eyes. "Little jockey boy been called up north. Card filled with rides, so he got to leave us. I know your Mr. Roy handling that as well."

Could it be? If so, it was a bust mouth tactic. Roy hadn't said anything to me, but he could recommend Rogelio to trainers up the coast, make sure the kid wasn't available for the Elkhorn. Flare would have to carry more weight without the five-pound bug boy allowance. But Alice wouldn't have any trouble signing a top pro for the ride. A lot of them would be here for the prep races before the Derby. Still, she would know Roy was out there, hacking away. Making her look bad to the Stronheims.

"Good for Rogelio," I said, carefully. "He deserves it."

"You next," Reno whispered. "I believe Mr. Roy worked that up, too."

I didn't say a word. Somewhere far away my leg throbbed.

"She'll want you up on my horse and it shall come to pass." His voice was level and gentle now, as if he knew the end to all of the tales he'd started me with. "Alice Piersall this minute fighting for her soul in ways you don't know. Don't care."

Was it craziness? Pure stress craziness? Or was there a warning in his words I could handle? "Tell her I came by. Please." I leaked the plea in one breath. "I'm sorry for whatever's going wrong."

"Want me to take you in there so you can report like you supposed to?" He moved as if to unlatch Flare's gate.

"I know what I'd see, Reno. Nothing. You hear me? Nothing for nobody. I'd see a Piersall horse training for his race good."

He dropped his lids so that his eyes were nearly closed, though he kept his unseeing face aimed right at me. "Don't matter what you say to me. What's right is for you to stay out of

Alice Piersall's business. What's right is you never touch my horse unless you for her."

I'm for her. I tried to say the words aloud. But I couldn't quite do it. As I choked on my silence, Reno went back down the powdery aisle toward invisibility, his laced, ever-polished boots giving off no sound I could hear.

CHAPTER 19

*R*eno was on the money about Rogelio. By morning our jock had packed his boots and soccer jerseys and sweat-washed helmets. He'd found a basement flat in the Bronx where he could rent couch space. He told me he'd been signed for three rides at Aqueduct on the day of the Wood Memorial, which was damn good for a green stick apprentice. He also assumed I'd be plucking his exercise rides. Speaking in a low, hinky voice as though there were dozens of secrets he'd loan me if we had the time, he told me to watch Flare's leads. He said Twilight Flare was like a yacht-sized Buick he'd driven in Miami. Belonged to so-and-so's cousin. Gas pedal and steer like a crazy bitch.

I wished him good luck in New York.

Rogelio assumed I'd throw a leg over the big horse, but nobody else did. Alice was still missing, without explanation. I worked every critter in the string, getting plans from Jenny that I wanted to believe she'd gotten from Alice. A sickle-hocked three-year-old Alice had claimed at Ellis Park was scratched from his six-furlong race for no reason anybody cared to give me. Flare stayed in his stall. The phone in the tack room rang for long periods of time, but nobody answered it.

When I'd ridden the last horse, Jenny finally confided in me. Reno wouldn't talk. He'd said what he had to say the night before and seemed determined to let his predictions speak for him. Jenny said all she knew about Alice was that there was an illness somewhere, and she'd only gotten that much because a doctor's office had called the barn by mistake. "She either aims to give it up," Jenny said, looking down the long barrel of the aisle toward a beveled square of sun, "or she means for us to go on ahead until she makes it back." Us. She meant Reno and herself, how they'd have to come to some understanding. I thought about it for half a minute. They couldn't sign the bills or paper the horses in their races. Even with Dawg's help they wouldn't last very damn long.

"Are you asking if I can help?" I felt the distance between us like it was walled in Sheetrock.

"I don't know," she said. "I barely know how to be like that. You're riding for Alice, that's how I think about it. He's leaving me a lot of decisions—rope to hang myself on, I reckon. He's making me ask you about that gelding, for one. Acts like he'd rather not have the horse worked at all. I'd take your opinion."

Jenny scratched a hand under the waistband of her pants. I felt a guitar twang across my chest as I realized how tough it was for her. She knew her way around trouble, maybe better than most. The woes from some kind of scorched-earth past were with her, right across her scar-straight mouth, and I could tell she was aware how close the edge of that pit still was. She didn't like being near it.

"My honest opinion is we ought to go roughshod and right.

Day by day. In the Piersall tradition." That just about made her laugh, and I realized I'd said a few words I really liked.

"Piersall would say to get your butt on that big racehorse."

I grinned. "Piersall would."

Fifteen minutes later Jenny legged me up on Flare and laid out exactly the kind of workout Alice loved. Dawg held the horse like he was a hinge on a swinging gate. Reno stood under the heat-banged eaves rolling bandages, his face wood grained with sweat and watchfulness. Another prediction had come true. I felt like the man's bad luck sideshow. Dawg whispered across Flare's wet eye, then strummed a hand over a nostril while I settled into the saddle. Backbone flexed beneath me. I felt the impatient ribs fill and spread. Yet the thing I watched as Dawg looped us out of the yard was Jenny and the way she looked sending us up the hill. Her shoulders tilted left under her pine-tarred shirt. Her brown corduroys needed another hitch. She gripped her hair at the base of her skull while I floated away on the best horse we had, and I saw how she hoped what she'd hoisted her life onto this time wouldn't come to a broken axle stop. She'd suffered enough of those. Pressing my weight hard into my boot heels, I tried to convince myself I hadn't made her any promises I couldn't keep.

Flare was stiff and uncertain about me, so I didn't push him. That meant the front end of the workout was lousy, with him cantering like he was two halves of two different horses. He didn't like it when somebody streaked past us either. His mule ears went flat against his head. His teeth snapped together in front of the snaffle. He was rank, out of rhythm, and so was I. When I finally cracked down on him, it felt good. I used spurs and a stick to drive him into a set bit. He broncoed and gave a bullshit quarter turn into the rail like he'd been spooked, but I knew better. I could see a whiskey-colored eye rimmed in naughty white. He wasn't afraid. Come on, I said as I yoked him between the reins, let's get to understanding business.

I won't say he was fine after that because he wasn't. No one but Rogelio had been on his back for quite a while. The hand gallop we laid out was fitful and distracted. But we were talking, the big fellow and I were, and it unfurled something inside me to realize that. I don't know exactly how to explain it. I saw robins grubbing in the gray mud inside the rail. I saw where a white-hearted branch had been sheared off a field oak in a recent storm, and a new calendar page tore itself off behind my eyes. I knew that when I could do this with Sunny, I'd be myself again.

I drew Flare back into a slack parade canter well short of the seven-eighths pole and let him drop his head into another stubborn buck. I could see Billy T. standing with Jerry Michaels, a publicity guy for the state racing commission, and Dwight Anselm, a retired trainer who spent too much of his time chicken-scratching for tips on his bets. Billy's hands were stuffed into the side pockets of a ratty quilted jacket, and he appeared to be watching for horses coming into sight on the backstretch as they cleared the obstruction of the tote board. He stood easy, a friend among friends, and I thought again of what Eric would look like when he came for me. He'd have the right man-child clothes on his body and the wrong damn prayer in his eyes.

Moving both reins to my left hand, I jammed my stick through the belt of my chaps so that it waved above me like a radio antenna. Then I scanned the balloon faces of the small, milling crowd for my husband. No dark-haired, chisel-boned, hopped-up Ballard boy. Dwight Anselm had his binoculars to his eyes now and the red cord of a stopwatch snaked around one wrist. He and Jerry and Billy didn't notice me. In fact, since Jenny didn't have the time to come watch us train, no one was there for me. I stood high and ballasted in the stirrups, feeling Flare's natural spirit rise in waves of heat and steam. I admired the horses filtering in through the gate. I was about to hurl myself back into my husband's ugly business, yet all I could think to ask for was that my last seconds on this planet—whenever they might be—would kindle themselves in a morning place just like this.

CHAPTER 20

After we split some cheap sandwiches for lunch, Jenny asked if I wanted to go to the ball game they were having behind the sheds. I was in no mood to play, but it seemed all right to sit on a bucket for a few minutes and nibble at the afternoon. Two other women dropped by to see about the game. I didn't know them. They worked for an Oklahoma trainer who ran a big public stable. Jenny asked them to settle in, so they brought out a couple of the giant beers they had wrapped in paper bags and made places to sit.

It took one of them about three seconds to start complaining about a groom who kept putting his flat hand on her butt when she was picking hooves or doing other chores that left her back turned. She'd told the boss about it, she said, even though he never did a goddamn thing. "He looks at me," she said, "with his supervising eyes all open like he's listening when I know he's not, and then he tells me to take care of it myself, how that's the best direct way. Like he wants me to put a pitchfork through the guy's balls and it's okay." The woman's friend, a shaggy blonde with a wine stain birthmark on her cheek, laughed and cracked into a beer. "I know it's not okay," the woman continued. "He don't want me to do nothing."

"Get Jenny to do it for you." The woman with the birthmark gave her friend a loose, jiggling hug. "Or tell him you and me are lezzies. He wants to think that anyway."

"That'll just turn on the bastard's high heat. You know how it goes. What I need is to get the foreman mad at him. That's all I got to do."

I watched Jenny, figuring she'd have something to say—probably something short—since her name had been called into it. I'd never thought of her as the kind of person you'd go to for backup rage, but it was possible. She'd been showing all kinds of strength during the troubles around Alice's barn. She tugged at the stalks of hay brushing against her shins and only started talking when the other two wound down. "Take that hoof pick right at his knee before he knows. Whip it sharp at the cap part. Then don't say nothing if you can help it. He won't go tattling; the foreman don't need to get into it at all."

I leaned over to catch Jenny's moving jaw beneath the fringe of her hair. Her eyes blinked double time while she talked at the ground. The woman who'd started the complaining, a round-shouldered gal with clippered gray-black hair, let a tiny, satisfied smile sidle onto her face. She didn't say anything to Jenny, as though it was understood she didn't have to.

"Hey." The birthmark woman nudged my shoulder with a hard fist that held a beer. "Aren't you the one got rolled by Maria Dolores and her man, if you don't mind my asking?"

The rattle of a kicked bucket ricocheted in my ears. For some reason I thought of Kevin and the hard, henpecking way he went at conversations. Then I took the beer because it had been offered.

"She might mind you asking," Jenny said, spidering her hands through the hay. "It's private, if you didn't know."

"Sorry," the woman said. The udder-shaped stain on her cheek speckled with blood. "Just something I heard."

"You know Maria?" I couldn't seem to hold back. I wanted to be able to imagine Danny in the big-engine car he'd told Dawg about, going in a direction he'd chosen. I wanted to be able to imagine that and not feel anything about it.

"Anita here does. Right? You know her?"

The short-haired woman shrugged. "Like you know anybody at this place. They can all stab you in the back. But I wouldn't have picked Maria Dolores for nothing bad. She's got a sweet face, you know? Speaks English good. Did her job."

Birthmark woman set down her beer can and clutched her fingers at her throat for my benefit. "Sweet? This girl lost all her money. All of it. I thought you said she had to be the one planned it."

"I said there was a man in it and I didn't think he was no planner like she was."

"Maybe we can shut up about it, if you don't mind." Jenny's head came up and she talked from behind a stubborn jut of teeth. "Kerry's right here listening."

"She asked, didn't she?"

Jenny swung my way, and I saw her brown eyes set bright and troubled in her face. She was worried about me. "You answered the question. You said you know Maria."

"What I should have said was she'd been with the guy awhile, they just didn't let on about it. Maybe now we know why."

"That makes sense," I blurted. "I'd like to know how I got taken." My words made everybody angle their bodies away.

"So we helped you out," said birthmark woman as she got to

her feet. "Now I'm gonna get to that damn ball field before I get too drunk to play right."

"Can't get drunk on this bat piss," her friend Anita said. "Won't be no excuses."

They walked as far as the white gate, all three of them, before two guys from Lazy L Stables stopped in the road and stretched over the fence, trying to talk Anita out of her one extra beer. I could hear what they were saying—I was maybe fifteen feet away—even though I wasn't part of it. The boys spread a little gossip, mostly about what a hot rod operation the Lazy L was and how its professional shine was rubbing off on them and their wallets.

Anita gave one of them—a bucktooth fellow with dun-colored hair and long sideburns—the beer, and I tried not to listen when the other one scootched close to Jenny and worked on sweet-talking her. The bucktooth guy wandered off after he drained the beer. Anita and her friend started to make tracks, too. The other boy stayed close, lolling near Jenny as though his body had something oozing out of it that had to be rubbed off. He told a loud, choppy version of a story Jenny and I knew, the one about the rogue horse that bit the boob off a newlywed bride, corsage and all. He tried hard to impress Jenny with the gory details, then seemed to realize he might have made a poor choice of tales. Jenny had stopped listening to him.

"Y'all ain't got much pep, do you?" the boy said. "Not as much as that black man you work for. They say he's been rolling craps like crazy come nights. Won't tell me where the game is, though, Lawrence won't. Says I ain't invited down there." It was a bad sign, I thought, him whining this early in the afternoon.

"Reno don't have time for craps," I said loudly. "He's on the row every night."

"Not what I hear." The boy squinted at Jenny instead of me. I could see his puffy tongue running like a fingertip across the uneven ends of his teeth.

"They don't let you in the game because you're not black," I said. "Live with it."

Then I thought for a second. Realized the braggart in front of me might be useful. I had some night business to attend to. He could be my cover. "Maybe we can settle this sometime." I got myself in a crouch, letting Lazy L know he was on the hook. "There's a game tonight. It might not be Lawrence's or whoever's, but I can find you a way to spend your money."

"Sure." Lazy L spread a horny grin across his face. "I'll go for that."

"Meet in front of the kitchen at nine and don't waste my time." I must have looked witchy enough because he smacked the dirt from his knees, said he'd be there, then took off. Jenny believed I'd made the offer only to get rid of the jerk. She cross-tracked her eyebrows again when I told her I was serious.

"I reckon you do like to play cards and gamble, but I don't see why you'd want to do it around that ass. He's not worth nothing."

"I don't," I said, wondering again how she'd face the heavy load of Alice's operation with just Reno and Dawg to help. Wondering where Alice was. "But sometimes a ass can make a regular girl look good."

*L*azy L boy was late. He showed up spitting chaw juice and working a hand through his front pocket like he hoped to renovate his crotch. First thing he checked with me was his money, $450 in rolled cash. Second thing he wanted to nail down was my boyfriend status.

"Married," I said, giving the kind of glossy smile that could only confuse him. Impatience had sharpened my tongue.

"Huh. Didn't see no ring."

"Don't need one. I know what I like." Then I asked him to get rid of his chew as I didn't want him splatting inside my car.

"You all got your rules, don't you?" He dipped his head so he could look at my body in a way he thought was secret. "I could get a cup in yonder to hold it."

"No cups," I said. "It's a short ride. And if you're not serious about getting to the table—"

"I'm serious." He skirted his lip over a slanty canine tooth. "I am, and I ain't stupid. Just thought maybe we could get along some."

I slid into the car. "Maybe," I said. "Winning might make me feel less married." What I really hoped was the winning—or the losing—would get me close to the right people. It was time to spring Sunny.

The setup at this game was different, more what you'd expect to find in the middle of a race meet when trackers are thinking about payouts before thrills. Lazy L hadn't brought his own bottle, so I stopped at Wildcat's and made him get some. Nobody would be spotting drinks on this night. Lazy L went for a bottle of Seagram's and a twelve-pack of Bud Light to chase. I had a bottle of Wild Turkey, eighty proof, to keep my sinuses clear.

We went to a tenant house on a broodmare farm just this side of Versailles. Two guys shared the house—and they treated it like crap—but there was room for two tables in the front part, and the refrigerator more or less worked. One table was already playing when we walked in. Thomas was there, and an old friend of his they called Polo, and two men I didn't know. The fifth was Marty Salazar, a former trainer who'd hooked himself up pretty good as a broker for the international crowd. There was a woman I didn't recognize hammering at a bag of ice on the pitted countertop near the fridge. She was tall and pointy around the edges, with dyed black hair that looked like it was about to leak onto her neck. The air smelled of smoke and unflushed piss, maybe a spill of pizza. Lazy L was smart enough to recognize he was out of his crowd. He pushed in closer to me, the bottle of Seagram's tapping his flat thigh, but he didn't say a word.

The second game set up quickly. Most of the guys were white since it was known to be an open game and Lawrence Twitchell's gig—wherever it was—was not. Thomas would get to Lawrence's later if he didn't go bust. I told Lazy L to sit across the table from me, just to keep our situation clear. Bobby, one of the guys who lived in the house, wanted to play pit boss, which was fine with me. Two-dollar ante, one dollar raises, a round of straight seven-card before we opened the door to chaos. Bobby, a pinkish pork slab man with a few days' growth on his face and bleary, bored eyes, insisted on the deal. He asked the woman from the counter to step over and cut the cards, and she did, looking as uninterested as he did. I checked them off as a pair to watch, even though she wasn't playing, then I anted up.

Bobby, a man who said to call him Moon, Derrold from Shamrock Stables, Lazy L boy, a kid named Jim, and me. The group didn't appear all that promising, but you never could tell. Money was money. My stepdaddy, Cliff, had made sure to pound that into my young head. Play it smart and you could fill your jar, even on a church night. Problem was, what I needed just now was something other than money.

Thomas was on a roll at the other end of the room. He was smoking a menthol, pouring quick shots into a can of Coke, laughing like a pinched cat. Went on about some green-broke filly Roy had his eye on down in Florida, hoping to get her cheap. Marty tried to grease a name from him—it was their dance, the two of them—but Thomas wouldn't give it up. "Brown baby," he chuckled. "Female. Fast as a grandmama's slap."

That got Polo going about the best mares he'd ever seen and how he wished they could foal as good as they ran. "I ain't hearing no argument," he said. "Genuine Risk was the best heart I ever saw in a gal." Polo must have been fifty, oak colored, gentle, a keeper in a business that didn't see fit to keep much. He'd worked for the Hancocks, one branch of the family or another, for years, and word had it they paid him every cent he was worth.

"Who want to argue with you?" Thomas snorted. "That's moldy old news. Call the bet and quit distracting."

Marty Salazar allowed as how Genuine Risk was a battler, though he liked raw speed when he saw it in a mare, he really did. His partner, he said, was trying like hell to bring an Argentine stud to stand in Kentucky because he stamped his get, colt and filly, with sizzle. It was just like Marty to plug his business at every turn.

"Call or fold," Bobby said to me. I hadn't been paying attention.

"Fold. I'm light." It was best to look weak early. Besides, I could tell Lazy L was holding something worthwhile because he'd finally taken his eyes off the black-haired woman's stand-up tits. He eventually laid down three tens and took the pot from Moon, who didn't seem bothered. We all knew the same thing: Lazy L would eventually be parted from his money.

We played for an hour straight. I lost $95. When Thomas's table took a break, Bobby shut us down too. "Gotta take a leak," he moaned, prodding at his back like it hurt him. "Which y'all need to do outside. Toilet's busted." Moon and Jim scuffed off for fresh air. I followed Marty to the grimy fridge for some ice. Thomas moved in behind us looking for a fresh Coke.

"How they hanging, Kerry? You robbed old Bobby yet?" Marty liked to swim with the lower life when he could find the stream, primarily to remind himself where he came from. Tonight he had on baggy khakis that looked like they'd been stained with Betadine and a stretched-at-the-tails golf shirt. Loafers, no socks, no belt. I knew the Lexus parked in the yard was his.

"Nobody's ever robbed Bobby, you think?"

"Not likely," Marty said. "Let me pour you some of that Turkey before you get parched." He gave a country club smile, and I could see from the cloudy edges of his eyes that he was drunk. Relaxed and polite, but drunk. He wondered who I was sleeping with—that ticker tape was easy to read—and when he handed me two fingers of whiskey in a flowered Dixie cup, I gave a half wink that let him know I'd read his mind. Marty'd always been in a pretty good marriage. But that hadn't kept the dog in us from sniffing.

"Eric at Belmont?" He opened his throat to the liquor.

"I hope to hell," I said.

"I heard he was having a patch of trouble, so maybe we won't talk about that." Marty focused the sober center of his pupils on me. "How about you get me tied to that horse you were on today? I'm feeling all kind of static about him."

"You mean Gem's Admiral?" I named a lunky four-year-old Alice was trying to rehab.

"Shit, Kerry." He flicked his Dixie cup into the crowded sink. The others were milling about the tables; my best moment was marching by. "You know the horse I'm talking about. The Twilight one. If he still had his nuts, I could get a couple million for him. As it is, I can get Piersall two firm offers in a day."

I lined up my words like glass beads. Thomas was standing too close for comfort. "Piersall don't own him. Besides, he's not training that well."

"Say that if you want." Marty scratched the inside of a forearm, sighting Polo, who was sorting coins at the table, down his hawkish nose. "Owner is one of those deathbed midwest widows, right? The kind with a smart accountant. Alice calls the shots on the horse."

"So the horse isn't for sale. Ask anybody."

"Every horse is for sale. Every trainer. Every jock. Even if the coinage isn't U.S. greenback money." He sighed to let me know he expected less petty bullshit from me.

"Not Twilight Flare. You know how Alice is with her clients."

"Alice Piersall thinks she's different," Marty said. "That don't make it so. Anyhow, we should talk more later."

"I'd like that," I said, nodding. "Believe I've got an even sweeter deal for you."

He gave me a long, slow shrug, then turned back to his table. I sucked some ice from my cup, hoping it would break through the firewall in my belly. I'd seen the spasm at the corner of Marty's damp and reddened mouth. He was ready for all kinds of business.

Bobby hollered at Jim to deal whether I had my butt in a chair or not. He'd opened a new deck of red cards and was restless to go. I sat down, but Lazy L was nowhere in sight, and neither was the woman. It wasn't hard to imagine the scam. Lazy L would be back in ten minutes, maybe less, with his rocks off and his wallet a little lighter. And that was only the beginning.

I won a small pot of five-card draw from Jim. Lazy L came back with pink blotches on his face and neck. He didn't say a word, but the fact that he kept clucking his tongue in his wet throat was almost worse. The woman seemed to have disappeared. She had her effect, however. Three deals later Lazy L was down $100 to both Bobby and Moon. Bobby, who had what looked like cigar ash hand stamped down the front of his shirt, still managed to act sullen.

Moon went crazy on a round of high-low that I survived. One of the men from Thomas's table left, and Thomas made like he would leave soon after, but he didn't. Marty acted like I didn't exist. Almost two hours later, Lazy L was pretty much busted and mad about it, so Bobby shoved his chair back and said he was hungry. Then he lumbered down the pipeline hallway to the rear of the house. It was his way of giving pissants a chance.

"You might want to catch a ride," I said to Lazy L, taking him aside. He'd served his purpose.

"Hell, no." The words fractured just above his sharp Adam's apple. "Still got seventy dollars. I'm staying."

"You're not staying. Jim's leaving, and they'll go to one table soon as they can. I'll have to sit out, too."

"Nobody's rousting me," he said. "Money's good. Ain't that drunk. Take your own girly ass home if you want."

"Hey," I said, closing in on him near a thicket of collapsed TV trays. "Get the signal. You're gone. That's what Bobby was saying."

"Bobby ain't shit. He's got to give me a chance to win back. That's fair play."

"What she's telling you"—we both heard Bobby's voice rasp down the tunnel from the bedrooms—"is how to stay out of trouble. Get the fuck gone. You suck at poker."

"And your dick ain't nothing to behold, neither," added a tired drawl that had to belong to the woman, though how she'd gotten back into the house I didn't know.

That did it. Lazy L was a lapdog, a fact he couldn't overcome. He tore out of the house, punching at a screen door that had no screen, swearing like a trucker. Jim said he'd get him back to the track, or as close as he could stand to drive him.

It was true that I'd sit out the new game. I didn't have the chops or the inclination to stay in. My concentration wasn't worth a dime. What surprised me was Marty's declaration that he was done. Everybody had assumed he was in for the duration.

"Go home to my sweet wife. Or some cable television." He yawned when he spoke and stretched his arms over his head until I could see the powder blue waistband of his boxers and the hanging lip of his furred belly. "Y'all make sure to sell me your best weanlings," he said, and Bobby and Polo laughed. They might give him some tips on the babies they were raising. They might not.

I followed him out to his car.

"When you back to New York?" Marty leaned himself against the moon-rimmed fender of the Lexus.

"Maybe not ever. If you can help me out."

He manufactured a sandy cough, then wiped his lips on his hand. "I've heard a little. Hoped you hadn't been dragged into it."

"I have. I wouldn't be talking to you otherwise."

"Yeah. Sure." He raised his chin to work out some sort of kink in his neck. "What I know is Hideo is gonna chap my white ass tomorrow unless I'm at the hotel by five-thirty."

He was stalling. Waiting for me to make the move.

"I'm glad Hideo's in town, Marty. I'd like for you all to make an offer on Sunsquall."

He coughed again to cover his surprise. "Shit," he said, looking at me, "you're serious."

"I am."

"Eric know about this?"

"He'll know when you make the offer. You tried to buy her eight months ago for George Patriarchos, remember? I squelched the deal. Now I want to unsquelch it."

"But you don't want your name or fingerprints all over it, huh? Otherwise we'd be doing this in suits and ties."

I performed an imitation of his earlier shrug. "I get my mare out from under some bookie thugs you don't need to hear about. That's all that's in it for me this late in the game. I'd like to sell her to someone who has a home barn in Kentucky, but I may not get that lucky." I waited. I could just see the dark logo of Marty's golf shirt, its stickman threads.

"Eric'll sign off?"

"He will if you and Hideo offer enough. She's worth it, I swear. She'll vet out perfect, the whole bit."

He paused, breathing through his nose like he'd find the answer he needed in the cold night air. "Patriarchos will still take her, I'm sure of that. He asks about her all the time. But I think Hideo ought to keep her for himself. At least for the summer. If she's healthy, she's that good."

I could barely hear his compliment through the gale force wind that had begun to blow through my head. Gone, gone, gone.

"I'll lock it up with the man over his rice and tea in the morning. Then we'll pin down Eric. Your name won't come up."

I nodded. Waited to see if lightning would strike.

"Good. Just give me a shake then." He reached out, his pale hand floating upward like ash. I smelled the sourness of sweat and drink on both of us. The bitter lubrication of deals.

"One last thing."

"What? More favors?" Marty flushed a little humor into his wary laugh. "I'm not even into my hangover yet."

"Lay off Twilight Flare. You don't know what he means to Alice right now, to her barn."

Another chuff of laughter. "Good barn is more than one horse. I know you know that. What lasts in this biz can't be bought or stolen. I like that Flare horse, like him a lot." He wiped his face free of some trickle I couldn't see. "What I'll do is not mention him to Hideo for a day or two. Until he notices. And I'll recommend he hire you to work his new mare." Then he banged the long door of his Lexus open, drenching himself in a lousy cowhide light and me in shadow. He didn't wave good-bye.

The stab of his headlights was like a poke at a sleeping beehive. Thomas was out the door looking for me before Marty was off the property.

"Huh. Wasn't sure you'd be here." He was both relieved and ticked and willing to show it.

"I'm still around." I felt scaled and peeled, only able to speak at half speed. "They're going to buy Sunny. I've got to hope Eric's sane enough to go with the offer."

"Well, good. You tell Marty to forget about that gelding of Piersall's, the one my boss wants to buy? Y'all was talking about him awful hard in there." He was whipping his key ring from hand to hand. I could hear it slice air.

"I did. But not for Roy's sake." He knew that was the truth.

"So you scalded me with my boss. Maybe you ought to get this night over with and spit right in my face."

A wrenching moment, one I hadn't prepared for. It seemed I could only solve one problem by creating another. "I needed to do it, Thomas. For Alice, for something . . . I don't know. It probably won't work. Roy will have his chance at Flare."

Thomas shushed through his teeth—a wet, frustrated sound. He didn't care what I needed. He needed plenty of things. And he'd seen too many trackers shredded and dumped by what they thought they had to have. "If that's how you cover for a friend, it's gonna take me until high sunrise to see it." He shushed again, and jerked his head. I had to swallow the sad water pooling under my tongue.

"There's not a horse yet that can get between real friends," I said. He was watching me, I knew, but I couldn't begin to predict this face. "Maybe I'm a failure to you right now. But I'll keep trying, I swear."

And he didn't deny what I said. Even as he showed me his back under the blue chip moon, he didn't do that.

CHAPTER 22

i knew Kevin would come back. Coyote to a carcass is what I told him, and he had the brass balls to tell me words like that hurt his feelings.

He found me on Alice's aisle, cleaning tack in the last white thumbnail of sun. I'd hunkered down with Piersall's crew to wait for a phone call from Marty. We were doing what we could to keep the barn going. Jenny had hired Burkie, a new hot-walker, with money from her own pocket. Burkie was a beefy, balding man with the possum-set eyes and low-action gait of someone who's spent time on dry tongue doses of Thorazine. He didn't click for me, but I could see he had some kind of Sunday school respect for Jenny. He wasn't Reno's type either, but Reno hadn't been consulted.

"You got the sense of a junkie thief," I said. I saw Kevin from a distance—the cocked head, the silent, snapping fingers—so I had time to varnish a little spite over the ax blade of my anger. "Don't show up here all droopy asking to be forgiven."

"I'm not," he said. But he was. I could see that in the heel-to-

toe caution of his step. "I'm down moving some horses, wanted to tell you—"

"Sometimes, there's nothing else in a story to tell. Talk isn't good forever, Kevin. It loses its edges. Like sawteeth." I plunged my arms into a bucket of water on the rail, trying to rinse them. "You tattled to Eric, probably for money. There's not a thing you can say to fix what you did."

"Eric would've found out anyway. And it's not like he wants all this bad shit to happen to you. He—"

That's when I called him a coyote and worse.

"You don't know what he'll do, Kev. Neither do I. He's not exactly rational these days. And it doesn't matter that some other slug would've dropped the dime. What matters is you did it first. You jumped at the chance."

He'd come dressed in a chest-hugging orange shirt with a zipper front and black jeans. Two of the ear cuffs were on. And a studded leather bracelet. He looked like a retail punk, lost in fresh air.

"He said you stole some things. Nice things. When I tried to clue you in on the way to Paris, when we were together, it was like you refused to hear what I was saying."

I gathered a few crumbly sponges. Anything I could organize. His words set off an irritating itch in my ears. "You claiming you tried to warn me? You think either of us got anything out of that trip but a teenage memory high? You think sitting in a car with me and having a few nice thoughts flip-flops the situation?"

"No. Look. All right." He twisted away from me with some kind of soft sound on his tongue, then moved out into the yard and craned his neck so he appeared to be studying the checkerboard of stalls, the abandoned water pump. The veins on his arms stood out so clearly they cast shadows. When he faced me again, his copper eyes looked almost concave with a feeling I wanted to call sadness. "I want to straighten out what I can, before more happens. Eric didn't, like, paint me the whole picture, okay? The real story of you two. He didn't talk about the junk he pulled. The loans. The dead horse stuff. Maybe I should've expected that."

"Man who hangs out with Doral Hughes should expect everything."

One side of his thin body flinched at my words. "What I'm saying, Kerry, is I'd like to help out. Unfuck things up."

I looked at his fitful, decorated face. There were portraits there I could keep for my mental scrapbook, snapshots that would remind me of the life in him that was all his own. I wouldn't deny what he meant to me, even when he posed and lied right in front of me. But there was no way I was letting him jack off his guilt.

"Problem is, like you say, things *are* happening." I tipped one of the wash buckets off the rail. The greasy, lukewarm water fountained onto the ground, soaking both of us from the knees down. "And I can't stop them. Change them if I'm lucky, but not stop them. I wanted to get the hell away from my problems, my problems followed me down here. So now I'm facing a shitload of music I don't like the sound of. I'm *facing* it. You need to do the same."

He knew better than to step back, or complain. I'd as much as called him a coward. Being witty or bitchy wouldn't help with that.

"I would like . . . ," he said, "I would like to rewind this video to a happier day. Driving and spliffing. Talking without worrying about what it all means. We used to have these pure times to-

gether, remember? We flowed, we learned stuff, we had this harmony, like, that nobody could mess with. A person doesn't out-
grow that, okay? I didn't think I was being such a bad boy. You've
never been one for hang-ups. I thought you'd get over it."

I moved toward him until our wet pant legs touched and
drained together into a puddle of yellow mud. He smelled
strangely fresh, tangy and cool all at once. I remembered hitching trailers with him, fixing flats, sharing dollar bills and coins.
Complaining about the monkey back problems of our lives that
would disappear when we grew up. Neither of us had grown
very far, though. The tattoos ringing Kevin's lashes made him
look younger, and retrievable. I wondered how they'd fade with
age.

"Kevin," I said, cupping my hands over the tight, child-soft
skin behind his cuffed ears, "I *will* get over it. But you won't be
here to see it happen. Go on now. Please."

"You don't want to hear my news?"

I slit my eyes, waited for some kind of final plea.

"Eric's here. I just trailered horses down for him, including
Sunny. She looks good. Aren't you happy to know that?"

Like a hammer to an anvil.

"I thought I ought to tell you." With a split lip smile, fingers
grappled onto the seams of his pockets. Impish.

"Well, I'm told." Words spoken from the bottom of some
well.

"And I can say this. Straight up. He's mad and mean to win
some money, but I don't think he's come to kill you. I'd say if I
thought he was." Kevin swayed a little, an unconvincing cobra.
"I've seen guys like that. I'd been here sooner if I thought he
was in that mood."

"Thanks."

He seemed happy with that one syllable, as flat as it was. "Yeah, look, I'll go now. I hope we're sort of even." And he leaned in for something, a brush of skin, a happy breath of kiss, and I gave up a version of that, thinking, *Even, not even, we're not,* never letting him know what a ruin I thought he'd come to.

*d*idn't dare go looking for her. Couldn't bear to leave the place where she was. I bivouacked in the car for the night, hemming myself into a short, ragged sleeve of sleep with thoughts about my mare.

Jenny had scheduled Flare's workout early, which is what Alice would have done. He was due to race shortly. The clockers wanted an official time on him—something to print in the papers—and they'd try damn hard to get it. But the footing was heavy at six o'clock and the visibility was bogus, which almost guaranteed a slow time. Jenny spread her feet and gave me a detailed description of the run she expected to see. Conservative, dull, safe. I liked listening to her orders. They were the only shelter I'd had for a while.

I took Flare up to the track in the company of a pony and rider from Marlou's barn. Jenny insisted on that. The girl on the buckskin pony was young and way too talkative for her job, although I understood her enthusiasm. She still believed it would always be like this, days blending from dark to light on horseback. I told her she ought to leave me at the gate because

I'd bet her $5 that my guy would go after her buckskin with his teeth if he wasn't given his space once he saw the track. She was reluctant to take my advice. She didn't want to look like she was afraid of a little bump and grind.

"Don't fret it," I told her. "I'm right about this. We'll go better on our own." The girl nodded until her safety helmet slipped over the bandanna she'd tied above her ears for warmth. She unclipped the lead from Flare's bridle and neck-reined the buckskin in a semicircle to our left. Getting rid of her relaxed me an important notch. This was a ride I wanted to go right.

I was forced to wait in the new mud and sawdust at the gate because there was a logjam of horses, so Pete, the assistant clocker, tapped me just like we'd expected.

"Who's that?" he asked, wiping a nylon sleeve across his platter face. The chill made his nose run. "Is that Piersall's rug?"

I said yes, it was Alice Piersall's saddle pad, though the monogram was so torn and faded even I had trouble vouching for that. I said I was on Twilight Flare, which Pete knew anyway. He just wanted to hear me say it. Then he picked up his beige phone and relayed the information. Pete didn't particularly care that he'd netted me; it was all the same to him on a long, cold morning. But there were people up in the grandstand who cared plenty.

Charlie eyed me carefully as he shook a cigarette free of a fresh, uncrumpled pack. He wore his hunter green windbreaker, and a pair of goggles were snapped crookedly across the front of his helmet. He knew about Rogelio's move up the coast because he knew nearly everything. He didn't know the truth of Alice's absence, none of us did, but the fact she wasn't standing where she should be got his attention. Something was afoot. He hoped to smell it off me the way a doctor smells infection from a wound.

"On your own this morning?"

"Almost," I said, giving nothing away. "Alice will be around."

"Heh." Charlie loaded his cigarette between his lips as a sort of grin. "You know who's on her way up here, what I heard from Sally Chisholm?"

I knew. Sally Chisholm was an old friend of Dean Ballard's. Eric would stable with her, use her riders.

"Yep." And I let Charlie see where things were grim with me. "But you know how I stay out of everybody's way."

He made a rude hawking sound over the plastic lighter cupped in his hands. He knew otherwise. "Watch your muck inside three-sixteenths. It's deep. Take it easy."

"Always do," I said, standing in the stirrups to work the knots out of my spine. Flare quivered beneath me. He was more than ready.

"Where you want it from?" Pete needed to know how I wanted to be timed.

"The last half mile," I said. And we left it at that. I trotted my boy clear of the open gate. He was high on the muscle already, bunched tight but not rigid, his long bones sliding and grouping beneath me. He'd go good. He seemed to like it bleak and dreary, which made him a throwback to his game Irish grand-sire in more ways than one. I reminded him of that as we scooted along the outside rail, talking to him as I hadn't the day before, just talking. I needed to concentrate. To pretend like nothing—no person, no other horse—had a piece of me. I barely noticed the shallow disks of the satellite arrays or the dull tan square of the test barn. There were dripping, blooming cherry trees and the thin, torn grass of the hillside. There was the red curl of the lower track filled with manic, barely broke two-year-olds, then nothing more than the hard belt of the rail. I could almost imagine we were about to run free across open fields, the way they still did around the stables in Europe. I shifted left to right to double-check the snugness of the girth, then stove the handle of my black-braided whip into the back pocket of my jeans. I wouldn't need it.

Jenny had been silver bell clear about what I was supposed to do. I was to set my horse up smartly with a half mile canter. Not give him his head but not coddle him either. Then I was to gallop four furlongs, coming in a shade under fifty seconds. I wasn't to press, I wasn't to hook up with anybody, I wasn't to hug the rail. "Outside him," Jenny said. "Drift him wide. That's how Reno says she does it." The point was to give Pete and his number crunchers exactly nothing. An average workout at an average pace. Our boy's odds would probably drift up to close to ten to one and no one would know if he was sharp or not, not even his new exercise rider.

I started to do my duty. We trotted. We cantered. I worked hard to get the long-backed bay to engage his hindquarters by collecting his stride. He limbered up beautifully and gave me a driven half-mile coast that felt like a ride in a full-sail boat. I stayed off the rail so Louisa Fett could putter by on a stumpy brown mare that belonged to Billy T. She made like she didn't see me, though Flare was more than seventeen hands high and impossible to miss. I was pleased to note that Louisa's butt looked like it was about to split out of the tight pants she had on.

I was setting my sights on the three-eighths pole when I saw her. She could be a hellion under saddle, cold jawed and stubborn when she caught a mood. But she never lacked that poise that comes from having power and knowing how to use it. Sunsquall. Red as the best Kentucky mud, red as a heated penny. The rider Sally and Eric had put on her barely looked up to the task.

I changed my plans, drew Flare back so Sunny would pass me. Pete and his clockers would have to wait. I just wanted to see . . . see what? If Marty was hanging over the rail like a proud papa? If I could breathe when I laid eyes on Eric? If Sally Chisholm would ignore me like she had every day before this one? Bad options. Surely, I'd had enough of those.

She was snorting as she went by, running a little head-heavy for my liking, but smooth. Her rider was small and unshaven, with broth yellow skin and fluid hands. He was strong enough, but he didn't look like he was having much fun. I tried to match an escaping sob to the pitch of air whistling through my helmet. Sunsquall. So close. So far from mine.

Let her go. That's what I started to do. I had a job to finish, and it didn't matter that my mare was showing me her damn gorgeous ass as she dwindled on that morning backstretch.

Except it did matter.

I bird-dogged her. Geared up a little and aimed for her outside flank. Her rider radared me pretty quickly, but he didn't pull up. Sunny was spry and quick and due to test her afterburners. Twilight Flare would be a damn good match.

I tried to ride it like a pro. Zoomed up on her heels and outsided her, pressing her toward the rail where we were both supposed to be in order to post an honest time. Then her rider gave me the look—that wicked, snotty, do-you-wanna-race look that's all curled mouth and goggled, squinting eyes. He made it easy, asking me to do the one thing I wanted. When my boy lowered his ugly Roman nose and we fell in with that charging mare, it was all over but the cussing.

Way the hell across the infield, far up in the frosty stands, the stems of a few stopwatches clicked.

What happened next deserves more than my words. More

than the queer music I hear after riding like the devil, when all the heart clanging and hoof beating finally catches up with me. I shortened the reins and dove into that gelding's stride in one sure motion. We hit the pole as a team. The only thing I can remember thinking is twelve; I dare you to take me under twelve.

He did, barely. Sunny was known for posting fancy fractions, but she eased into the first furlong. Maybe three ticks over eleven seconds, that was the guess I made in the quiet part of my mind that was floating somewhere above my possessed body. We could do it again. I knew we could. And we'd attract attention if we did.

One tick over. That was my guess for the next eighth mile. Sunny was as smooth as a gliding gull next to us, her small copper-maned head bobbing evenly in the corner of my eye. The rider began to press her some as we leaned through the turn, but he'd be careful there, I was sure of it. He wouldn't ask those slashing hooves for a big move. My mare was primarily a sprinter; she was known to draw off the lead steadily, with a fine hiss of speed. She wasn't a route horse like my boy, who was used to bulldogging his way out of the pack, often on the uphill sweep of a deep turf course. Our advantage was size and smooth-gear tactical speed.

Flare was the one who made the final call, I swear to God. It happened off the turn, three-sixteenths to go, well past the point he would usually sense a need to go to the front. I felt a quiet hitch, almost like bomber doors were opening beneath me, and boom. I had to pump my arms forward, and pump, and pump, just to keep up with the bit he'd seized in his teeth. Yet instead of flattening his stride like the good ones do when they're tired but too game to give up, I felt lifted a couple of inches, like we were hydroplaning down the stretch on pure energy. Sunny's rider saw it. As we drew a half length in front I watched him nestle his hands above Sun's sweat-mapped neck. He wouldn't drive the mare now, or drop her. He'd come off the speed the way he'd step off a tightrope, all grace and timing. He'd let me go. There was no need to grind out a win. It wasn't what he was after.

I rode the last sixteenth without thinking about it. The horse I was on needed me, and I gave him what I had in an honest, gut-busting effort. He had to believe there was nothing half-hearted about such a time. No half hearts. As we swept past the finish line and the clumps of bettors, tourists, and hungover pros dawdling along the rail, I didn't need to do much math. Sunny was right on our tail, two lengths back. It took me fifty yards to get my gelding in hand. When I looked back to see Sunny's rider high in his stirrups with the hood of his jacket parachuting behind him, I could see him smiling that crazy kind of smile you can't fake. Under forty-five seconds. Two furlongs in eleven apiece.

"Oh God. Oh God." I was sort of hiccuping as he cantered up alongside, Sunny snatching hard at the bit to let us all know she wasn't dead yet. "Maybe we should try that more often."

"No chance," he said. "Trainer want a hot three only." I was high in the stirrups now too, my hamstrings unclamping, my arms completely numb from elbow to glove. Horses on the rail moved aside for us, allowing us to cool down. I couldn't be sure whether the guy knew who I was or not. Couldn't tell if Sunny recognized my voice.

"I'd be skinned and gutted but my boss isn't around. Won't have to explain this until the numbers go up."

The guy shrugged. He had a few shy black hairs on his chin, looked too young to drive. "Your horse running good."

"Better than I knew." I realized suddenly that I'd done the whole thing—run my future up alongside that classy mare—without daydreaming I was riding her.

"Your boss around," he said. "I know her by my eyes. She like the one bench, wear a pink coat like usual."

I tried not to act surprised as my stomach split and sank into my soaked boots. Alice was back. I went momentarily blind in the blotted sunlight as Sunny and her rider rocked on past me. It was barely past breakfast time, and I had to tell Alice Piersall I'd pan-fried her money horse. Not that she didn't already know. I cooled out another half mile trying to inhale enough leftover fog to get my mouth wet. What the hell had gotten into me? Did I really think I could make a statement about *my* future on *her* best horse? I'd find out soon enough. I slapped Flare on his hot, foamy shoulder and tried to tell myself that at least the two of us still recognized a jailbreak run. We'd gone unfettered on the one path in the world where that was still the rule. We'd done it good.

Alice was nowhere in sight when Charlie shuttled the buckskin pony through the gate so it could accompany us back to the barn. But Roy was. And he looked hot collared. Flare gave us a snatchy time with the shank—he practically sat on the rail to avoid being clipped—so the pony rider and I were both pretty hassled by the time Roy got to us. It didn't help that Pete, as goofy as he meant it, announced real loud that we'd zipped off a forty-four and four-fifths charge that was guaranteed to make us the flavor of the day. Charlie gave me some gloved applause until Roy got close enough to crab-claw Flare's bridle.

"You got the devil up your ass?" Roy croaked. He looked like he hadn't slept, although his sunlamp tan was still even all the way down into the V of his jonquil yellow sweater.

"What the hell was that about?" he repeated, squeezing my boot hard with his left hand while he kept my horse from pivoting into him with his right.

"That was about working for Alice." I leaned over like I needed to adjust the martingale and yanked my foot free. "We're having a time here, Roy. You might want to stand clear."

"Don't you cross me, you bitch. I got a deal for this horse. You can't blow him out like that and try to change the situation. We have an agreement." He didn't seem to care how it looked for him to be cornering me when I was on another trainer's horse. I could tell other people were watching us, listening. Bad form. Bad politics. It wasn't his usual style.

"Save it for the bank, Roy." I gave Flare a little spur, and he hopped like he'd been zapped by a peeled wire. The pony girl tried to keep herself close. "I don't owe you any favors. You must have got that wrong."

"Those New York guys will take it out of your hide if you're not protected. I swear to that." The words boiled out of his mouth.

"Maybe. I'm not owed much safety in this life. Nobody is."

He stepped back then, the rage drawing him up straight. His eyes went to bloodshot splinters. I noticed how he didn't have a shirt on under his sweater, wasn't wearing his Rolex either, and I wondered if I'd pushed the wrong button too hard. I'd staged a kid fool run on a horse too many people were watching. Now Roy was making a public asshole run at me. It was hard to say which was riskier, or more stupid.

I told the pony girl to circle us out of there. We managed to jig our lathered gelding past the guard shack before he kicked anybody. As Roy fell out of sight, I let the reins go loose for the first time in a while.

"He go good?" the pony girl asked me as she sat butt-tight on her creaky western saddle. She was just making noise talk, but I didn't take it that way. I gave her the once-over, measuring her freckled, buttermilk arms and gawky smile against the future I could imagine for her. I'd been like her not so long ago, docile, laced with cheer. "Like a dream," I said in a sawmill way she couldn't miss. "Like the frigging perfect victory dream you almost wish you'd never had."

*a*lice did her version of the Queen of the Nile, and even though I was so tense I could barely move my head on my neck, I was thankful to see it. She'd caught a ride downhill on one of the groundskeeper's electric carts. By the time I got to the yard, she had the driver backing up as close to the tack room door as he could get, fussing all the time about what a giant pig disgrace to humanity she was. "But I don't want to walk," she shouted. "I feel too weak for it. So get me up to my chair before y'all leave off for wherever."

It was like someone had come and overcranked every creature in the barn, even the horses. Especially the horses. Flatiron heads bobbed and weaved in the stalls. Dawg froze for a moment with a feed tub in his hands, then stormed up the aisle like a roofing nail had been jammed under his skin. Reno, who'd been waiting for me to lumber home on his horse, stopped short of grabbing the lead away from Marlou's pony girl. He just stopped. Jenny came hustling from the far side of the building once she heard the news from Dawg, though she tried not to rush it. Only Burkie was unaffected. He went on scooping and piling manure like it needed to be done.

Alice got herself off the sagging rear of the cart and into the red director's chair we'd set up for her every morning. "Jenny," she wheezed, looking high into the cobwebbed rafters, "it looks like you done good with all the professionals I left you with. I apologize for missing so much school. It couldn't be helped. Now I'm back, and that can't be helped either."

Reno eased in and took hold of Flare, never once glancing at his boss. I dismounted, unbuckled the soaked girth. Reno could tell I'd slungshot his gelding home, and he knew what to do about it. He draped Flare in a blue sweat sheet and got him moving. I watched the great rump muscles gather and release under the glove-thin hide.

"Kerry, how many more hay rides you got?" Alice had her feet stuck straight out in front of her, work boots waggling. I held up four fingers. "Then I won't beat your dumb ass until you're done. Just promise you won't cause any more heart attacks with your fast riding this morning. I saw Niall Riordan up yonder, and his Irish gills were gray. He's still trying to keep his pants clean." And that was it. Half a minute later I was on my way to breeze another horse another mile. I didn't know what to think. Worse yet, I couldn't begin to tell what Alice was in the mood to believe.

We wrapped up just after ten when Alice chased Dawg and Burkie down to the kitchen for a long drink of coffee, which she paid for. She asked Jenny to come sit in the aisle next to her with the books, all of them. She told me to stand close by. As far as I knew, she hadn't exchanged a single word with Reno, or he with her, though we could all hear him stirring one of his poultices in the end stall, where the tatty rooster was kicking up dust in front of the door. That's how their forward life worked. No

compliments, no special notice of any kind. They blended together with business.

"We'll start with the easy stuff." Alice held out a hand for the
workout book, which Jenny gave to her. "You tell me which of
these nags is still on at least three legs and we'll go from there."

Jenny did it quickly, summarizing the status of each horse
without adding a lot of optimistic, mush-mouth opinion. Alice
closed her eyes once or twice when Jenny spelled out some middling bad news about a sore leg or a cough, but mostly she kept
silent. I remembered the day she'd hired me, how she'd sat in
her toy chair so solid and battling. She was going for the same
effect now, sarcastic and untouchable, but it wasn't quite working.

"You agree with all that hooey? Being the expert you are?" Alice leveled a finger at me. I started to say yes, but didn't. "I
wanted to put the dark filly in a bar shoe, and Jenny didn't go for
it. She wanted to rest her. I think that's what you would've done."

"Thought about me, did you, Kerry? That's nice. Were you
thinking of me this morning when you showcased my turf
horse?"

"No." I hesitated, fingers curled against the tendons of my
palms. "I was being stupid out there."

"Could be your special stock in trade." Alice rubbed a hand
along her neck, and I saw how dull her hair had gotten, how
frayed. "You must've had Jenny hire the new man, by the way.
He's so ugly, he couldn't begin to get you into trouble."

There it was. Alice getting back in the ring by sucker punching me. I could tell she needed a knockout; I could practically
taste the hot spit on her tongue. Something had happened to
her while she was gone and she needed a knockout bad.

"Jenny's got me too busy hauling shit and cleaning sheaths to
get into real trouble."

Jenny gave half a smile.

Alice paused, then sank in her chair until the hinges creaked. "Well, maybe that's true. Now do y'all want my story, or do we go on with this everyday nonsense us kitchen-headed women are so good at? I stopped to see Phil Kronce first thing, and he tells me we got horses marked to run."

"We do." Jenny opened a green folder on her lap, one she must have bought at a drugstore somewhere, and pushed some papers toward Alice, who waved them away.

"All right. They owe me up there, so we'll pretend we're running a regular, sanitary, grade-A racing barn here. But according to the thin topsoil of decency that still covers my true nature, I ought to give you all at least five words of a reasonable explanation. I'm not going to tell Reno one good goddamn thing because what happened is about forty percent his fault.

"Jenny," she continued, "go squirt me some faucet water in a glass so I can deliver my speech." Jenny got up and went into the bunk room, which had become her place since Danny had left. While she was getting the water, Alice waved me around in front of her. "Your husband hasn't lovey-doveyed you yet, has he?" I shook my head. "He's slower off the mark than I figured. Do me a favor, will you, and let me know when you hear from his lying mouth." I saw it again, a weary, caustic swell in her throat.

She gulped the water Jenny brought and went on. "There are two good reasons for me to talk. I need to and I want to. I only ask that you both clamp it shut long enough to suffer that."

I watched Jenny lower her eyes.

"The main fact," Alice continued, "is that Walt Simpson died on me two days ago. Walt, as Kerry may kindly remember, ran my farm over at home when he was up to it. The easy stuff—

mowing, patching fences, plumbing, turning out mares. He'd been with me, and my daddy before, nearly thirty years."

I listened to each word come around the bend like a tightly coupled freight car. Whatever Alice was owning up to, the delivery had been rehearsed. It was true that I'd met Walt once or twice. A white-haired, dim-faced man who liked to stay to himself and meddle with farm machinery.

"What I can hardly explain is how Walt's passing hit me. He'd been lingering with the cancer, but I thought bringing in the hospice nurse was as bad as it would get. He'd been in the metal-sided bed since February.

"So, ladies, I'm admitting to a temporary collapse. A failure. An absence from duty. Walt and I got married once a hundred years ago, which I don't want to talk about, and we never managed to undo that mess, not the formal way anyhow. Then he died. I was by his sour mattress when it happened. End of story."

I blinked. Looked as high as Alice's frozen face and began to tell her I was sorry.

"I'm pitiful sorry too," she interrupted. "I don't have much of an opinion about marriage since mine was as useful as a rubber glove and not that long-lasting. We rolled in the sack about ten months, got it out of our systems. Then we did what we needed to do. It worked a certain way for us, our not being housekeeping people and all." She looked up at me—into me—until my face began to heat up. "Now I've got a business to run, *if* I can find the meanness to run it. Kept telling myself that I needed to be on that farm, and Reno kept chanting at me the same thing like my eternal soul would chase a dead man to hell if I wasn't there to see his last green puke. Where I should have been was right here, busting heads at this spring meet. Claiming horses,

taking names. And I wasn't. Pretended there was another calling in my life—another life—and there is not, God damn it, not
for me. Not even when I wanted there to be. Which I found out
in a shitty way. There is nothing uglier than a good man on
tubes and a catheter."

Jenny dropped her chin so low her hair parted along her
white neck. Alice's words seemed to be taking her somewhere
she'd been before.

"Walt wouldn't have cared if I'd left him," Alice said. I could
tell by the mucus slide of her words that she was as close to tears
as she could get. "He didn't care. He liked to hear how the
horses were going, liked his liquor, liked a bush-hogged field. I
never knew a man so easy to please."

I waited three or four beats before I made a slow memorial
break to the left. I didn't know how to stand next to this version
of Alice Piersall. I wanted out of there.

"Not done yet, Kerry, if your raisin heart can stand it." Alice
aimed her broken eyebrows at me. "Jenny here's simpatico, as I
can see. You, on the other hand, put some kind of choke hold on
Roy Delvecchio this morning, and you used my horse to do it. I
ought to know what that's about."

How could I tell her it was about the last few things I cared
for? "I used Flare to hook up my old mare," I said, tasting the
cotton on my tongue. "He's been running like a field pony, and
I thought it might help him. But it was mainly selfish."

"You know you posted the best of thirty-eight workouts?" Alice scootched upright, her voice restoking itself like a boiler.
Out of one corner of my eye I saw that it was now Jenny who
hoped to break free.

"Sounds about right." I wanted to be apologetic.

"How many times you think my horses have posted a best
workout?"

"Probably none."

"None is right. Not on this track. Now that my horse is famous, you want to tell me and Miss Jenny both why your old lover boy was so jammed up?"

Which lies to tell? What truths? "Roy wants Flare in his barn. He told me that. He wanted me to keep him informed even before I got the ride, how Flare was eating and so forth. Claims he's got a deal with the Stronheim kids."

"And you sold me out?"

"He tried to bribe me." I let the blade fall just like that.

Alice threw the rest of her water in the air toward my face. "No faith. No loyalty. You ought to get set up in politics." She shifted toward Jenny like she couldn't stand to look at me any longer. "Are the vets scheduled?" Jenny told her they were, with elbows sticking out as she spoke like she'd survived a hurricane wind. I thought about how Jenny would be better for Alice in so many ways. Jenny could stand being heaped on—or maybe even cared about—in ways that I couldn't.

Alice came back at me, her eyes cobbled with feeling and heat. "All right. I got some bullshit to equal yours, young lady. See how you like it." She stood, and I saw how the past days had worn scaly patches on her skin. The back of one hand was cracked and sore. "That stunt this morning may have helped me in a assbackward way."

I held my breath. Waited. Alice looked at me as if she expected me to spring a leak.

"It's true. That gelding has been on the sales block. Mrs. Stronheim is real old. Her sons could give a flying fig about a five-year-old horse who doesn't even have his balls. They want to unload him. But Mrs. Stronheim likes me, much as I hate to admit it. Your flight to freedom proves I've got him in shape for the Elkhorn. That might be enough to keep him in this barn."

She cornered away from me, one hand on a hip as though she almost felt in charge again. "If the widow Stronheim truly knew how good that horse is, she'd be tempted to send him to a splashier barn. But I've got her convinced he needs old-fashioned, old-maid care. I iced the cake when I told her my brother—that's what I called Walt because I wasn't sure she'd cozy up to the husband thing—was near to dying. The widow's big on sentiment. I doled some out."

"Then he'll stay here." My voice sounded crepey and dry.

"Signed and sealed last I checked. Although I probably ought to make some nice phone calls to be triple sure. Downside is the press will hotseat my boy and that sheik horse of Niall's so they've got something to hype for race day. And rumor has it your mare will join the fray. My odds'll come down. Which I hadn't planned on."

She focused across the gate at the road, where a graceful blood bay was being led to his barn. Assessing one more horse. Always assessing. I'd been right about Flare and how much she wanted to keep him. Still, what I'd done might cost her some serious money on the tote board. If the medical bills were half what I imagined. . . . She wasn't whining, though. She was showing me—and herself—what couldn't be taken away from her. She watched that elegant horse until it was out of sight.

"It's almost a wicked favor, your riding like that. First, you got Delvecchio stomping like Rumpelstiltskin. Second, I got no choice now but to run the big nag straight out. Can't hide *him* under his bushel, either. I've just about got the feeling you were sticking up for me in a crazy, sky-dive way. Any chance of that?"

My knees were shaking, it was that bad. The kind of hope that scalloped Alice Piersall's words was the terrible, soaring kind.

"Let me ask about yourself." She peered into my face, brassy eyes so steady they were hypnotic. Trying to give me something she wouldn't name. "That husband is coming around. I can feel it like bad weather in an achy back. You're going to have to settle out with him. Level it all. Which reminds me again of what I never had to lance and drain with Walt." She looked at me even harder. "I can see how you might have the guff now, Kerry. The backbone. Don't let me down."

She went on up the aisle without me, breaking the link. Stopped at every stall and spoke quietly with the creatures that met her there. They nudged and butted her shoulders, smelling her, assuring themselves of a pattern they hadn't forgotten. She lifted fingers peeled raw by medicines and disinfectants to touch their odd cowlicks, their stars and blazes of white. Birds swooped above her in the dense air of the loft. A pair of bandages bannered along a rail in the wind. She was alone, and silent, and on this day of return, unbeatable. There was no way to consider her beyond that.

CHAPTER 25

*L*ouisa Fett got to me that night, right about the time it got dark enough to trip over your own toes if you weren't paying attention. I wasn't paying attention. The way I put it together later is that Louisa and her friend picked me up after I stopped by my car to grab my ditty bag and towel. I thought of Louisa whenever I visited the Chevy since I fully expected her to smash the windshield with a set of hoof trimmers. She owed me one. But she hadn't been worth much extra worry since I had plenty else on my mind. What I was worth to Louisa—well, she decided that for herself, and our paths crossed as they had to.

The redhead bulled in behind me just after I cut around a molting forsythia bush on the back way to the shower. She shoved me forward first, a rude junior high push into the shadows, then bear-hugged me from behind. She was stronger than I'd guessed, but I didn't fight her much. She wasn't from Eric, so smelling her powdery Orphan Annie smell was a kind of relief.

Louisa came down the chipped concrete steps that led to the bathrooms. She looked glittering and miffed, and I could see she was disappointed she hadn't had the chance to toss me over a high railing. We weren't quite alone. I heard split, ricocheted voices and the standard hiss of the showers even as I understood I'd have to handle this brand of trouble on my own.

"Bitch." Louisa was so into her soap opera mode that she walked right up and slapped me. She forgot the blow was likely to hurt her some. I saw the wet flinch in her eyes as my left ear began to buzz and swell. "Troublemaking bitch." She put her weight behind the next one, which was hard enough to make me struggle. Redhead clawed one of her hands into the tender hair at the base of my neck to hold me still.

"You're not getting out of this one," she panted.

"Think you can come in here like a rich whore—which you aren't—and take Billy back. I know what you're after, you and Chantal." Louisa dug her fingers behind one side of my collarbone and pulled. I kicked at her, but she was ready. She levered a low, fast punch at my stomach. When I twisted into it to soften the blow, I heard my hair tear free in the redhead's fist.

"I'm not after Billy. Ask him."

"You want to fuck your way back into his barn. Everybody knows that. It's what you did with Ballard." She smacked me across the mouth with a hand that had rings on it. "Everybody knows what you are."

Redhead kidney-punched me about then, and I went to my knees, where I didn't want to be. They could kick me to pieces down there.

"Wrong," I said, as if I was used to talking through my own blood. "Who I been riding for?"

"Fatso Alice." Louisa looked like she wanted to take a knife blade to parts of my face. I hoped she didn't have one.

"Roy D.," she answered again.

"The man with the favors, you got it." I sniffed and coughed, trying to keep my head clear for the opportunity I needed. The snot and stuff was really flowing. "I don't need Billy, except that he's nice . . . better looking. He already said he won't take me back. Ask him. Maybe he can be yours."

Louisa socketed the sharp toe of her cowboy boot between two of my ribs, checking her aim. Redhead breathed harder, raspier, as if the excitement of holding me down gave her that much. "I got better gigs going with Roy. Money. Big owners. You know how it is."

She kicked me close to where Eric had bunged up those same ribs. I went blind with what felt more like ground fire than pain. Couldn't breathe, couldn't talk. Which was fine with them.

"You are full of total dog shit. I'm done putting up with you."

Redhead slammed me in the tailbone, then pancaked me with a foot to the spine. I covered my head with my arms, believing it couldn't last long no matter how bad it got. Louisa was a braggart. I was lucky in that. She had something to say every time she hit me, which slowed her down and gave me time to serve up a story. There was a tiny chance it would work.

"You want the scheme," I gasped. "I'll give it up. Easy money, easy work."

"I'm fixing it so you won't ride for nobody for a long time." They both chased me with the hard curl of their boots, one on each side. I rolled when I could. It was like dodging scorpions.

"I do threesies . . . for Roy. With clients' wives . . . or whoever. Keeps . . . every . . . happy." It hurt to say the words. They did the job, though, and stopped Louisa long enough for me to get my back to the hedge. There was a siren somewhere between my ears, and the rush of running liquid. I crawled to my knees but Redhead flattened me before I got both legs working.

"Check it," I spit. And I named some of the right names. It

was good enough to get Redhead laughing. We all knew plenty of people who'd pay the hired help for just about anything.

"I will," said Louisa. "You keep your hands off Billy T. like I say. Me and him got plans." She went for a slow roundhouse at my head. I shucked it onto my shoulder, which went dead numb. Through the throb, I realized that Louisa didn't have Billy where she wanted him. Not yet. Which meant she hadn't gotten him into bed. My head cleared a little as I considered that, then I heard Redhead say something urgent, then say something again. I toppled and somebody stepped hard on one of my fish-flopping hands. It was all I could do to keep breathing with my face in the dirt.

"Get out there. Get . . . come on." Voices roller-coasted above me. "God damn . . . what you . . . what?" Then came a floating mattress time, when I convinced myself I was asleep. Passed out, maybe. Probably. Then hands on me, trying to prop me up while I gagged from trying to move too much. I went to jelly again, following a looped line of cusswords around and down into darkness. It took me a while to understand that somebody was asking if I was all right.

I opened one flank steak eye and tried to draw a bead on the face that looked too far away to be any help to me. Dawg.

"Somebody at you bad. You all right? Know your name? At you bad. First I thought it was some of them biker men work at the barns. Then I seen it was girls coming out of there, looking all hurried up. So I busted through. Didn't have to throw no shots, though." Dawg shook his head to slow down the speed of his own talk, and I could see the clear sweat rivering in front of his ear. I tried to follow his fast, jitterbug voice. "You owe money? Reno, he say some people been watching you, but he didn't exactly say to be ready for the girl hoodlums. Damn."

I sat up and gagged again. "Reno got you . . . looking out for me?" My teeth were okay. I hawked all kinds of goo out of my mouth after I checked them.

"Not exactly. No." Dawg rolled one half of his mouth down like I wasn't getting it. "He looking out for everything. You know how it is. I'm gonna miss the shuttle now. Need to find a ride to town unless you want me to walk you to Piersall's." It was all he could think of. How somebody else needed to tend to me. I shook my head.

"Got . . . things here somewhere," I said. Dawg glanced around until he found my towel and my bag under a bush. He tried to hand them to me, but I couldn't quite seem to take them.

"We got to get you up to a office or something. You look bad."

I balanced myself over my anvil feet and shook my head again. "Help me to the steps," I said. "I'll be okay when I clean up."

He believed me because he wanted to believe me. I clutched the towel to my chest like it was a captured flag, and Dawg steered me upward, one step at a time. What I needed was ice and a good, safe bed. What I'd get was a cold shower, alone. Louisa hadn't broken anything. The inside of my busted mouth could go without stitches. I was right at lucky.

Dawg shuffled with me to the crumbly entrance of the ladies' room. "Is that what they was into you for? Gambling money?" He pushed his long fingers across his temple, spreading his sweat in wide streaks. Ever since the Danny business, he'd thought of me as jinxed.

"No. That was only about a man, if you can believe it."

"Don't know about that. Don't want to know." He shrugged into his giant T-shirt and gave me the starched, neutral look he practiced at the barns. It didn't work. I snagged his fingers with mine, thanked him. Told him he'd saved me a load of trouble and maybe some time in the hospital. That he was a brave and righteous man, one we could all learn from. I embarrassed him. The dark threads in his eyes got darker, and I could tell nobody had said those words to him before. He wanted to disappear down the steps like a dropped rock. And he did.

CHAPTER 26

i came out of the shower deaf from the roar of water, scoured, sleepy. Louisa Fett had settled her accounts—I felt that in every joint and soft part I had—but in some way I couldn't put a tongue to she'd also resolved something for me. I no longer felt a black winch line pulling me back into the muck of my history. Riding alongside Sunny that morning had released something in me. I was settling out, just like Alice had declared I should. I looked awful but halfway decided that was all right too. I could cut my hair, get a tan. Drink milk shakes until my mouth healed. I'd taken the punches. Now I'd scramble to my feet.

The first thing I had to do was walk, and keep walking, or I'd be too stiff to get on a horse the next morning, and I didn't want Louisa to have that satisfaction. I toweled off while the two other women waiting for the shower kept a tight rein on their eyes and pretended I didn't look like an underfed wife who's been thrown through the wall of her house trailer. I had a hard time getting into my jeans. The women kept their backs to me the way people do in a shared hospital room. I combed what hair I could reach and ponytailed it away from my face. One of my cheekbones felt like it had been chipped off, but it hadn't. The swelling wasn't bad enough for that.

I stepped out into the deadish glow cast by the security lights high on their tarred poles. There was a near-full moon, which made the barns go flat and plastic against the dark. It was spooky, but only if you didn't know the ghosts. I limped away from the sheds. Crossed in front of Preston Patchen's barn, where I greeted the yellow-eyed shepherd dog and turned onto the gravel toward the lower track that the consigned two-year-olds had been tearing up while they learned to work under saddle. I'd been dumped down there a few times in my career, thrown crown first in the mud while I tried to convince a four-footed toddler to run in regular circles. It was deserted now and looked like every off-season oval I'd ever been on: lonely, spindly, cheap.

I saw the orange embers of cigarettes high on the far bank where some grooms were taking a break. Lovers, I thought. Or the backside banger version of such. There weren't any voices, though. It wasn't the kind of night that drew out talk.

I don't know how long he'd been with me. Five minutes. An hour. Maybe the whole lifetime-in-a-day. I became aware of him as I scrabbled up a dirt path toward the barns on the ridge, falling to my hands in the slick clay more than once. A pair of terriers set to yapping, the kind Danny had called stew dogs, and I turned to catch some gray splinters of movement behind me. Someone was trailing me fifty, maybe sixty yards back. I knew who it was. And I knew he wouldn't have let me see him if he hadn't been ready. Eric had always been good at choosing his spots. I didn't stop, just kept walking the circuit, massaging fresh blood through my bruises and feeling the sharp edges of the cage around my heart.

He followed me all the way to my Chevy, the last bit of turf I had. Kept his distance until then, through the bleached gates, past the nestled cars and the close, moist heat of sleeping horses. We weren't alone, but it felt that way, like we were connected by a long, unkinked lifeline in a place suddenly gone moon-surfaced and stark. I watched him as he closed the gap. He didn't look different despite the fact his hair had begun to grow over his ears and neck. His wasn't a body interested in change. Experience maybe, but never change. He didn't know how to hang a head or drop a smile. I didn't think he ever would.

I found my keys and pronged them among my cold fingers. Delayed reaction.

"Am I allowed near you?" It was all he said.

"You shouldn't be, but what can I do?" The words came up mossy and tired, and I didn't try to make them more than that. The big feelings weren't there, not the anger or the ache. I turned to fumble at the trunk latch like there was some reason I needed it open.

"I wanted to see you, Kerry. To apologize." He paused awhile. "I've been out of control. We both have. And I couldn't get you on the damn phone . . ."

A laugh screwed its way into my mouth. "Because you can't ever find a racetracker," I interrupted, "not when you need him."

He saw where I was headed with that remark and cut himself off. Waited.

"I told you I was out of things." Which was easy for me to say with my back to him.

He took two shallow breaths I could hear. "I'm not sure you're out of shit. If you were, you'd be down with Cliff and your mama trying to be a cocktail waitress." He moved closer, toward my elbow, though not close enough to touch me. He was wearing a boxy jacket I didn't recognize with a black T-shirt underneath. Wedding ring, water-resistant watch, musky after-shave, stealth. I had the distant thought that he might try to hit me again, but I couldn't summon up much concern. Pain had moved way down my worry list. There wasn't much Eric Ballard could take from me now that wasn't mine—just mine—to give.

"I guess I should thank you for sending my own friend to bloodhound for you."

"He was easy about it, Kevin was. Thought he could find you. He knows I just want a chance to work things out."

"Kevin's ignorant."

"Could be." Eric fluttered a few fingers in front of his face like he needed to keep his own attention. "I'd have made it here soon enough anyway. I heard from that hardline-type foreman, what's he go by—"

"Reno. You didn't. He never gave me up."

"Have it your way. I took a few calls from down here. You weren't exactly hiding and people here weren't exactly doing the hiding for you."

I made myself travel the map of his face. The high forehead, the squared cheekbones and jaw that should have meant real strength, the bright deep-set eyes you couldn't appreciate except in daylight. It was a good face, and I was sorry I still felt that way about it.

"I need you. I'm going to run Sunny big."

"More of your bullshit, Eric. I don't have money or anything else you need. It's a mistake to try her out so soon." I opened the hatchback and shoved the lid upward until it screeched.

He grabbed me then, pressed the round bones of my wrist against the gaping edge of the lid. Pulled my other arm behind me like a cop would, using his weight to flatten my thighs against the back of the car. He grunted at a higher and higher pitch and didn't seem happy until I was stretched and swaying in his grip like a butchered side of meat. I didn't struggle, didn't speak. Wasn't planning on giving him the satisfaction.

"Have you made it your job in life to make me mad? To smart-mouth me into something we'll both regret?" He ground my wrist into the bite of the metal until he found just the right crease. The pressure radiated down my arm and into my body until my clenched jaw shook. I wondered if the old, soothing lover-wife strategies would work on this version of the man I was bound to. I doubted it.

"Get ahold." I ground the syllables through millstones of hurt, treating him just like I'd treat a stud horse that pinned me in a stall. "Ahold there. Come on."

It seemed to work. The guttural bluntness of it. Eric let go of the arm flexed behind my back, and while he didn't completely release me, the force of his body was less punishing, more kneading and sexual. After a passage of time I measured by the hard throb of light behind my eyelids, he released me, shrinking under the shoulder pads of his jacket, his head rocking smoothly on his neck as though it was searching for a new balance.

"Damn me." I heard him reel in a flimsy line of words. "I . . . is it still that bad?"

He meant my beaten face, which he could finally see in the dome-light gleam of the car. It captivated him even though he didn't remember that he hadn't hit me there.

"Got this tonight." I touched my swollen cheek before I could stop myself. "I healed up quick after you . . . ambushed me." I braced for a slap that didn't come. Told myself to ratchet down the provocations.

"Kerry." He ignored what I'd said and unpacked my name like it was wrapped in good memories. "Let's start over. Let me start over. I never meant to hit you, I still can't believe it happened. But it happened. I remember it as the worst thing I've ever done."

I watched his bundled lashes close over his eyes as they did when he was thinking about himself. "You want to tell me you only did it because you were cranked? Want to serve that one up as usual?"

The crease beneath his soft mouth deepened. I wasn't giving him enough room, though even he seemed unsure of his limits—or whether he had any left. "I *was* cranked. I'm clean now—except for these . . . episodes . . . but I'd be lying if I told you I think it's for good."

"Get your mother to send you to Betty Ford," I said, rooting among my clothes and bags just to feel them. "She likes to talk about it."

"Let's not get into that, Kerry. I want to go back and—"

"Yeah, back to the so-called deal you made that killed Stevie. I was your dumb-ass sweetheart there. Go wherever you want, Eric. Just go without me."

I waited for him to wag his handsome head and say I wasn't being fair, that I didn't understand. That I was wrong. He didn't oblige.

"I fucked it up. Don't think I don't know that." He stepped backward as if there was something that needed to pass between us other than the licking wind. His hands rested in his pockets, almost benign. "I brought you these," he said, and he held something out to me that barely filled his white palm. It was a box. The velvety, satin-lined kind with the tight, hidden hinges. The kind that holds jewelry. I snapped it open. The clustered diamonds winked at me and spun.

"You forgot them," he said with a chip of a smile. "They go with the necklace. Since I want both of us to get out of this as neatly as we can, maybe we can go someplace and talk. Makes me nervous standing out here like I'm haggling for a score."

The box that held the earrings seemed to burrow into my hand. I pocketed it, slammed the car shut so hard I buzzed the pulse that was beating in my neck. This was new territory, this bargaining. "We can walk. I need to keep the stiffness out."

"No walking here," he said. "I know too many people."

His car was one of the Mercedes sedans leased by his father's development firm. He'd driven down, he said, to keep his hands busy and get his mind right. Airplane flights made him want to drink vodka out of tiny, lady-shouldered bottles, as if I didn't know. I slipped cautiously into the passenger side, checking out the triangle shadows in the backseat. I still wasn't sure he'd come after me alone. The way he'd stretched and swung my body was too real, too possible. But there was no one there. At my feet were close to a dozen empty diet drink cans. Eric mentioned he'd drunk the stuff all the way down, warm.

"Remind you of old Dean to sit in a successmobile that still smells like the dealership? Want to start with that?" He gave the hollow puppet-son laugh, first time that night.

"I'd rather end a few things," I said.

He sat with his hands on the steering wheel, not gripping but stroking the wrapped leather, soothing it. It was possible then to recall what we'd been good at: culling yearlings, sorting bills over coffee or gourmet pizza, training a few handpicked horses while we waltzed the waltz of the young who have promise. We'd woven what we knew and what we were willing to risk. Now, like then, Eric wanted me to be the bad news, the heavy freight.

"Do you want to talk about us?"

"Not that. Not yet." He flung himself back in the bucket

seat, irritated. "You always go for the serious big picture first. I'm not ready for it."

"Then what the hell are you here for? I don't have the money I took. Even if I did, it's not enough to bail you out."

"I don't know that, do I? I hear otherwise." He leaned over, eyes fastened on me. The high beam of a threat spilled over the edges of his pupils. "I know what you clicked out of the safe, though God in hell knows how you got the combination. I heard about your big track score. Don't try to scam me, my love. Remember who you're dealing with."

I sat still in my seat. It might have been the penitentiary's electric chair, as free as I felt to leave it. I hoped he wasn't going to ask for the necklace.

He broke before he got to that point, panted to a halt. "Damn it." Shoved his wild, curled hair back with both hands. "I might as well be having fucking acid flashbacks to be talking like this. I've got to stay focused. I came down here . . . I came down," he gulped, "to give you these," and he slid two fingers over the knot in my pocket that was the velvet box, the first time he'd touched me gently, "and to run Sunny. I thought we could have it out. I thought being down here might get my head straight. I need that. I'm under the gun."

My thigh burned against the shape of his hand. Eric dipped his forehead to the arm of his silk jacket and wiped it dry. "What else can I say except that a big drink would be excellent right now."

I tried to get a tough, raspy sound to come through my nose. When he didn't respond, I took my chance. "We have to sell Sunny."

"That *would* put me in the grinder, which is probably where you want me. I've heard from Smarty Marty Salazar and his guy. Nice offer, but my bankers won't wait." His words sounded paved in ice.

"Give them these." I took the earrings out of my pocket and held them level with his chin. "They can have the necklace, they can have my car, tell them—"

"No." He swatted my hand out of the air. "Don't try that again. You know what this is about, you've always known. That's why you took off and left. This is about me being grown up, accountable. Right now I'm just trying to find the courage to do what I need."

"You're thinking about taking Marty's deal?" A fast, sweet pain pooled in my jaw, my eyes.

"Yeah. I am. Seeing you again . . . that's the difference. I pay the price for any delays. A hard price. But I'll get to saddle Sunny one more time in that stakes race, then who knows? They won't kill me. I'm not worth that. I'm hoping they leave enough of me behind so I can get to work finding my next Breeders Cup horse. Recovery is my game, right? It would help if you'd tell me it's a good idea." He gave a haunted, fractured shrug beneath his jacket. He'd talked himself into a corner he wouldn't be able to defend. He finally wanted it that way.

"I think it's good, but—"

"Nothing else." He walled me off with his hands. "I want to remember it this way."

He had the sale papers in the glove compartment. I signed where he told me to. He told me I could come to Sally's barn in the morning if I wanted, to give Sunny her exercise. I told him I'd try to do that.

When it was done we both seemed unable to move, stuck sweaty to our seats, surrounded by steamed windows and the Armor All stink of the car. My kicked tailbone throbbed. My face was puffy and hot. The Eric who sat beside me now was perversely familiar, almost comfortable. I broke the rickety silence by asking him for aspirin. He always carried it.

"In the trunk," he said. "I'll get them. Valium, too, if you want. The doctor and I decided they don't count against me."

He left his door open when he returned with three pills for me and a warm soda to sip from. If he popped his own tablets, he did it out of my sight. The fresh, ordinary air that smelled of dew and straw revived us both a little, and I realized we were headed into that awkward cul-de-sac you come to at the end of a bad date. Or a good date that's scared you.

Eric sat sideways with his long legs outside the car. He didn't know how to do this part either. He asked who'd hit me, I didn't tell. He said he was sorry he'd started the evening so rough, he'd forgotten how to react to me. "You know," he said when I still wouldn't answer, "my divorced friends always tell me the sex is hot when a marriage crashes, like they finally get to do it on tables after the settlement conferences. It's a crazy head rush, they say. Last chance to get everything in."

"You believe that?" I knew how he could. I saw myself straddling him, slamming Dean's goddamn Mercedes to pieces with what was left of us.

"One guy, Jacob from the Hamptons somewhere, you met him, he said he and his ex fucked perfectly when they had to visit some in-law's grave. What do you think? You think that's sick?"

"Eric," I said, focusing on the dashboard, where Sunny's papers lay slashed by my signature. "I was in . . . I cared about you. Never stinted on that, but—"

"Don't say it. You're talking to Mr. Poor Impulse Control. I know. This is where we agree to separate and say we've had a few good times." He swiveled then and caught my shoulder, searched my eyes, really searched them, for something under all the fatigue, and giving up. Then he kissed me, and it was long and careful and secret and meant too many things at once. All of the undeniables. He curved a hand below my neck and molded it downward until it was between my thighs. But he broke the kiss. Stopped it. And I could see from his blistered, pleading irises that even that had not taken him where he wanted to be.

"Good luck in the race," I said, looking away, tasting him everywhere inside me. "And later."

"Thanks." He straightened himself, got out of the car again. It was harder for me. I knew I wouldn't see him again for a long while, and that somehow made me move more slowly. I was getting what I'd wished for when I first hit the track—a clean slate, bare platter—and it made me feel purely empty. What was left? A flesh sack who could ride fast and hang on? Memories I could sort like old postcards?

"I can send you the necklace," I said. "I only wanted my money."

Hearing those words and the faith they implied seemed to pluck at him a little, my rakish, raked-over boy. "Horseshit." He said it carefully, as though he wanted to make a happy sound. Like we still shared some spirit. "You enjoy the necklace when you have the time. Make sure you think of me."

CHAPTER 27

i made it through Sunny's half-mile breeze before Sally Chisholm saw me dry heave into my gloves and pulled me out of the saddle. Somebody else would have to prep Hideo Hidashi's mare for the stakes race. Sally had noticed my pumpkin face first thing that morning; everybody had. Now I had to tell her my tailbone was probably broken and would she please get me over to Alice Piersall's where I could get fixed up. Alice told me to lie down in Jenny's room, which I did, though I gagged more air when I got there and recalled how I'd gotten all weak and widespread for Danny on that very same bed.

I fell asleep anyway, or close to it, something I hadn't been able to do after I watched Eric nose his soundless black car toward the highway the night before. Jenny had a blue-checkered quilt on her bed that smelled of somebody's hot, dry attic. That helped. I woke up when Jenny stuck her head in the door and whispered my name.

"I'm sorry." She said it twice. "I know you ain't feeling up to par, but I think you ought to hear this."

Just trying to straighten my legs sent shooting pains up my back. "What? What's wrong?" I was groggy.

"Nothing dangerous," and I could see Jenny was trying to give me my privacy by not barging farther into her own room. But something was up. She kept checking over her shoulder. "Come out when you can."

I lurched to the door like an arthritic dog, braced against the door frame, and willed my hips and shoulders to move in all directions. Bull riders felt this bad at least once a week, I told myself, which maybe explained why there were so few of them and why they were so stinking mean.

I bowlegged out to the aisle where Jenny was waiting. "Your friend's here." She crooked her head to where Thomas was talking to Reno in the vicinity of Flare's stall. Someone else had ridden Flare that morning. I hoped everything was all right. "Heavy shit going down. More of it." Jenny's lips were off her teeth like she was ready to laugh, but the rest of her was dead serious. "You go hear what he's saying."

Thomas was motor-mouthing to Reno, talking horses, always horses, with his big body slumped like a grain sack against the barn wall. Reno was running the oiled strap of a lead line between his fingers as he listened. They'd known each other—respected each other—for a long time, and I knew they were saying a lot right then that wasn't coming across in words. The language of men used to being dealt out. When he saw me, Reno began running that strap through his fingers in the other direction. Thomas stopped in the middle of whatever opinion he was delivering and turned my way. He wasn't unhappy to see me, that much rinsed clear across his face, but I couldn't be sure I'd been completely forgiven.

"Hey, woman." He took a long medical-doctor look at me.

"You took it right bad. The boy there"—he meant Dawg—"said you got set upon. How you feeling?"

"Sore," I said. "Ugly. What's up? I know you got more to do than waste time with us down at this little barn." Reno hung the lead line on a fat nail head and ducked into Flare's stall, where I knew he could still hear us.

"Yeah, well it's a damn busy time like always. Just wanted to check on you, is all." He dug his hands into the back pockets of his pressed pants, which made his broad chest go broader.

"You want to know who did this?" I pointed to my blackened eye. "Is that it?"

"Believe I know who did that. Not hard to figure, especially after what went down at the clubhouse this morning." Thomas's flattish nose was still flared with worry, but like Jenny, he seemed on the verge of hawking up a laugh.

"Lord God in heaven help me." He shook his head. "I was there for the first of it, like I was telling Reno here. Mr. D. on his way to the elevator to go up to one of them rooms for breakfast. Had the Talbotts with him, you know the man with the spiky-headed London wife my grooms can't understand a word she says. They're all dressed up and talking nice when Selby James, works consignments with Mr. Camp, you know who I mean, he comes walking over to keep Mr. D. from getting on that elevator. I can't hear what he says; I'm way over toward trackside with the clockers waiting to pick up a horse, but I can tell he's making Mr. D. mad right in front of the Talbotts. Mr. D. gets all fussy, looks like he's swatting at bees when he gets angry in his good clothes. Gets rid of Selby, though—Selby don't get on the elevator—so I don't think about it no more. I know Selby has this good-looking new wife—Sondra something-or-other she used to be; you probably rode with her—but I don't think about that either. All I wonder is whether Mr. D. ever backed off on a high bid for one of Selby's horses, which is the kind of business might make a man like that hot enough to bother."

Thomas stopped, dug in a front pocket for his handkerchief because he was starting to sweat. What was left of my stomach felt like it wanted to turn inside out.

"I heard the rest later, after Mr. Delvecchio was so late coming back to the barn, and Freddy from security drops by in the van to brag on all he knows. Which he says he got straight from the other officers and from young Beverly, pretty black sister who waits on them tables up there. Mr. D. starts his breakfast, see, settling down with the Talbotts and their tomato drinks. He's wanting them to buy another horse. He's smooth, got the manners firing like always, already tipped Beverly five dollars for getting the drinks. Then Freddy says two white women come over from somewhere up yonder, maybe the Bluegrass Room. Don't know who they were exactly, owner wives is what I guess. They got the fine makeup and hair, anyway, and they come over and cut into Mr. D. right away, real loud." Thomas wiped his face and wheezed into his hands. His face got dark with laughter. He could hardly keep going.

"Way I hear it . . ." He wheezed again. "Way I hear it . . . those gals took up some eggs and toast and grapefruits before they was done. Ham. Potatoes. Threw it all over Mr. D. Hit that fancy Mrs. Talbott, too, then she got into it long enough for security to see. Food everywhere, just all over, is what Freddy said. And nasty screaming too. I guess they hollered out things like people up there never heard. Somebody poking the wrong somebodies. Wrong husbands. Wrong gals. The women saying Mr. D. told what he shouldn't have, how they all had trust, and him denying it, and everybody shouting to sue everybody else. They finally shut up except for crying when the cops rolled in. Freddy comes by after I haven't seen Mr. D. for the longest time and asks me how my boss runs such a big, fast barn when it's clear his dick ain't hardly ever in his own pants."

I held my arms against my tightening ribs, tried not to laugh along with him. "That's not news, Thomas. Why are you telling me this?" But I knew why. Louisa and her red friend had blabbed my story until it got into some ears that believed it. And Thomas knew how to follow a snake to its hole.

" 'Cause it's funny as shit." He blew his nose, then looked at the few painted boards that were the only things separating the two of us from Reno. " 'Cause you busted this horse out yesterday, and I thought it was my important business. I can't worry about Mr. D.'s high life, I got nothing to say on that. I worry about my horses and my job. What y'all need to understand is that the move Mr. D. was putting on this horse won't fly. He tried to void the deal Piersall made, thought he had his way again with the owner's sons, but we ain't getting the horse. After this mess, we'll be lucky not to lose a chunk of what we already have."

I started to explain, to say how it was never supposed to involve his job.

"Be quiet. You got nothing I want to hear." His face under its cinnamon freckles was yellowy pale again. "Me and my barn will be all right. Roy Delvecchio gets pulled in half like a old night crawler all the time. But y'all got to tell Miz Piersall how we're out of it."

"Reno will tell her," I said, planting a shaky hand on the wall. "She probably knows anyway."

"Probably she does." Thomas threw his shoulders back and tucked his official black polo shirt under his belt. "That's a good horse," he said, rolling his head to where Flare stood snoozing.

"Tell preacher man I bet him one fine pit of Missouri barbecue that he won't win tomorrow. Tell him that."

"What if he don't bet barbecue?"

"He will." Thomas took three long, rolling strides away from me. The mischief piped high in his voice. "He'll do it 'cause I say so. That's how it works."

I dropped my pounding forehead against the half door to Flare's stall, waited until Thomas was out of sight. I heard the gelding's sleepy breath and the light whisper of a brush—a refrain to human motion I couldn't see. "You catch all that?" I asked. I stepped to the side until I could see the entire bruise of my shadow on the whitewashed plank wall. "I know you believe in every hard thing you've done, Reno. So do I. I'd just like to say some of our priorities are the same."

He didn't reply. I didn't expect him to. If we were toe to toe at all, it was because I'd spoken in my way.

Jenny came up behind me while I listened to the rooster scratch at the dirt for grubs. She asked me if I wanted to use her room some more. I told her I didn't. "Don't ever make too much happen around here," I said. "It's not worth figuring the odds."

She shrugged, not listening. I thanked her for letting me mess up her bed.

"You ought to have it," she said. "Being more senior and all that."

"Didn't want it. Couldn't stand it now. Let me straighten up in there, though, before I leave."

"No reason to." Jenny raised her arm to block me. "I'm clearing out. Alice has got this room off her kitchen at the farm. It's warmer, better for me."

Sweet, solid Jenny with the fine blonde hairs at her sideburns, the pinked pits on her chin. Dear Jenny, who knew how to duck, how to be there for other people. I looked at her and said I'd seen the place, it was plenty nice, and that going out there with Alice was probably a good idea for her career and all. I acted like I didn't notice that she was trying to tell me she was scared.

"You can't tell he was in there for so long. I mean, Alice had the hospital bed and all that cleaned up. It don't smell like nothing. I hope to get a piece of carpet for the floor—Alice has been real nice about that idea—and I'll have a truck to drive to Churchill Downs when the racing moves that way."

"It's okay." I gave her a straight-up grin. "You don't have to act like you feel bad. You're doing the right thing. Alice needs somebody she can trust."

Dawg roared by about then to say there were all sorts of sleazy stories about me at the track kitchen, too many to believe unless I was a bad-ass nudie movie star. "One of them's got you cracking whips at a bunch of rich men's bare butts." Dawg split his wide mouth and showed teeth. "I told them I hadn't seen you handle one man normal who liked it."

"They need more to talk about down there." I held my face smooth as paper. "Better horses."

"Hell, yeah." Dawg wiped his hands clean across the front of his baseball jersey. "They all telling me to put my paycheck on that rapper's horse in the Blue Grass race, and I ain't doing it, except maybe in a wheel."

"Don't believe what you hear, Dawg."

"Not what I see or read about neither. I know." He puffed his young, brown cheeks. "I ain't believe in nothing around this place."

CHAPTER 2 8

*b*ustle. Military faces. Hooves pawing at crushed straw. It had rained for maybe an hour after midnight, but the morning had hung itself up to dry. The track was fast. The turf course would be deep and wet, especially on the dipping backstretch, but that was good for us.

Alice asked me to pony three horses to the gate, that was it. No workouts. My ass wasn't well enough to stick in the air at high speed, she said, so she split the work between Grace Albert, a long-wristed woman who caught most of her rides from Marlou, and another bug boy Red Flora had on display, Canadian kid named Auguste. Grace had hit the track on Flare that morning at 6:01. I'd gone up to see it. She'd jogged him only half a mile, just enough to let him know the best was yet to come. Niall Riordan was there too, ponying his smaller black horse around one turn himself, the horse working up a necktie of foam just doing that. There would be nine horses in the grass race, including two down from New York and one thick-ankled English-bred trained by Roy. And Sunny. Riordan's sheik horse had the overnight odds of five to two. Flare was holding at a very cashable eight to one. Sunny was the unknown.

Charlie gave me hell for being grounded. He knew I'd earned my whipping but said he hoped I'd be sailing through the candy wrappers at Churchill Downs the following week. I told him I didn't think I'd be there right away. Some R&R might be in order. He tilted over the shiny horn of his saddle when I said that, held out his insulated coffee mug as if to share.

"Don't know if I've ever seen a funnier mess than the one you caused." He flicked his tongue between his lips, testing the air. He meant the Roy sex scandal business.

"I didn't cause a thing," I said. It was weird to be on the ground looking up at him. Made me a little dizzy.

"Course you didn't. What I should've said is I hear tell you make a pretty lie and a pretty payback both." He dug into his boot top for a cigarette while he snickered. "People around here need to learn not to treat each other so bad. Laziest dogs got sharp teeth."

I let Charlie think his thoughts, then asked him what his call was on the Elkhorn. He said he liked Alice's boy, but he'd like him even more at a mile and a half. Told me Sunsquall was a complete mystery to him, just like another gal he knew. "I'll lay down on that Calumet colt," he admitted, "because I'm weak and like to live in the past. Can't see those red and blue silks come onto this track without my eyes halfway crying." He kicked his sorrel mare forward so he could play usher to a rank horse. "Old man," he said, not looking back at me. "Throwing away my money."

Grace Albert did fine on Flare as much as it mattered. It was Sunny I watched. She jogged like she was full of fire. Her rider nodded when he saw me on the rail. I could tell he'd be laying money on her number that afternoon. It would be impossible not to.

As I walked down the hill to pony up, still limping more on my left side than my right, I saw Louisa Fett in a ridiculous orange sweatshirt that made her hair look like pink insulation. She was aboard a bay with washboard ribs, and Billy T. was at her knee, nodding at his own words and making circular motions with the one hand that wasn't near his horse's bridle. They listened to each other. Communicated. The horse overstepped and clipped his own heels every third or fourth step. I slipped off the road, not hiding exactly but getting out of the way. Pretended there were other horses to see. When they were safely past, I wondered how he did it, how he ran a barn full of crazies without being crazy himself. He didn't care for Louisa—I wouldn't ever allow that scene in my movie—but he could work with her and have her believe she was good at what she did. Which only made her better. A man like that might do the same for me, I thought. Silvery Billy. When my time came.

Back at Alice's shed row the panic was contained. Everybody was battle eyed and busy, even possumy Burkie, who had taken to feeding Flare's rooster out of his ticklish, spade-sized hand. I took my best chance. Crept into Jenny's tidy room that she'd decided to occupy one final night. There were her extra shoes, the sneakers for softball. There were the plastic bags from the mall that held her clothes, one for clean, one for dirty. A box for her hairbrush and shampoo. She'd wiped off the high, dusty window, and it let in a smothered golden light that broke into squares across her bed. I sat quietly on the mattress, tracing the patient curlicue trail of the tiny stitches on that checkered quilt. Then I slid the velvet box with the Ballard family earrings underneath the pillow. No note. This time no one needed a note. Jenny would know who the box was from. She might not know why it was hers, why I'd done such a thing, but I'd let her make up the answer she could live with.

Before I left I noticed how Jenny had put an old towel on the concrete floor to break up the gray space. She'd also shoved the small brown refrigerator to the far, far corner. The bunk room didn't belong to her—it would never belong to anybody—but she had changed it in the few ways she had.

Shimmery afternoon. I walked in a slow, distorted circle and touched a piece of tack or a prickly muzzle at every stall in the barn. My car was packed since it had never really been unpacked. Mama didn't know to expect me, but it wouldn't surprise her to see me at the door. I'd tell her about the necklace that was in the package she'd kept, tell her it was hers in exchange for a few days' rent and plenty of sangria. She'd like that. I'd stay with her until horses returned to my night dreams. Then I'd come back to my bluegrass home. The ruckus would die down as it always did. I'd go to a farm somewhere so I could enjoy the sass and bounty of thoroughbreds learning to run, or I'd catch on at Churchill Downs for a bit. It wouldn't be long before I was sweat in the saddle again.

I paid special attention to Alice's red filly when I got to her stall. She wouldn't try to break her maiden until the fall. I told her I'd be here to see it happen.

When it came time to rig Twilight Flare, we all gathered around in a way we usually didn't. Marlou was there. And Grace Albert. Burkie, who was wearing a clean shirt for the afternoon. Jenny. Dawg. Reno had braided the gelding's cowlicked mane in tight black thread that didn't show. He'd been preaching an on-again, off-again lesson to the animal since dawn, and he kept it up when he took him out of the stall. It was up to Dawg to shoo the rooster back into its webbed corner, and it was up to him to make sure the bridle, the martingale, and the girth had been cleaned, and cleaned again. We were admiring the big fellow with his ramrod forehead and his plackets of shifting muscle when Alice stepped out of the tack room. She had changed into a pale blue skirt and vest over a basic saleslady blouse. Her hair was down. She had panty hose on, and flat red canvas shoes for her feet. Except for all of the things hidden in the satchel of her face, she looked almost unremarkable.

She and Reno staged one last quarrel over whether to tie Flare's tongue down to help his breathing. They decided not to do it.

Then we made our own parade. All except Jenny and Burkie, who would stay and listen to the race on Dawg's radio because someone had to be in the barn and Jenny wanted it that way. Alice and Marlou went first, followed by Reno and Dawg, who each had a chain lead wrapped over the nose of their irrepressible horse. I was last, where I should have been.

I peeled off before they swung under the stone arch that took them into the saddling area. Marlou would stand with Alice as family. There would be no entourage like the sheik's or the one that still flailed around Roy even though he was smelling pretty strongly of skunk. Eric would saddle Sunny with Marty Salazar's help, and somewhere in the crowd a restless New York connection or two would be watching. My place was elsewhere.

I left them as they waded into the sea of competition.

I ambled through the grandstand to see the post parade because I'd always liked that part. Charlie and his crew in dark green hunting jackets, velvet caps, boots, and britches. The metallic wail of the horn. The horses so glad to be out of the pit. One of the New York horses had drawn the post. He looked relaxed, ready to concentrate. Roy's entry didn't move real pretty, and he'd soaked his flanks he was so nervous. I could practically hear Roy swearing from his box up in the grandstand. He needed a slow early pace to have a chance, and the sheik horse, smaller and perfectly proportioned, wasn't likely to give it to him. For my part, I thought Flare looked the strongest and grabbiest of the group, Sunny the most agile and fleet. Her jockey didn't have her attention yet—I could see her wandering eye as they jogged past—but he'd have it when the time came. When they moved onto the summery sponge of the turf course, my mare would change as the surface beneath her hooves changed. I somehow knew it.

As the uneven daisy chain of horses and balloon-colored jocks wrapped back on itself, I found myself near the rail next to a short, jowly man in a brown houndstooth jacket. A patron. A bettor. A man filled with surefire numbers of his own making. When he saw my ID clip, he asked me if one of mine was out there for the race. He took me for a groom.

I told him I rode Twilight Flare when I was needed. I didn't feel the need to mention Sunny.

He puckered his shiny mouth over his coffee-stained teeth, checked his program, which was lousy with calculations, some of them in two colors of ink. "Twilight Flare. Twilight," he muttered, then jerked his head up like he might catch me off guard. "Down to seven to one, about right. You mean you don't see Palace Nightwatch taking it all?"

I shrugged. "Nightwatch is better at a mile. Course is damp. My guy's a stayer. You'll need a stayer with all this front end speed."

"Speed?"

"Nightwatch. And the Sunsquall mare. You never know what the blend will be."

"No recent Beyer number on the mare. I keep track of my Beyers." The man wanted a discussion, maybe even an argument, to keep his mind off the money he'd already laid to rest.

"I can only say she's fresh. Fit. And Flare's beat Nightwatch before."

The man gave a grunt, flipped his program to the next page, and commenced adding more numbers in the margins there. "I got him in one exacta," he said. "Maybe I ought to factor her in."

"Good luck," I said.

"You too," went the reply.

I pushed back through the thickening, hope-wrung crowd to higher ground. None of us knew what would happen. Not the number-weaving touts. Not the high hat trainers. Not the princes or the thieves. I stood on my tiptoes so I could see the dark shapes of faces and helmets through the green sieve of the gate. Somewhere in there an assistant starter was pinching Flare's long ear to hold him steady. And a good jock was whispering to Sunny with love. Somewhere eighteen hearts were beating even louder than my own.

It came in an instant. The unannounced trill of the bell. The soft chunk of doors thrown open. The great swipe of forelegs at the sun, the surge of necks into a wide river of earth that was always promised before them. It was done. We were off.

ACKNOWLEDGMENTS

My thanks to Lois Rosenthal of *Story* magazine and Mitch Wieland of *The Idaho Review* for printing excerpts from this novel in somewhat different form. Thanks also to Eileen Pollack, Elwood Reid, Michael Paterniti, Sara Corbett, Janet Holmes, and Beth Haas for reading early drafts. To Gail Hochman for her belief. To Lois and Jerry Thompson for their racing stories. To Kris Taveggia for dragging me to my first morning workout at Keeneland. To Denise Roy for being what all writers wish for—a bright and shining editor.

Thanks to my father, who bought the first pony, and to Eileen Beckman, who taught me how to ride her.

Above all, to RWS, who was there during the lost bets, long nights, and all other gambles.